# MARS CHILD

by
CYRIL JUDD

I0616968

ARMCHAIR FICTION
PO Box 4369, Medford, Oregon   97501-0168

*For more information about Armchair Books and products, visit our
website at...*

**www.armchairfiction.com**

*Or email us at...*

**armchairfiction@yahoo.com**

# THEY ARRIVED ON MARS TO ESCAPE FROM A DYING PLANET

The man-made colony on Mars had no real need for heroes. What it needed were people who knew how to solve the problems of simple survival. The Sun Laker colonists had tried just about everything to save their colony from eventual extinction: hard work, political pull, prayer, and even good old-fashioned stubbornness. But when they found themselves at the mercy of a corrupt drug manufacturer, it seemed the only thing left to hope for was a miracle itself. That miracle soon arrived in the form of a newborn baby boy, the first child successfully conceived on the red planet. This infant soon became the hope and inspiration of a people fighting against seemingly impossible odds. However, more than anything else, the Martian colony wanted independence from a doomed Earth—and it abruptly found itself in deadly danger of succeeding!

# CAST OF CHARACTERS

## DR. TONY HELLMAN
*Disillusioned and lonely—could the good doctor renew his hope in humanity while on a distant planet?*

## ANNA WILLENDORF
*This beautiful woman came to Mars with the strange talent of being there before you even knew you needed her.*

## POLLY KANDRO
*Unable to carry a child to term on Earth, would her newborn son be able to survive the harsh enviroment of Mars?*

## "SUNNY" KANDRO
*Hope and anxiety surrounded the arrival of this newborn boy. There had been only one other child concieved on Mars…and it did not survive.*

## DOUGLAS GRAMHAM
*This famed author was both admired and hated—and his writings could either bolster the Martian colony or spell its doom.*

## HUGO BRENNER
*A notorious wealthy drug manufacturer—his plot to gain the Colony's Lab facilities for his own use could result in bankruptcy and ruin for the Martian settlers.*

# CHAPTER ONE

JIM KANDRO couldn't pace the corridors, because there weren't any. The Colony's hospital was simply an extra room built onto the doctor's rammed-earth house. They still called it "earth," though it was the rust-reddened soil of Mars.

The narrow space between bed and wall cramped his restless legs; the monotonous motion wearied his arm. But Jim stayed on, doggedly determined to see the thing through, rubbing his wife's back and whispering reassurances, as much to himself as to her.

"Why don't you let me take over for a while?" the doctor suggested. Jim's usefulness was over now; the man was only communicating his own panic to his wife. "Go in the other room and lie down, or take a walk outside if you want to. Nothing's going to happen for a while yet."

"Doc…" The man's voice was rough with anxiety, but he held back the frantic questions. "Please, Tony," he said simply, "I'd rather stick around." He fixed a smile to his face as he bent over Polly again.

Anna came in before Tony had quite decided to call her. It was a talent she seemed to have, one of the reasons why he had chosen her for his assistant.

"I think Jim needs a cup of coffee," he told her firmly.

Kandro straightened up awkwardly. "All right, Doc." He was trying hard to be matter-of-fact. "You'll call me if anything—when there's news?"

"Of course he will." Anna's quick assurance forestalled Tony's exasperated retort. She put her hand on Kandro's arm, and smiled down at the woman on the bed. "Not much longer now, Polly," she said with quiet certainty. "Come on, Jim."

As the door closed behind them, Tony turned to his patient, and was surprised by a brief smile on her lips. "You mustn't mind," she explained, almost apologetically. "He's so worried."

She had no breath for more. She twisted suddenly on the narrow bed and clutched at the air till Tony gave her his hand to squeeze on. Every other form of physical labor, he reflected unhappily, was made easier by the light gravity of Mars; but the labor of childbirth was eternally the same. And there was nothing he could do right now, except to offer her the reassurance of his presence. He stood and waited, gooseflesh cascading from the nape of his neck down his spine as she ground her teeth against the pain.

When it was gone and she released his hand, he turned to the sterilizer for a fresh glove. One more examination, he decided. Something should be happening by now.

He heard her deep inhalation behind him.

"Anna's so nice," she sighed.

HE HEARD the difference before he turned and saw it. Polly was lying back, completely relaxed, making the most of the time before the pain returned.

"Yes, she is," Tony said. He dropped the glove on the table; another examination wasn't going to do any good, for her or for him. Quit the damned fiddling, he told himself. Sit and wait. You let that poor son-of-a-gun get you down. If she can wait, you can too. Be the doctor you would have been in Pittsburgh or Springfield—any Springfield on Earth. So you're on Mars. So what? Sit and wait.

He got a chair and put it next to the high bed, dropped his hand casually on the sheet where Polly could see it, where she could grab it again when she wanted to. He leaned back and forced himself, muscle by unwilling muscle, to relax.

\*    \*    \*

ON THE other side of the door, Jim raised his "coffee" cup for the fourth time to his lips, and for the fourth time put it down again untasted.

"But what do you *think*, Anna?" he burst out. "How does it look to you? You'd know if there was anything…*wrong.*"

"It looks all right to me," she said again, gently. "It looks like a normal delivery."

"But she's been—she started at six o'clock this morning! Why should it take so long?"

"Sometimes it does. That doesn't mean there's anything wrong. It's hard work that's all. It takes time." It was useless to tell him not to worry. She went over to the work counter that ran the length of the rectangular room. "I don't think it'll be much longer now, Jim.

Do you want to try and get some sleep while you wait? Or if you're going to stay up, could you give me a hand here?" She pulled out materials quickly.

"Sure." He got up, still holding the cup as though he didn't even know it was in his hand. "I mean, I'll be glad to help." He let Anna relieve him of the cup, and accepted an alky torch, never wondering why she should choose to start a job at half-past midnight.

"Look," he said desperately. "You would tell me, wouldn't you, if it wasn't going right? He—Tony wouldn't want to keep me from knowing, would he? She never got this far before, you know."

"Believe me, Jim, if there were anything wrong, Tony would tell you. And I don't know any more than you do. You were in there longer than I was. Here, hold the flame down this way, will you?"

For just a minute, he turned his attention to the work. "But why wouldn't he *tell* me anything?"

"Because there was nothing to tell, I imagine." Even Anna's patience could wear thin. Deftly, she removed the torch from his hand before the down-turned flame could do any damage.

Kandro wanted to yell: *you don't know, none of you know, twelve years we've been married and a man and a woman wants kids, and none of you know how we want kids and all she does is get so sick you'd think she's dying and she never got this far before and you just don't know...*

He saw in Anna's eyes that he didn't have to say it that she did understand. Her arms went out a little, and the big, rawboned man flopped on his knees before the plain little woman and sobbed with his head awkwardly pillowed against her.

\*　　\*　　\*

AT 3:37 A. M., Dr. Tony Hellman adjusted a tiny oxygen mask over the red button nose of a newborn infant, wiped it and wrapped it, and returned his attention to the mother. He reached for the buzzer that would summon Anna from the other room to help; but he didn't push it. Kandro was sure to come storming in with her, and Polly was too wakeful and excited as it was. Then, too, there was a certain perverse satisfaction in doing the whole job himself, even the messy wiping up operations that would be left to a student nurse back on Earth.

WHEN he had finished, he overrode Polly's plan to stay awake and stare at her baby. He gave her a stiff shot of sedative to make certain, then decided to give her her OxEn pill for the next day as well, hoping she would sleep through till late morning.

Only since the development of the magic pink pellets, containing the so-called "oxygen enzyme," had it been possible for most human beings to live a normal life on Mars. Before that, anyone who did not have the rare good luck to possess naturally Mars-worthy lungs lived permanently in an oxygen mask. Now masks were needed only for babies too small to tolerate the pill.

The miracle enzyme made the air of Mars as useful to human lungs as the native atmosphere of Earth…always provided the human in question took his pill religiously every day. Let thirty hours go by without renewing the treatment, and he would be dying, within minutes, of anoxemia.

Tony took a last look at the baby, made sure the tiny mask was properly adjusted, and checked the oxy tank for proper flow. Polly was already half-asleep. He went quietly past her bed, and opened the door to his living room.

"Shh!" Anna turned from her workbench, her face warm and cheerful. She pointed to the bunk where Jim, fully dressed in tunic and sand boots, lay fast asleep.

"Everything all right?"

Tony nodded. "Damn sight better than I expected." After the glaring light of the hospital room, the quiet dark in here was good. More than that, Anna's untroubled presence served to dissolve all the nervous tension of the hours before. Suddenly too fatigued even to talk, he finished briefly, "Boy—five pounds two ounces, Earth weight—good color—strong too."

"Good." Anna returned her attention to the work. "I'll finish this up and then go sit with her. I'll call you if she needs anything."

"What about him?"

Anna glanced at Jim's sprawled figure. "He'll be all right." she smiled. "He can wait a few hours to meet his son."

For just a moment more the doctor stood there, watching her, fascinated as always by her delicate art. A puff on the tube, a twist as it reddened in the flame, a spin against an iron tool, another puff. All of it casual, seemingly random, and then, somehow, there was a finished piece of work—part of the intricate glass tubing always needed at the Lab, a fragile-looking piece of stemware for some new colonist's household, a precise hypodermic syringe for himself.

He watched till his weary eyes refused the bright spot of light where the pale flame washed over the glowing glass. Then he stumbled into the adjoining bedroom and slept.

## CHAPTER TWO

THE Lab was the cash drop of Sun Lake. Mars had a slight case of radioactivity, nothing you couldn't live with, but enough to enable Sun Lake City Colony to concentrate and isolate radioisotopes and radioactive organics for sale on Earth at better than competitive prices, even after the stiff tariff for transport.

The materials handled were only mildly dangerous, but it was the doctor's job to render them effectively not dangerous at all. Twice a day, before work started in the morning and again before quitting time, Tony geigered the whole place. On this precaution the whole community depended, not only for safeguarding their sole source of income, but for their very lives. Every adult member of the Colony did work at least indirectly connected with the Lab; all of them spent some time there.

Among other things, it was the only building with a large enough room to serve for social functions. And it offered the only possible change from mud-colored walls; from isomorphic rooms, all just 15x15, from cement floors and wall bunks. The Lab had everything the other buildings lacked—steel frame work and alumalloy wall sheathing; copper tubing and running hot water; built-in power outlets, Earth-made furniture; even the blessings of an Earth-import air filtering system.

The one-kilometer walk out to the Lab in the early morning always infused the doctor with a glowing sense of confidence and well being. In a year on Mars, he had lost little of his first pleasure in the buoyancy afforded by the low gravity. Walking was effortless; and, in the thin air, an hour's sunlight was enough to clear the night's chill from the open spaces. At noon, the sun would be too bright; in the evening, the cold would return as suddenly as it had departed. Now, in the first part of the morning, it was like a perfect autumn day on Earth.

Behind him, in the houses that lined both sides of the colony's single curved street, people were dressing hurriedly, eating, making plans, getting ready for the day's work. Ahead, the shining blue walls of the Lab were set off against the magnificent backdrop of *Lacus Solis* itself. The ancient seabed was alive again with color as the early sun's rays glinted off millions of tiny particles, the salts and minerals of Mars deposited by long-dried waters in millenia past. The clean lines of the new building against that sparkling expanse constituted at once a challenge and a reassurance—this is what man can do; here is everything he needs to do it with.

*If we can...a second chance for man, if we can learn how to use it...*

Tony unlocked the storage cabinet built into the massive lead-lined door of the Lab. He took out his suit of protective armor—probably the only Earth-import wearing apparel ever bought and paid for by the Colony—but before he got into it, he turned to look back just once at the little huddle of houses where, a few hours ago, Polly Kandro had affirmed her faith in Sun Lake's future in the most emphatic personal manner.

THE solidity of the Lab was a disagreeable symbol of the Colony's present status; it was still the only decent structure Sun Lake had to show. Halfway up the almost imperceptible three-kilometer slope from "canal" bed at his left to "sea" level at his right sat the Colony, lumpishly. Every building, like Tony's own home-and-hospital, was tamped native dirt. The arc of dull rust-brown huts squatting close to the ground and close to each other presented to Tony a monotonous row of identical plastic-windowed backsides.

Behind them, fields A, B, C, and D showed, even from the Lab, the work of Sun Lake's "mudkickers"—the agronomists who, using tools as ancient as the harrow and as modern as the mutation-creating particles that stream from a cyclotron, were changing Mars plants into things that could nourish an Earth animal, and changing Earth plants into things that could draw nourishment from the grudging Martian soil.

Mutated bean plants whose ancestors had been a button-bearing Mars cactus dotted field A. Mutated cauliflowers—the size of apples, dark brown and still manufacturing in themselves too much potassium cyanide to be edible—darkened field B; another few plant-generations and they would be food for the Colony table, though tasting somewhat of the neutralized cyanide bitter almonds.

Ten kilometers beyond the fields of bastard Earth-Mars vegetation, there had been beauty only recently—the fantastically eroded Rimrock Hills. Five months ago, however, the first pre-fab shacks had gone up in the camp on the other side of the hills. Three months ago the first furnace had been fired at Pittco Three: Pittsburgh Coal, Coke and Iron Company's Mars Metal Refining Plant Number Three. Now a dirty shroud of yellow-stained smoke draped the peaks from dawn to dark.

With a feeling of intense distaste, Tony started climbing into his suit of armor. *A second chance for man...*

His own high-flown thoughts mocked him. Another chance to do exactly as they had done on Earth. Already the clean air of Mars was thickening with the eructations of Earth's commerce. Nor was the camp beyond the hill a lone offender. Even Sun Lake, to survive at all, had to maintain a cash crop economy—and the Lab was the potentially deadly crop.

Tony made sure that every flap on his suit was zippered and closed, and the last adjustments made on the helmet. He picked up the hand counter from the bottom of the compartment and worked the screw around to calibrate out Mars' naturally heavy background "noise." The needle eased to zero on the dial. Only then did he open the heavy door of the lab itself and begin his slow trip of inspection through the building.

ALL areas were well under the threshold of danger, as usual, except for a hot patch in the isotope room. Tony chalked a yellow line around the spot and marked the door of the room with a bright yellow cross. Finished, he headed straight for the clean-up room and checked the condition of the exterior of his suit against the bigger stationary radiation counter that was kept there.

Not until he was sure he hadn't picked up anything on gloves or boots did he remove his suit and dump it down the chute for routine de-radiation. He hated to take time for the rest of the procedure today: He had to check with the men who were working in the hot spot; he had to get back to the hospital to see Polly; he had a patient, Joan Radcliff, who worried him badly. What was more, he'd slept too late to eat breakfast at the communal table shared by most unmarried Colony members; he hadn't even had "coffee"—and he missed it. But after the number of times he'd nagged the others about skimping on

11

safety precautions, he couldn't pass up any of them himself.

He stripped and dumped his clothes down another chute, sand-scrubbed himself, and holding his breath, walked through the stinking alcohol spray. Methyl alcohol, cheaper and easier to produce in the lab than water, and sand for soap made bathing an ordeal instead of the pleasant ritual it had been on Earth.

Tony moved fast, but by the time he had put on a fresh tunic and boots and emerged into the central hall, the Lab was already full of people getting set for the day's work. He edged past a knot of busy conversationalists in the corridor.

"Hey, Doc..."

He paused, and that was his undoing.

"How's Polly? Tony, hold on—how's the baby? Are they all right? Doc, wait a minute. Did everything go all right? Where are they? What is it...?"

HE ANSWERED the same questions a dozen times. It seemed that half the population of Sun Lake was in the corridor with him, and they all wanted to know the same thing. Finally, despairing of getting through until he had satisfied them all, Tony climbed up on a chair and addressed the crowd.

"Five pounds, two ounces, Earth weight—a boy—wrigglingest baby I ever saw. Plenty lively, and he looks just like his old man. What else do you want to know?"

"How's Polly?"

"Fine. So's Jim." The hoary joke got its inevitable laugh.

Then one of the chemists said, "I make a motion for a birthday present. Let's build that other room onto the Kandro house right now."

It was an offer that had been made months before, and that Polly, hesitant and slightly superstitious, had refused. "There'll be time enough after the baby's born," she had told them, and stuck to it.

Tony knew why; knew about the first time, eleven years before, when she had carried a child for seven months, and then had to pack away all the things she had lovingly collected for its birth. They had stayed in their cartons for four more years, and two more miscarriages, before she gave them tearfully to a luckier woman.

"When is she going home, Doc?" one of the electronics men asked. "How much time have we got?"

"I don't know. Maybe tomorrow morning," Tony told them. "She's in pretty good shape. It's just a matter of where she'll be most comfortable. I don't imagine she'll want to stay in the hospital very long... After all, it's not exactly designed for luxurious convalescence." They were all familiar with the crowded little room; he waited for a dutiful laugh to die down, and added, "I think tomorrow will be about right...not later than the day after."

"We better get started then," Mimi Jonathan, the pert black-haired lab administrator, spoke up. "Suppose I make up some work parties, and we get things going?"

She produced a pencil and paper and began taking down the names and abilities of everyone whose lab work was not too pressing. Two groups of volunteers left promptly, to collect soil from the old "canal" bottom, and to set up the frames for ramming. Others would have to stay in the lab to set up the machinery for work on the synthetics that would paint the new room, build the new furniture, and clothe the new baby. While Mimi plunged into the complexities of reassigning work space and job time, the doctor managed to get away from the enthusiastic crowd.

He made his way to the isotopes room, and was happy to find Sam Flexner, the chemist in charge, waiting for him at the yellow-chalked door. Apparently his harping on safety rules had penetrated in at least one case; Sam knew enough to stay on the spot even in the midst of the sudden excitement over the baby.

TONY opened the door and pointed out the ragged chalked circle on the floor. "Any idea what it is?"

"We were running some radio-phosphorus," Sam said doubtfully. "But there was no trouble on the run. Must be spillage." The chemist had a young open face, and Tony liked him. He began to fill in the necessary report.

"What reason?" Spillage was unusual.

"It's a bigger order than we usually handle—must have been a hundred kilograms." Sam looked up sharply. "It was all right yesterday, wasn't it? The afternoon checkup?"

Tony nodded.

"Then it must have been at closing. I...well, I left a few minutes early yesterday. Figured the boys could close up all right, but I guess one of them took a lazy man's load in his tote box...filled it up too high to save himself a trip. I'll check on it and tell them in a nice way, all right?"

"That should do it. But I better have a look at the checkout tubes."

Sam brought over a tray of tubes resting in numbered grooves. He was wearing one like them pinned to his own lapel. The content of the tubes was its normal dirty white. Purple would have meant "too close to hot stuff too long."

"Okay," said Tony, checking his form. "That hot spot there, I think you'd better chisel it out and get one of the suppliers to take it way out and dump it."

"Old Learoyd was here with a load of vanadium dirt. He'll do it when he leaves for Pittco."

"Fine. Get it done. And tell Learoyd to put the stuff in the back of his rig. I don't think you could kill any of those old boys with anything subtler than a meat ax, but I wouldn't want him to sit next to it for a ten-hour trip." He dated and timed off the form. "That's that. Only you better stick around till close-up after this." He smiled and put a stop to the young chemist's attempt at explanation. "How's Verna, anyhow? Something better happen soon, if it's going to make all this trouble."

SAM grinned back. "You may hear something soon," he admitted. "But please don't—uh—"

"Doctors don't gossip," Tony said. "One thing about this place," he added, "we can't help making history every time we turn around. Have a baby, and it's the first baby; have another baby, and it's the first girl born; slice out an appendix, and it's the first abdominal surgery. Let's see—you and Verna will be the first marriage between a drop-in chemical engineer and a share-holding agronomist—if she'll have you."

"Sounds like one of those weather records," complained Sam. "The coldest 3:00 P. M. reading at the corner of Spruce and Juice on a January 16th since 2107."

"It's your place in history," Tony assured him. "We'll all be footnotes. I'll see you this afternoon."

# CHAPTER THREE

TONY stepped out with springs in his knees, and, feeling the waxing heat of the morning threw back the hood of his parka. The marvelous clear air of an hour earlier was fast disappearing, as the mineral trash that covered Mars' surface began to heat and roil the atmosphere. He looked off toward the Rimrock Hills, mourning their vanished beauty; then he stopped in surprise, squinting at the enigmatic black bugs crawling back and forth within the shadow of the hills.

He stood there, watching, as the seemingly random pattern of motion trended gradually in the direction of the Colony.

Who would be out on the desert afoot? He stopped and shielded his eyes. There were about twenty of them, and they were humped with carbines and oxy masks.

The military!

But why? There'd never been a visit from Commissioner Bell's little intercolony police force before; never been any occasion for it. Each colony handled its own internal policing.

It was a year now since Bell's boys had been out for anything except routine administrative work, such as guard mount over the rocket; the last time was when an ace foundryman for Mars Machine Tool was rightly suspected of committing mayhem on a Marsport shopkeeper. Mars Machine Tool's colony administration insisted on being unimpressed by the evidence and refused to surrender him to Marsport. Bell's boys had simply walked in and taken him away for his trial and conviction.

But Sun Lakers weren't given to mayhem.

Tony headed back for the lab as the crooked trail of the soldiers straightened out into a beeline for the same place. He had his patients, but he was also a member of the Colony Council and this looked like Council business.

In the Lab he went straight to the front office and asked Mimi: "Did Harve ever get that recorder put together?"

"Last week," she said. "It's been a blessing too. Why?"

"I think Bell's boys are paying us a call." He told her what he'd seen outside. "It might be useful to have a record of it."

Mimi nodded thoughtfully, and flipped a lever at the side of her desk. "That'll register anywhere in the office," she explained. "I'm a pacer—Harve set it up so I could walk all over the office while I talk, and still have it record."

Sam Flexner was also there. He put down a completed report form on the spillage in his department to ask: "What do they want?"

"I don't know," Tony told him. "But I think we'd better put in an intercom call for Joe Gracey to come on out here. He ought to be tending his seedling in C Area. Phone the South End to send a runner and get him out here on the double."

Gracey was the senior agronomist, and, like Mimi and Tony, a member of the Colony Council. The fourth member, and most recent addition, was Nick Cantrella; in only six months' time since his arrival at Sun Lake, Nick had risen from junior setup man to bossing all maintenance and procurement for the Lab. At the moment he was home with a nasty chemical burn on his arm. It wasn't really so bad that he couldn't be called in for an emergency, but Tony hesitated to do so, and he noticed that Mimi didn't suggest it either. Nick had a red-hot temper and practically no inhibitions.

"No," the doctor said to the questioners that began to press around him, "I don't think we ought to go out and meet them. Better just go ahead and work and get the new room for the Kandros put together. Flexner, will you stick around? It may be some damn thing or other about our atomics—some technical precaution we may have missed."

"No, sir," said another man emphatically. It was O'Donnell, who had ditched a law career to become a sweeper and then a maintenance man and then a good jury-rig physicist. It was his job to see that no daylight showed between the Colony's atomics practice and the law.

"Hmp," said the doctor. "You stick around too."

THERE was a thudding on the door and a self-conscious calling of an archaic formula: "Open in the name of the law!"

The delegation was a half-platoon of soldiers with their carbines and cumbersome oxygen masks and tanks—a choice bit of military conservatism, since a pocketful of OxEn pills weighed a hundredth as much and would keep them alive a hundred times longer. There were two civilians and an officer—Lieutenant Ed Nealey.

Tony was relieved to see him; they were fellow-members of a subscription club that split the heavy postage on Earthside scientific periodicals, and Tony knew Nealey to be a conscientious and levelheaded young career officer.

The doctor was extending his hand to Nealey when he remembered his protocol: One of the civilians was unknown to him, but the other was Hamilton Bell, Commissioner of Interplanetary Affairs.

"I'm Tony Hellman, Commissioner," he said. "I don't know if you remember me. I'm the doctor here and a member of our Colony's Council."

The commissioner was a small man, tending somewhat to pompous frailty. He looked like the kind of person rumor made him out to be: a never very important functionary who got the dreary Mars post when a very ordinary graft ring of which he was a prominent member was "exposed." The exposure followed only reasonably quickly on the heels of his bolt from the Insurantist Senate minority in the Panamerican World Federation. In the interval between the news accounts of Bell's political switch, and the spectacular news stories of graft corruption in which he was involved, there had been just time for the minority to become a majority...

"Can you speak for the Colony?" he asked abruptly, ignoring Tony's hand.

THE doctor cast a bewildered look at Lt. Nealey, whose eyes were front and whose face was set... Tony noticed he carried in a canvas scabbard the disassembled dipole and handle of an electronic "Bloodhound."

"I'm a council member," Tony said. "So is Miss Jonathan here. Another council member's ill and the third is on his way. The two of us can speak for the Colony. Now, what can we do for you?"

"It's a police matter. Do you care to make a statement before I have to drag the situation out into the open?"

"Let me take it," muttered O'Donnell. Tony nodded. The lawyer-turned-physicist firmly told the commissioner: "I want to remind you that we are a chartered colony, and, under the charter, are entitled to police ourselves. And I also want to say that we are not going to respond to any fishing expeditions until we hear what the complaint is."

"Suit yourself," grunted the commissioner. "But you're not self-policing when you steal from another colony. Mr. Brenner, tell your story."

Eyes swiveled to the other civilian, Brenner of Brenner Pharmaceuticals. *So that*, thought Tony, *is what a trillionaire looks like*. Younger than anyone could reasonably expect, and somehow looking comfortably conservative even in a parka of orange-red mutation mink. The best of food, plenty of rest, and the most careful attention to his bodily needs were combining to cover the prominent bones of his face with deceptive pads of soft flesh; but he still wore the countenance of a lean and questing man: a perplexing expression of bland good humor or of permanent inner amusement.

Brenner shrugged and smiled a little uncomfortably. "I had no choice, Doctor," he said. "A hundred kilos of my marcaine—bulk micron dust, you understand—was stolen yesterday."

SOMEBODY gasped. A hundred kilograms of marcaine, principal product of Brenner's works, was a small fortune on Mars—and a large fortune on Earth, if it could be diverted from medical use and channeled into one of the innumerable pipelines to addicts.

"Naturally I reported it," Brenner explained. "And of course Commissioner Bell had to order a Bloodhound search. It brought us here."

"Ed," Tony appealed to the grim-faced lieutenant, "did you operate the Bloodhound? Will you give me your personal word that it led to the Colony?"

"Answer him, Lieutenant," Bell ordered.

"I'm sorry to...Dr. Hellman," Nealey said stiffly. "I checked the machine three times, myself. Strong scent from Brenner's storeroom to the Rimrocks, then some confusion in the Rimrock caves, and a weakening scent from the Rimrocks to here. It doesn't actually stand up all the way here, but it doesn't go anywhere else. That's definite."

"Please, Dr. Hellman," said Brenner kindly. "You needn't look so stricken. All it means is that there's a rotten apple in your barrel. That happens."

Gracey hurried in, a spindle-shanked ex-professor of low-temperature agronomy from Nome University. He addressed himself directly to Brenner: "What are *you* doing here?"

"Mr. Brenner has sworn out an intercolony complaint of grand theft," said the commissioner. "You're Gracey? You needn't waste your breath trying to blacken Mr. Brenner's character. He's already informed me that there was a disagreement between you, which you've taken to heart." His meager smile showed that what he meant was "become a little cracked over."

"He hasn't got any character to blacken," growled the agronomist. "He tried to get me to breed marcaine weeds for higher production of his hell-dust and I wanted to know why. Wasn't that naive of me? I checked on Earth and I found out that maybe ten percent of his marcaine goes into medical hands and the rest—"

The commissioner shut him up with a decisive: "That's enough. I will *not* listen to random accusations based on newspaper gossip. I don't doubt that after marcaine arrives on Earth some of it is diverted. The world has its weak-willed people. But Mr. Brenner is a responsible manufacturer and you people…I respect your ideals but I'm afraid I can't say much for your performance. The business of Mars is business. And a major theft from one of our leading industrial colonies is very serious indeed."

"Gentlemen," said Brenner, "I *can't* ignore it. I'd like to, simply to spare the unpleasantness, but the amount involved is too important financially. And there's always the danger that some quantity might get into illegal channels."

GRACEY snarled, looked as though he wanted to spit on the immaculate floor of the Lab.

"What exactly do you intend to do?" Tony asked hastily, anxious to forestall an eruption from the irritable agronomist.

"It should be quite clear by now," Bell replied, "that it is my duty to conduct a search of these premises."

"You'll keep your grabbing little hands off our equipment!" Unexpectedly, it was Flexner who exploded. "It's all nonsense, and you know it. What would we steal from that *drug peddler*?"

Brenner's quiet laugh rasped into the appalled silence that followed. Flexner, enraged, took just one belligerent step toward the trillionaire and the commissioner.

"Sergeant!" barked Lieutenant Nealey, and a noncom, unslinging his carbine like an automaton, aimed from the hip at the chemist. Flexner stopped in his tracks, red-faced with anger, and said bitterly: "So he can make the damned stuff and welcome, but all hell breaks loose if somebody hooks it."

"For the last time—" began Bell, exasperatedly, and then interrupted himself. He drew a paper from his parka and handed it to Tony. "The warrant," he said shortly.

Tony passed it to O'Donnell and there was a long, foot-tapping minute while the ex-lawyer studied the document.

At last O'Donnell said, "According to this, you plan to open our shipping crates and break into our process ovens. Is that correct?" He was pale with anger and worry.

"Correct," said the commissioner, while Brenner shrugged helplessly. "Marcaine could, of course, be concealed from the Bloodhound in lead-insulated containers."

"Then you *are* aware," said Tony, "that we manufacture radioactive materials?"

"I am."

"And you realize that there are certain procedures required by law for the handling of such materials?"

"*Doctor* Hellman! Has it slipped your mind that I represent the law you're speaking of?"

"Not at all." Tony was determined not to lose his temper. "But I could hardly expect you to carry in your mind all the time the innumerable petty details that must come under your administration. And it happens that I represent, here in the Colony, the observance of the laws under which our radioactives license was granted. I think that as chief radiological monitor for the Colony, I should be permitted to accompany your men in any search.

"That's out of the question." The commissioner dismissed the request impatiently. "The license you spoke of is, as we both know, a grade-B atomics license, permitting you to handle only materials well below the safety level, so I see no reason for any unnecessary fuss. Lieutenant..."

"Just a minute, please, Commissioner," Tony interrupted frantically. It was perfectly true that as the direct representative on Mars of the Panamerican World Federation, Bell was judge, jury, and corner cop, all rolled into one. Redress was as far away as Earth, and the road to Earth was the rocket from which Bell had the power to bar them.

"Don't you realize," Tony pleaded, "that our materials stay below the safety level only because we have a well-established monitoring procedure? If you insist on breaking into process ovens and opening crates without my supervision, Sun Lake cannot assume responsibility for any dangerous radioactivity."

"I understand that, Doctor," Bell answered crisply. "Any handling of radioactives in my presence is obviously done on *my* responsibility, not yours. The commission, oddly enough, is supplied with its own monitors. I do not believe we will require your assistance. Carry on, Lieutenant."

NEALEY took a reluctant step forward. Choking back his anger, Tony said flatly: "In my opinion you are exceeding your authority. Your men will interfere with our processing and break open our shipment crates. Our machinery is so delicately adjusted that any kind of handling by untrained people could easily destroy it. And we've spent the last month packing our outgoing shipments for the next rocket. You know what the law is for packing radioactives. If you broke open our shipments, the rocket would be here and gone before we had the stuff decontaminated and repacked. It would be ruinous for the Colony."

He saw out of the corner of his eye that O'Donnell was unwillingly shaking this head. Bell was the law on Mars. And Bell wasn't even bothering to answer.

"At least give us a chance to look into it," urged the doctor. "Maybe we have got a bad apple. We'll find him if we do. You can't wreck us just on suspicion."

"More than suspicion is involved here," said Bell. "The findings of the Ground Tracing Device, M-27, known as the Bloodhound, when operated by a qualified commissioned officer, are accepted as completely legal evidence in all authorized world courts."

They watched bleakly as the lieutenant began to assemble the dipole handle, power pack and meters of the Bloodhound.

"I have a suggestion," said Brenner. "Under Title Fifteen of the Interplanetary Affairs Act—"

"*No,*" said O'Donnell. "We don't want it."

Brenner said persuasively, "If you're clean, there's nothing to worry about."

"Title Fifteen was never meant to be applicable to a case like this," O'Donnell crossfired. "It's one of those shotgun laws, like a conspiracy count—"

"That's enough," said the commissioner. "You can't have it both ways. As long as Mr. Brenner's willing, this is your notice; I'll confirm it in writing. Under Title Fifteen of the Interplanetary Affairs Act, I advise the Sun Lake Colony that you have until the next Shipment Day to produce the marcaine thief and the stolen marcaine or evidence of its disposal. If you fail to do so I will instruct the military to seal off Sun Lake Colony and a suitable surrounding area for a period of six months so that a thorough search can be conducted. Lieutenant, move your men out of here."

NEALEY snapped the half-platoon to attention and marched them through the Lab door. The unmilitary figures of the commissioner and the tall, angular drug maker followed them.

O'Donnell's face was grim. "It was written in the old days of one ship a year and never revised," he said. "'Sealed off means just that—nothing and nobody in, nothing and nobody out."

"But we're geared for four ships a year," said Flexner complainingly. "Shipment Day's only three weeks off. Rocket's due in ten days, two days unloading, one week overhaul and off she goes. We'd miss the next two rockets!"

"*We'd miss the next two rockets,*" Tony repeated, dazed. "Half a year without shipments coming in, half a year with out goods going out."

"He's trying to strangle us."

"It can't be legal," objected Flexner.

"It is. By the time it could be changed, the Colony'd be dead anyway."

"Even if we pulled through, we'd be poison to Earthside buyers— shipments arriving there half a year late."

"He's trying to strangle us," O'Donnell insisted doggedly.

"*How many OxEn pills have we got?*"

"What's Bell's angle? What's Brenner out for?"

"Bell's crooked. Everybody knows that."

"That's why they sent him to Mars."

"But what's his angle?"

Tony was still a doctor. To no one in particular he muttered, "I've got to check on the baby," and started out again on the road from the Lab to the huts with the spring gone from his knees.

# CHAPTER FOUR

THE living room was empty. Someone had tidied it, straightened the wall bunk where Jim had slept, and cleaned up the dirty dishes. Anna's long work-counter was bare, all the tools and materials stored away now in cupboards underneath. That alone made the room look deserted.

Tony wouldn't talk to the women about the commissioner and his trap. He'd try not to think about it; he'd tell himself it would work out somehow in the three weeks of grace they had—

The door to the hospital was open, but no sounds came from the other side. Polly was asleep then, and Anna had gone out.

Tony drew a cup of water from the tap on the plastic keg, and set it to boil on the stove with a pinch of "coffee" makings—the ground, dried husks of a cactus-like plant that grew in some abundance on the desert. At its best the stuff had approximately the flavor of a five-day old brew of Earth-import brick coffee, made double strength to start with and many times reheated. It did contain a substance resembling caffeine, but to Tony it often seemed the greatest single drawback to human life on Mars.

Automatically he checked the time; the stuff was completely undrinkable if it brewed even a fraction of a minute too long. Before he put any food on to cook, he stepped into the hospital half of his hut for a look at Polly.

"Well!"

"Hello, Tony." Anna barely looked up to acknowledge his presence. She had moved the baby's basket next to Polly's bed and was bending over, peering into it.

"We were watching the baby," she unnecessarily told him, and promptly returned to that fascinating occupation.

"Just what is there to watch so hard?" the doctor demanded.

"He's..." Anna finally transferred her attention; she made a helpless little gesture and smiled with an irritating air of mystery. "He's very interesting," she said finally.

"Women," Tony exploded. "Sit for hours watching a baby sleep."

"But he's not sleeping," Anna protested.

"He's hardly slept all morning," Polly added proudly. "I've never seen such a lively baby!"

"And how would *you* know what he was doing all morning? When I left here you were asleep yourself, and Anna was all ready to go home and do likewise. Where's Jim?"

"He wanted to go to work," Anna explained. "He was—embarrassed, I guess, about staying out. I told him I'd stay. I wasn't really sleepy anyhow."

"You weren't sleepy? After twenty-six hours awake?" He tried hard to be stern. "So you sent Jim off to work to give him a chance to brag about his baby. You weren't sleepy, and neither was Polly, and strangely enough, neither was the newcomer here. Well, as of now, all three of you are just too sleepy to stay awake, you understand?"

Purposefully, he moved the basket to the far side of the room. What they said was true, he noticed; young Kandro was wide awake and kicking, apparently perfectly content. Not even crying. Strange behavior for a newborn.

"Come on, Anna, clear out." He put the baby down, and turned to Polly. "I'll give you ten minutes to get to sleep before I stuff some more sedative into you," he informed her. "Didn't anybody ever tell you you're supposed to be tired now?"

"All right." Polly refused to be ruffled. "He's an awfully nice baby, Tony." She settled herself more comfortably under the thin cover, and was asleep almost before they left the room.

"Now go on home," Tony told Anna. "I'm going to make myself some breakfast. Wait a minute. Did you eat anything?"

"I did, thanks." Abruptly she turned toward him, and made a conscious effort at concentration. The abstracted look left her eyes and she was brisk and alert as usual. "What about Polly? Don't you have to go out again? Somebody should be here."

"I'll get hold of Gladys when I leave. Don't worry about it."

"All right." She smiled at his impatient tone. "You don't have to push me. I'll go." She picked up the heavy parka she had worn on her way over there, in the early morning hours the day before. At the door, she turned back. "You're still coming over for dinner tomorrow night?"

"You couldn't keep me away," he assured her.

She came back into the room, and took a ration slip from the drawer where Tony kept them. "You pay in advance, you see," she added, smiling.

"And well worth it." Tony held the door for her, a habit he never quite lost even in the atmosphere of determined sexual equality that pervaded the Colony. Not until she was gone did he remember the coffee he'd started.

It was ruined, of course, and now he'd have to do without it. Water was too scarce, still, to waste because of carelessness. But coffee or no, he was hungry. He found a dish of barley gruel, left over from a lunch he'd cooked for himself two days ago, heated it, and spooned it down hastily. Then, with a final check to make sure Polly was really asleep, he set out for the Poroskys' house to find Gladys.

At fourteen, Gladys was the oldest child in the Colony—none of the adult members were over thirty-five years—and her status was halfway between that of a full working member and the errand-girl position her younger sister occupied. She was old enough to assist almost anybody at anything, still too young to take full responsibility for a job. Now, Tony found, she was over at the Radcliff's, sitting with Joan. It was his next stop anyhow.

\* \* \*

IF THEY did have to leave Mars, it would have at least one good effect: the life of Joan Radcliff would be saved. But, the doctor reflected, she'd die of a broken heart as surely as she was dying on Mars of...whatever it was. His star patient, the thin, intense girl lived only for the success of the colony on Mars. And life on Mars was killing her.

When he knew what she had, maybe, Tony would know how to cure it. Meanwhile, all he could do was make a faithful record of its symptoms and try out treatments till he found one that would work. Or until he was sure none of them worked.

It was like an allergy and it was like heart disease and it was like fungus infection where you couldn't put your finger on the parasite. The biochem boys back on Earth would lick it some day as they had licked dozens of others, but right now Tony didn't even have a name to tag it by.

Joan came down with it two days after she and her husband, Hank, arrived on the shuttle rocket. If the doctor didn't find some relief for her soon, it looked as though she would have to go back on the next one.

Tony bit hard on the stem of his empty pipe, slipped it into a pocket, and walked into the bedroom of the Radcliff house.

"How's it going?" He put his bag on the table and sat down on the edge of Joan's bunk.

"Not so good." She had to work for a smile; a good colonist is always cheerful. "I just can't seem to get settled. It's as if the bed was full of stale cracker crumbs and broken shells..."

She began to cough, short dry barks that rattled her thin body, feather-light on Mars, against the bed.

*Cracker crumbs and seashells!*

Sometimes it seemed that the damned condition reached her mind too. It was hard to distinguish between the delirium of fever, the depression of fatigue and confinement and the distortions of mental disease.

The spasm had passed. She battled the itch to cough again and counter-irritate her raw, constricted throat. Tony, watching, knew the guts it took. He had told her that a cough can be controlled that she should control it because the spasms endangered her already overtaxed heart. But even before he warned her, she was fighting: a good colonist guarded her health; it was a colony asset.

Everything for the Colony. And for Henry, her husband. Joan was one of those thin, intense young people who give their lunch money to Causes. It had taken a lot of skipped lunches to get her and Henry to Mars as shareholders, Tony realized. But she could never have been satisfied with less—the non-voting position of "drop-in," for instance. She had to identify herself with a heroic unpopular abstraction, or life wasn't worth living.

Tony had more than a touch of it himself. All of them in the Colony did. But the doctor doubted that he had enough of it to fight against the brief, delusive relief of a coughing fit in order to get well imperceptibly sooner and go back to work for the Colony.

*If* she got well.

Tony opened his little black bag ritually, his mind flashing back to the intern days when he had perfected the gesture: the grave and kindly set of face, the brooding moment of introspection over the open mouth of the learned tool chest. Too bad; too bad you couldn't cut whatever it was out of her suffering body and bury it; or bore a hole in her and let the poison run down a drain. There was no tool waiting for him in the open bag with which to stop the girl's own chemistry from fighting against her flesh.

JOAN whispered, "Got some magic in there for me?" A good colonist is always cheerful; the great days are ahead.

"Middling magic, anyhow." He put the thermometer in her dry mouth, and peeled back the blanket. There were new red bumps on her arms and legs; that was one phase of it he could treat. He smoothed on ointment, and changed the dressings on the old puffy sore spots.

"That's good," she whispered gratefully as he took the thermometer from her mouth. "So cool..." Her temperature was up another two-tenths over yesterday's 101.3 And the thermometer was not even moist.

Another injection, then. He hated to use them, as long as he wasn't sure of the nature of the disease, but one of his precious stores of anti-histamines seemed to give a little relief. It was temporary, of course, and he ardently hoped it was doing no permanent damage...but it did shrink the inflamed watery bladder that her throat lining had become under the action of killer-enzymes. She would be able to breathe more easily now, and to sleep. It might last as long as twenty-four hours.

One more day, and by that time Hank would be back with a little of the latest Earth-developed hormone fraction.

Tony had heard that Benoway, over at Mars Machine Tool, was using it with startlingly good results for serious burns and infections. It just might turn the trick; there was no way to know till they tried.

Joan's eyes closed and the doctor sat there staring at the parchment-like lids, her chapped and wrinkled lips. Tony grimaced; she was obviously being a fool.

He rose noiselessly and crossed the room to the water jug. When he came back he spoke her name softly: "Joan?"

Her eyes opened and he held out the glass.

"Here's some water."

"Oh, thank you..." She sighed dreamily, reaching out—but she snatched her hand back. "No, I don't need any." She was wide-awake now and she looked frightened. "I don't really want it," she pleaded, but her eyes never left the glass.

"Take it, drink it and don't be silly," he snapped at her. Then, gently, he propped up her shoulders with his arm and held the glass to her lips. She sipped hesitantly at first, then drank with noisy gulps.

"What are you trying to do to yourself? Didn't I order extra water rations for you?"

She nodded, shamefaced.

"I'm going to have some words with Hank when he comes back, to make sure you drink enough."

"It's not his fault," she said quickly. "I didn't tell him. Water's so precious and the rest of you are working and I'm just lying here. I don't *deserve* any extra water."

He handed her the glass, refilled, and propped her up again.

"Shut up and drink this."

She did, with a combination of guilt and delight plain on her face.

"That's better. Hank ought to be back tomorrow with the medication from Mars Machine Tool. *I'll* tell him about the water this time, and I don't want any nonsense from you about not drinking it. *You're* a lot more valuable to the Colony than a few quarts of water."

"ALL right, Doctor." her voice was very small. "Do you really think he'll be back tomorrow?"

Tony shrugged with calculated indecision. Mars Machine Tool was almost a thousand miles away, and allowing time for food and rest, Radcliff should be back before midday tomorrow. But Joan's question was so pathetically eager, he didn't dare sound too sure. It was even harder when she opened her eyes again, while he was closing his bag, to ask: "Doctor, will it do any good, do you think? You never told me the name of it."

"Oh," he answered vaguely, "it's just something new." Just as he knew about Hank, he knew perfectly well the sixteen-syllable name of the hormone fraction. But he was afraid that Joan would know it, too, from sensational press stories, and that she would expect a miracle. The doctor was expecting only another disappointment, another possibility ruled out, another step toward the day when he'd have to break the girl's heart by ordering her back to Earth.

"I won't be able to leave anyone with you for a while," he told her as he left. "I need Gladys to stay with Polly Kandro. But remember, if you need anything, or want anything, *use the intercom. Call somebody to do it for you.* Your heart isn't in any shape for exercise."

She nodded without lifting her head from the pillow, and smiled gratefully. Things would be better, Tony thought, when Hank was back.

The sun was beating down more strongly when he stepped outside. It was past mid-morning already, and he had to get over to Nick Cantrella's: give him official clearance on the burned arm, and talk to him about Bell's threat. But there were other patients, and they needed treatment more urgently than Nick. Better to get through with them first. Then when he got to Cantrella, they'd be able to buckle down to the quarantine problem.

## CHAPTER FIVE

A YOUNG girl's head was splitting with the agony of her infected supraorbital sinus, but she was no whiner and even managed a smile.

"I've got a present for you, Dorothy," he said. "It's from a girl who was your age a couple of centuries ago. Her name was Tracy. I don't know whether it was her last or first name, but she gave it to this stuff." He held up a hypo filled with golden fluid. "It's called bacitracin. They found out that this Tracy's body fought off some infections, so they discovered how it did the trick and wrapped it up in this stuff—a good, effective antibiotic."

She hardly noticed the needle. *Misdirection is as useful to a doctor as it is to a stage magician*, he thought wryly.

A middle-aged man who should have known better was recovering nicely from his hernia operation.

"I still say, Oscar, that you shouldn't have let me fix it up. You would have been a medical marvel—The Man Who Got Ruptured on Mars. I could have had you stuffed, got you a grand glass case right next to the door at some medical museum on Earth. Maybe a neon sign. You got a nice repair job, though I say it myself, but you're throwing away worldwide medical fame. The Man Who Tried to Lift a Lead Shipping Crate barehanded! I can see it now in all the textbooks. You sure you don't want me to undo you again?"

"All right, Doc," grinned Oscar, red-faced. "You made your point. If I see anybody even looking as though he's going to lift a gutbuster, I'll throw him down and sit on him until the crane arrives. Satisfy you?"

A not-quite-young woman suffered from headaches, lower back pains, sleeplessness and depression. Poker-faced, the doctor told her:

"Mrs. Beyles, you're the most difficult medical problem—a maladjusted person. I wouldn't be that direct if we were on Earth, but this is Sun Lake. We can't have you drinking our water and eating our food if you don't pay for it in work. What you want, whether or not you admit it to yourself, is to get off Mars, and I'm going to oblige you. If you knew what Joan Radcliff is going through to stay—never mind. No, I will not give you any sleeping pills. If you want to sleep, go out and work until you're too tired to do anything else."

Was he right? He wondered. He knew the woman would never believe him and would hate him forever, but it was another kind of surgery that had to be done—fortunately, not often. The woman would either change her attitude, thereby losing her ills and becoming the asset to the Colony that her strapping frame and muscles should make her, or out she would go. It was brutal, it was profit-and-loss, it was utterly necessary.

AND so to Nick Cantrella at last, thank Heaven. Heaven had often been thanked in the colony for Nick's arrival. He was the born leader, the inspired and unorthodox electronics man who hadn't garnered the sheaf of degrees needed for a halfway decent job on an Earth cluttered with bargain counter Ph.D.s.

In the Colony he had signed up as a maintenance and setup man, but spent so much of his time troubleshooting that he was finally relieved of the routine part of his work. Just recently he had been promoted to chief of maintenance, purchasing and repairs of all Lab equipment. His new dignity hadn't kept him out of trouble. He was home with a nasty chemical burn in his arm acquired far outside the line of duty.

Tony didn't know whether he was glad or sorry Nick had missed the session with Bell and Brenner. Nick could think on his feet, but it was an even chance that Brenner's oily sympathy and Bell's open contempt of the Colony would have goaded him into thinking with his fists.

"Tony!" Nick yelled as he came in the door. "Gracey was here with the news. It's the biggest thing that ever hit Sun Lake! It'll be the making of us!"

"Let's see the arm, Combustible," said Tony dryly. "Medicine first, politics later."

Nick fumed as the doctor removed the dressing and examined the site of the burn—now just a good scar, painless, non-disabling and uncomplicated, due to quick poulticing and a heavy coat of eschar.

Tony slapped Nick on the back. "Okay, Fearless," he said. "You can go back to work. Inhale chlorine. Drop pigs of osmium on your toes. Sit on a crateful of radiophosphorus and get a buttful of geigers. Stir nitric acid with your forefinger. There's *lots* of things you haven't tried yet; maybe you'll like them—who knows?"

"So it splashed," Nick grinned, flexing his arm. "Damn good thing I wasn't there this morning. I would've thrown those bums out. Do you realize that this is the biggest break we've ever had? Why, man, we should have been praying for something just like this to happen. We *never* would have cut the Earth tie on our own and given up luxuries like Earthside medicine. I'm glad Bell's kicking us into it. All we have to do is retool for OxEn." His face glowed. "What a beautiful job that's going to be. Those boys in the Lab can do anything—with my machinery, of course," he added.

"You can't do it, Nick." Tony shook his head ruefully. "Ask any of the biochem boys. I went on the guided tour through the Kelsey plant in Louisville while I was thinking over joining the Colony. It left me footsore and limping because that plant is ten stories high and covers four city blocks. They operate more than 500 stages of concentration and refinement to roll those little pink pills out of protoculture. And the first couple of hundred stages have to be remote-control sterile. There isn't as much glass on all of Mars as the Kelsey people had just in their protoculture tanks. It's out, boy. *Out.*"

"Hell, we'll rig up something. With all the crooks on Mars, we can make something they want and swap it for OxEn across Bell's search cordon. Don't worry about it, Tony. This should have happened a long time ago. On our own."

"You're missing something. What if we *do* catch a marcaine thief and the hoard and turn them over to Bell?"

NICK was thunderstruck. "You mean you think it wasn't a frame-up? One of our guys?"

"We can't rule it out until we've looked."

"Yeah, it *could* happen. Well, if you'll kindly write out my medical discharge, I'll get a majority together and put it in the form of a motion that we hold a shakedown inspection of the Colony."

"There's an easier way, maybe," Tony said. "Anybody who toted that much marcaine got gowed up on the stuff, whether he knows it or not. Its micron dust-fused ampoules are about the only thing that hold it without leakage, and this was in bulk. Also, the thief might be a regular marcaine addict as well as wanting the stuff to sell."

"So," Nick grinned, "we line everybody up and just see which one does this." He went into a comedy routine of tics and twitches and strange yapping noises. "You know that won't work," he wound up soberly. "There isn't any way to smell out a markie."

"*Practically* no way," Tony corrected him. "That's why Brenner's a trillionaire and that's why marcaine gives stiff competition to Earthside narcotics in spite of the extra cost. The damned stuff doesn't affect you so people notice. You become an addict, you take your belt as often as you please, and you can live in your own private sweet-dream world without anybody the wiser until—blooie!—you drop dead from failure of the cardiac node to keep your heart pumping."

"You said *practically* no way," Nick reminded him. "What's the catch? Have you got an angle?"

"I get my electroencephalograph out and read up on the characteristic brainwave patterns of marcaine users. Then I run the e.e.g. over everybody who could possibly have carried the stuff from Brenner to here. You want to line that up for me?"

Nick nodded glumly. "Sure," he said, "but you won't find any markies here. It's a frameup, I tell you... Hello, honey! What are you doing home at this hour of the day? What's all that junk for?"

TONY turned to see Marian Cantrella, Nick's blonde and beautiful wife, pushing her way through the door, her arms full of soft white cloth, scissors, heat-sealer, and paper patterns.

"You'll be witness, won't you, Tony, when I testify that I only left home because he didn't want me here?" Marian turned large violet eyes from the doctor to her husband and back again. "On second thought," she concluded, "you're no better than he is. *Could* either one of you big, *strong* men stop gaping and give me a hand with this—stuff?"

Nick jumped up and relieved her of some of her bundles. "What's it all about?" He fingered the fine cloth curiously.

"Baby shirts, nightgowns, and diapers," Marian said composedly. "Are you all through pawing it?"

"Oh, for the Kandro kid." But he didn't relinquish the material. "Where'd the cloth come from?"

"I think they just ran it off." Marian took the heat-sealer from him and plugged it in to the house battery to warm up. She cleared a space on the table and laid out the patterns to study. "What's the matter?" she asked. "Something wrong with it?"

"No, it's a nice job." He brought the bolt of cloth over to the table and spread it out, then carefully pulled a thread loose. "But they should have replaced the extrusion nozzle. See that line there—there on the side—where it looks irregular?"

Tony went over to look at the thread Nick was holding up to the light. He couldn't see anything wrong with it, and Marian confessed she couldn't, either.

"It's there," Nick told them. "It means a worn nozzle. But it's not a bad job. Who did the setup?"

"For heaven's sake," Marian exploded. "*I* don't know who did it! They handed it to me and said go home and make tiny garments, so I went."

"Okay, baby," Nick soothed her. "I just thought you might know." He turned to Tony as Marian began cutting off squares from the bolt for diapers. "I don't see how they had a machine free for it," he fretted. "Every piece of equipment in the shop was scheduled for full time until Shipment. Well—," he stopped himself. "I guess it doesn't matter anyhow. From here on out we can pretty much stop worrying every time we need to use a piece of the Lab for Colony goods. The days of plenty have arrived—extra underwear and new dinner plates all around."

"Sure," the doctor agreed sourly. "All the pajamas you want—and no OxEn. Tell me, Marian, what are the women saying about this marcaine business?"

"Same as the men, I guess." She tested the heat-sealer on a corner of the first diaper, and turned the dial for more heat. "It'll blow over. Even if this shipment does get held up, it'll straighten out. Kind of a shame if we're cordoned while the rocket's in, though."

SHE tried the sealer again, gave a small satisfied grunt, then began running it deftly along the cut edges, leaving a smooth perfect selvedge behind.

"I was hoping we'd get a look at Douglas Graham," she added. "I think he's *wonderful*."

"Hah?" demanded Nick, starting. "Oh, the *This Is* man. My rival. He should be honored to be my rival."

"What's going on?" asked Tony. "Is it a family joke?"

"Douglas Graham's a national joke," said Nick. "Now that he's going to gunth Mars, that makes him an interplanetary joke."

"Oh, the writer," Tony remembered. The rocket doctor had told him last trip that Graham would be aboard the next.

"He's wonderful," said Marian. "I just loved *This Is Eurasia*. All those dictators, and the Cham of Tartary and the history, he made it sound so exciting—just like a story."

*"This Is Mars,"* said Nick sonorously. "Chapter One, Page One, The Story of the Sun Lake Colony, or, A Milestone in the History of Mankind."

"Do you think he really will write us up?" asked Marian. "I mean if that silly marcaine business doesn't keep him away?"

"No, pet. We'll be ignored or maybe he'll take a few digs at us. His books run first as serials in *World Welfare*, and *World Welfare* isn't interested in co-op colonists. It is interested in Pittco #3 over the hill, I'll bet you, by the way Pittco advertises. He'll probably play up all the industrial colonies as big smash-hits for free enterprises and not mention things like the Pittco red-light house."

MARIAN'S lips tightened. "I don't think it's *decent*," she said.

"Right," agreed Nick soberly. "I'll tell Madame Rose tonight. Haven't been over for days. I'll tell her my wife doesn't understand me and doesn't think her girls are decent. Want to come along and make a night of it, Tony?"

"Ump," said Tony. If he was any judge, Marian's sense of humor didn't go that far.

"That's not what I meant," she cried indignantly. "I meant it wasn't decent for him to hide things like that and—oh, you're joking… Well, I don't believe he would do it. I've read his books and they're *good*."

"Have you got any of Graham's stuff around?" Tony asked hastily. "I don't think I ever read any."

"I shouldn't take time out," said Marian, a little sulkily, "but—"

SHE put down the sealer and shooed Tony off the trunk he'd been sitting on. A considerable quantity of wool socks and underwear turned up before she hit the right level. She handed over a conventional onionskin export edition.

Tony read at random:

The Cham's black eyes met mine with a gaze hypnotic in its intensity. The corners of his mouth drew up in a smile. The Cham spoke, and the front of his plum-colored silk robe embroidered with three-toed dragons in gold and silver thread rose and fell as he gestured for emphasis.

These are the words of the man who rules over the twenty-five million souls that hold the lifeline between America's frontier on the Yang-Tse Kian River and her allies in the Middle East: "Please convey to the people of your country my highest esteem and warmest assurances that the long peace between our nations shall never be broken without cause by me."

The significance of this—

Tony handed the book back. "I don't think I've been missing much," he said.

"When you've read one, you've read 'em all," Nick agreed. "All those gunthers are the same."

Marian was still digging through the trunk, fascinated at the forgotten things she was turning up. It was surprising how little used were most of the items they had found essential to include in their limited baggage when they left Earth.

"Here's something," she laughed. "I used to read it back on Earth, and I thought it would be so useful here..."

She held out an onionskin pamphlet titled in red: *The Wonders of Mars*, by Red Sand Jim Granata, Interplanetary Pioneer.

"I remember standing for the longest time with an extra lipstick in one hand and this in the other, and they both weighed exactly the same, and I decided..." She broke out in another peal of laughter. "I decided to be *practical* and take *this*. What I wouldn't give for that lipstick now."

Nick took the book from her and riffled through the pages with a reminiscent smile. "It's terrible, Tony," he said. "Get these chapter headings: 'Mining for Emeralds,' 'Trapped in a Sandstorm'—Red Sand Jim should wish the air on Earth was as clear as the heart of a Martian sandstorm—'Besieged by Brownies in the Rimrock Hills.'"

*"What?"* demanded the doctor, incredulously.

"'Besieged by Brownies in the Rimrock Hills.' If you don't believe me, look. The Brownies, it says here, were a constant menace to intrepid interplanetary pioneers like Red Sand Jim because they killed people and stole their babies and things like that. They didn't often see one—"

"Naturally."

"NATURALLY, Doctor, naturally. But they were little people who didn't wear shoes or clothes, it says here—*which* reminds me." He closed the book. "I was out at the caves yesterday—took a ride with one of the prospectors. We've never really looked into the caves, and I had nothing better to do while you were teaching me safety precautions, so I wandered around some, and found kids' footprints in the entrance to one of them."

"They take the goats out there to graze sometimes," Tony said.

"That's not it. Looks like they've been going barefoot, and I don't think they ought to be allowed—"

"They certainly shouldn't!" Marian was indignant. "Why, they could *hurt* themselves. And they shouldn't be allowed in those caves either."

"They're not," Tony said grimly. "They have strict orders to stay away from the caves. But I never thought they'd be screwy enough to try going barefoot. I'll have to tell them about it."

"Tell them good," Nick urged him. "There's a lot of rock out there, and a lot of dangerous surface salts."

"I wish I knew some way to make it stick," the doctor said, worriedly. "Once those kids get a notion in their heads—if they still hang around the caves after listening to old man Learoyd's horror stories—I don't know."

"Don't take it so hard." Nick couldn't stay serious long. "Maybe it wasn't the kids. Could be it's Brownies."

"Very funny. I'll pass the word to the mothers that there shouldn't be any barefoot boy stuff on Mars. I've got enough trouble without frostbitten toes, lacerations and mineral poisoning."

"'You better hope they're Brownie prints, Tony. That'd be easier to handle than teaching our pack of kids."

"Look who's talking. I'll thank you to line up that vote on an e.e.g. test for marcaine now while I dig up my medical references.

Also—" he got up briskly—"if there's more trouble coming, I better take care of myself while I can. Lunch'll be all gone if I don't get there soon."

Tony had small zest for the communal meals shared by most of the unmarried members of the settlement. Pooling rations and taking turns at the work did make it easier to get decent meals; but the atmosphere was, inevitably, one of noisy good-fellowship. The doctor would have preferred a quieter and more restful arrangement. He thought wistfully for a moment of the comradeship that existed between Nick and his wife. On second thought, it would hardly be worth it, having to get married in order to have his meals at home.

## CHAPTER SIX

FORTY years in the life of a planet is nothing at all, especially when the planet is ancient Mars. It had been that long since the first Earth rocket had crashed at the southern apex of *Syrtis Major*—and remained there, a shining, rustless memorial with only the broad fractures in it's fuel tanks to tell its story to those who came after.

Forty years, almost, since the first too-hopeful colonists followed, three thousand doomed souls. Their Earth-bred bodies, less durable than the flimsiest of their constructions, were already rotted to the skeletons when a belated relief ship came with the supplies without which they would have starved to death.

Forty years, now, of slow growth but rapid change, during, which a barren world had played host to successively, a handful of explorers; a few score prospectors and wanderers-at-large; a thousand or so latter-day homesteaders, with their lean, silent women; and finally—after OxEn—the new industrial colonies, none of them more than five years old.

The explorers had disappeared: gone back to Earth to lecture and write, or blended completely into the Martian scene; the prospectors and frontiersmen, most of them, had died; but the colonists, determined to stay on, drew fresh blood continually from the lifeline at Marsport—the quarterly rockets from Earth.

Sun Lake City Colony, alone among those who had come to Mars, wanted nothing more than to cut, once and forever that vital tie with Earth. But it was too soon, still too soon; the Colony was not yet strong enough to live if the umbilical cord were severed.

And the colonists knew it. After lunch they gathered in the Lab, every last man, woman, and child. Tony rose from the black box of the electroencephalograph to count heads.

"We're one over," he told Nick. "Polly's in the hospital, Joan's home, Hank's at Mars Machine Tool or on his way back. Tad's on radio shack. Who's the spare?"

"Learoyd," said Nick. "And I've got Tad messaging Machine Tool to confirm Hank's whereabouts for the last four days."

"Okay. I'll get Tad later."

A whiskery man who looked as though he was pushing 90 stormed up to the doctor.

"It ain't your business whether I take a sniff of marcaine now and again and it ain't for you to say I stole any hundred kilos if you do find I use it once in a way. *Bunch of greeners.*"

"Calm down, Learoyd," sighed the doctor.

"*Greener,*" taunted the old-timer. "Call yourself Marsmen…"

"You can call us anything you want, Learoyd," said the doctor. "Only we've got to straighten this thing out. When did you last take marcaine? It won't—"

"You don't even know where you are," quavered the old man, "Lake-us Sole-us, my eye. You're right on the edge of Ryan's Plain and you don't even know it. He was here first and he had a right to name it! Old Jim Ryan…"

PATIENTLY Tony tried to explain: "Brenner says somebody stole the hundred kilos of marcaine two days ago. It could have been any of us. You were around, so we've got to be able to tell Commissioner Bell—"

"Another greener—a politician greener. The Law on Mars." Learoyd's voice was heavily satirical. "When there was twenty, thirty of us, we didn't need no law; we didn't go around thieving. We got here ahead of you all, you and the farmers, too. What for did you have to come crowding in?"

"*When* did you take that last belt of marcaine?"

The old pork-and-beaner sighed brokenly. "It was more'n two years ago. I ain't got money for marcaine, I ain't a panhandler and I do a good job hauling for you, don't I?"

"Sure, Learoyd."

"Then why do you have to come bothering me? We was here

*first."* He collapsed into the chair by the black box, grieving for the past of the red planet, before this damn OxEn, when Marsworthy lungs were a man's passport to adventure where no man had ever been before, where a mountain range was your mountain range and nobody else's. Where Jim Ryan died in the middle of great, flat, spreading Ryan's Plain, starved to death out there when his half-track broke down.

Learoyd chuckled, not feeling the electrodes they were putting to his head. He'd got off a good one—five years on Mars and these ten greeners landed. They wanted to he heroes, the little greeners, but he told them. He sure told them.

"Call yourselves Marsmen? In six months half of you'll be dead. And the other half'll wish they was."

Jim Granata was in that bunch—a sly one, pumping him, making notes, making sketches, but he wasn't a Marsman. He went back to Earth and made him a pot full of money with books and—what did they call it? Granata's Combined Interplanetary Shows. Little Jim, he called himself Red Sand Jim Granata, but he was never a Marsman.

The Marsmen came first. Sam Welch surveyed Royal Range, the Palisades. Amby McCoy—he got killed by eating Mars plants; they found him with his food run out, curled up with the agony of poisoning. A thousand dollars a day they got then, when a thousand dollars was a thousand.

It was in '07 he told off those greeners twenty-eight years ago. Only one rocket every couple years then, and sometimes they didn't get through. Jim Granata, he never set foot on Mars after '18 with his money and all; he wasn't a Marsman. They were here first. Nobody could take that away from them.

Sam Welch, Amby McCoy, Jim Ryan. Why not die too? Learoyd wondered bitterly. A thousand dollars a day they paid him when a thousand dollars was a thousand, and look at him now. Where had it gone? Why was he living by hauling dirt for the greeners when he had been here first? His lip trembled and he wiped his mouth.

SOMEBODY was shaking his shoulder and saying: "That's all, Learoyd. You're in the clear. Nothing to worry about."

The old man slouched through the crowd and out of the Lab, shaking his head and muttering what sounded like curses.

Tony hadn't been very far from hoping that Learoyd would turn out to be the thief. The law would have to go easy on him and it would clean up the Colony's problem.

Colonist after colonist seated himself in the chair and cleared himself by revealing marcaine-negative brainwaves to the e.e.g. Tony didn't dare to think of what it meant. The last of them, the boy from the radio shack, was relieved to take his turn.

"That's the lot," Tony reported to Nick when young Tad, too, was cleared by the machine, and had gone back to his job.

Cantrella refused to share the doctor's gloom. "It's just what we needed," he insisted, smacking his fist into his palm. "Face it, man. There isn't any marcaine thief. Bell thinks he can run us off Mars by cutting off our import-export. *Let* them cut us off! We'll barter for OxEn. We'll damn well do without the Earthside enzymes and immunizers. We'll get tough with Mars, lick it on its own ground! We'll have to eventually; why not right now?"

"I don't know, Nick. I think you're going too fast," Tony demurred. "Look at old Learoyd—he's *us*, only a little worse."

"The pork-and-beaners imported their food, clothes, fuel, and look at them," Nick insisted. "They failed. They didn't strike roots. They didn't adapt."

"I don't know, Nick," the doctor repeated unhappily. "I've got to go see Polly and the baby now."

* * *

TONY lugged the e.e.g. back to his hospital-shack and found Anna holding the hand of a white, trembling, terrified Polly. Polly's other arm was around the baby, clutching the red-faced little thing as if it were on the edge of a precipice.

Without a word he took the child, snapped on his stethoscope and sounded its heart, which was normal. In spite of the red-faced creature's squirming, the minute oxygen mask was in place.

Baffled, he replaced the baby and demanded of the women: "What's wrong?"

"I have to work," said Anna abruptly. She patted Polly's hand and slipped out.

"I saw something," Polly whispered. Her eyes were crazy.

Tony sat on the side of the bed and picked up the hand Anna had been holding. It was cold.

"What did you see, Polly?" he asked kindly. "Spots on the baby? A rash?"

She disengaged her hand and pointed at the window in line with the bed and two meters from its foot.

"I saw a brownie. It wanted to steal my baby." She clutched the child again, not taking her eyes off the window.

Normally Tony would have been amused and not shown it. Under the strain of the day, he fought down a violent anger. The little idiot! At a time when the whole Colony was in real and deadly peril, she was making no effort to distinguish between a dream and reality.

"You must have drowsed off," he said, not as harshly as he felt. "It was just a nightmare. With your history, of *course* you're afraid that somehow you'll lose this baby, too. You've heard all this pork-and-beaner and homesteader nonsense about brownies, so in your dream your fear took that form. That's all there is to it."

Polly shook her head. "Gladys was staying with me," she recited monotonously, "and she had to go to that test in the Lab and she said she'd send somebody who'd been tested as soon as she got there. Just when I heard the door close, this face came up outside the window. It was a brownie face. It had big thin ears and big eyes, with thin eyebrows, and it was bald and leathery.

"It looked at me and then it looked at my baby. I screamed and screamed but it just looked at my baby. It wanted to steal my baby. And then it got down below the windowsill just before Anna came in. Even after she put my baby here with me, I couldn't stop shaking."

Anger was getting the better of him. "Do you realize that your story is perfectly ridiculous if you insist on claiming it really happened, but perfectly logical if you admit it was a dream?"

SHE began to cry and hug the baby. "I saw it! I saw it! I'm afraid…"

Tony relaxed; tears were the best medicine for her tension. To help them along, he rose and got her a sedative and a glass of water.

"Take this," he said, putting the capsule to her mouth.

"I don't want to go to sleep," she sniffled. But she swallowed it and in a minute or two felt under her pillow for a handkerchief.

When she had wiped her eyes and blown her nose, the doctor said quietly: "I can *prove* it was a dream. The brownies are just the kind of thing the pork-and-beaners and the homesteaders would invent to scare themselves with. And the myth got exploited in the Sunday supplements and on TV, of course. But there can't be any brownies because there isn't any animal life on Mars.

"We've been exploring this planet up, down and sideways for 40 years now. We found a weed you can make dope out of; we found you can make liquor out of Mars plants; we found a lot of ores and minerals. But not one trace of animal life. Think of it, Polly—40 years and *nobody has found any animal life on Mars.*"

She reasoned, a little fuzzy with the sedative: "Maybe brownies could stay out of people's way. If they're smart they could."

"That's right. But what did the brownies evolve from in that case? You know that if you have a higher form of life, it evolved from a lower form. Where are all the lower forms of life that evolved into brownies? There aren't any. Not so much as one puny little amoeba. So if there's no place the brownies could have come from, there are no brownies."

Her face relaxed a little, and Tony talked on doggedly. "You got a bad scare and no mistake. But you scared yourself, like the homesteaders that started this nonsense." A sudden notion struck him. He put it in the urgent file, and went on. "You were afraid your bad luck would catch up with you and take your baby away. This is Mars, so you symbolized it as a brownie. The vividness doesn't mean anything—you probably saw a scary picture in the papers of a baby-stealing Martian brownie and stored it in your memory, and out it popped at the right time."

Polly cracked a sleepy smile and said, "I'm sorry," and closed her eyes.

*She'll be all right,* thought Tony, *and it's a good thing it turned up to remind me of the homesteaders—Thaler? Toller?*

Whoever they were, the old couple on the wretched "farm" to the South. Toller, that was right. He hadn't seen them for a year, but he was going to see them today.

Anna was in the other, residential, half of the shack. "I think I talked her out of it," he said. "You'll stay here?"

"Yes. Where are you off for?" He was lugging the e.e.g. out again.

"That old couple, the Tollers. I wouldn't put the marcaine theft past them and they're close enough to our general area. Before the last dozen Sun Lakers arrived, I had enough time on my hands to run out and see how they were coming along. If I just tell them it's time for another checkup, I'm pretty sure I can persuade them to give me a brainwave reading. That may break the case."

He strapped the black box to his bicycle and set off.

*   *   *

THE Tollers were a different type from old Learoyd, and driven to Mars by a different urge. Learoyd had fancied himself an explorer and adventurer who would make a sudden strike and, after a suitably romantic life of adventure, retire to his wealth.

The Tollers laid the longer, slower-maturing plans of peasants: *In two years, when I have saved up seven schilling three groschen, I will buy Bauer's bull calf, which will service the cows of the village; Fritz by then will be big enough to take care of the work. Zimmerman, the drunkard, will go into debt to me for service of his cows and pledge his south strip, so Fritz need not marry his Eva. Schumacher's Gretel has a harelip but there's no escaping it—his west pasture adjoins mine...*

It hadn't worked out for the Tollers—the steady, upward trend of land values, the slow improvement of the soil, the dozen sons and daughters to work it, the growing village, town, city—

All that happened was they had scratched out a living, had one son and gone a little dotty from hardship. Both had Mars-worthy lungs. If she had not, Mrs. Toller would, like hundreds of other wives, have lived as matter-of-factly in an oxygen mask as her many-times-removed great-grandmother had lived in a sunbonnet.

The husband, by now, was stone-blind. Data from him and hundreds of others had helped to work out the protective shots against ultraviolet damage to the eyes, a tiny piece in the mosaic of research that had made real colonization at all possible.

Still, Tony dreaded visiting them. He didn't see their mangy goat, last of a herd that had been browsing wiregrass on his last trip. They must have slaughtered it to augment the scanty produce of their heavily manured kitchen garden.

He knocked on the door of the hut and went in, carrying the black box. Mrs. Toller was sitting in the dark, crammed little room's only chair. Toller was in bed.

"Why, it's Doctor Tony, Theron," the old lady explained to her husband. Not bad, thought Tony, since he hadn't been able to remember *their* names in a flash.

"Say hello to Doctor Tony, Theron. He brought us the mail."

"Mail? No, Mrs. Toller—" he began.

The old man started out of a light doze and demanded: "Did the boy write? Read me what he wrote."

"I didn't bring any mail," said Tony. "The rocket isn't due for two weeks."

"Junior will write in two weeks, Theron," she told her husband. "These are our letters to *him*," she said, producing three spacemailers from her bodice.

Tony started to protest, thought better of it, and glanced at them. All three were identical.

Our Dear Son,

How are you getting along? We are all well and hope you are well. We miss you here on the farm and hope that some day you will come back with a nice girl because one day it will all be yours when we are gone and it is a nice property in a growing section. Some day it will be all built up. Please write and tell us how you are getting along. We hope you are well and miss you.

Your Loving Parents

ON THE other side, the envelope side of spacemail blanks, Tony saw canceled fifty-dollar stamps and the address to "Theron Pogue Toller, Junior, R. F. D. Six, Texarkana, Texas, U. S. A., Earth." The return address was: "Mr. and Mrs. T. P. Toller, c/o Sun Lake City Colony, Mars." Stamped heavily on each was a large, red notice: "DIRECTORY SEARCHED, ADDRESSEE UNKNOWN, RETURNED TO SENDER."

The old man croaked, "Did the boy write?"

"I've come to give you a physical checkup," said Tony loudly, oppressed by the squalid walls and the senile dementia they housed.

"Isn't that nice of Doctor Tony, Theron?" asked Mrs. Toller, tucking the letters back into her dress. But the old man had fallen asleep again.

Tony dipped the electrodes on and joggled Toller awake for a reading. Marcaine-negative.

"We came in such a beautiful rocket ship," rambled Mrs. Toller as he put the e.e.g. on her. "It was quite an adventure, wasn't it, Theron? We were so young. Only 23 and 24, and we sold our place in

Missouri. It was such a lovely rocket we came in, a little one, not like the ones today, but this was before Mars got built up. We had quite a fright when one of the steering jets went bad while Mars was ahead, just like a big moon, and the poor crewmen had to go outside in their suits. It was quite an adventure, wasn't it, Theron?

"I often wonder, Doctor Tony, whether Junior has ever been back to the old place in Missouri. We had him our first year here, you know; he's 19. He wanted to see the Earth, didn't he, Theron? So when he was 17 we went all the way to Marsport to see him off. It was quite an adventure, wasn't it, Theron? And he sent us his address *right* away—"

Marcaine-negative brainwave.

He was too sickened to stay, and the bird-like chatter of Mrs. Toller never stopped as he said good-by and wheeled off to Sun Lake.

Their horrible deterioration during the past year into senility in the mid-forties answered Nick Cantrella's plan to establish the colony immediately as self-sustaining.

It simply couldn't be done. It was bad enough now—the damn dull, monotonous, primitive, regulated existence of the colony. How long was it now since he'd eaten an egg? How long since he'd drunk a cup of coffee, *real* coffee, with cream and sugar? How long since he had worn underclothes or had a real bath? How long since he'd had a highball after a good day's work? Or smoked his pipe without frantic puffing to keep it lit in the thin, cold, oxygen-poor air?

But life on Mars without even the minimum of supplies, immunization and adaptation shots was out of the question. If they asked his medical advice, his answer would have to be:

"If we are forbidden Earth supplies we must go back to Earth."

TONY groped in his pocket for his pipe, and clenched it between his teeth. All right then, he thought, go back to Earth—go back and get yourself a decent cup of coffee in the morning. Go back—

Back to what? To a clinic in an industrial town where he could give slapdash time-clocked attention to the most obvious ills of men, women, and children whose fears and deprivations began in the womb and ended in the grave? Cure a kid's pneumonia, then send him back to a drafty home again? Fix up an alcoholic factory-worker, and return him to the ugliness that will put him on dope or in the schizo ward next year? No, he'd tried the clinics already, and they wouldn't do.

Back to the office, maybe? An office like the one he'd had, briefly, in the penthouse of a New York apartment building. Take your patients one at a time, give them plenty of attention, they're easy to cure if you understand them—the ulcers and piles and false pregnancies, the thousand-and-one diseases of the body that grew out of the prevailing disease of the mind—fear.

Go back? He bit hard on his empty pipe. It would be consoling to stand again on Earth, and fill his pipe and light it, puff clouds of smoke—while he waited for the crowded, psychotic planet to blow itself up and put an end to man once and for all.

## CHAPTER SEVEN

HANK RADCLIFF shook Tony awake a little before dawn.

"I got the stuff, Doc," he grinned. "Just came in on foot from Pittco. The half-track broke down twenty miles out of Mars Machine on the way back, and I bummed a ride on a Pittco plane headed this way. The half-track's still at Rolling Mills and—"

The doctor shook his head groggily and thought of giving Hank hell for the abrupt awakening. But it was hard to stay mad at him, and Tony would have been roused by his alarm clock for the Lab check in a quarter-hour anyway. Did the Lab check matter? Did the medication for Joan matter? No. They were all heading back for Earth before long.

"Make me some coffee," he growled. "One minute by the clock."

He stretched, rolled out, shucked his pajama tops and gave himself a sponge bath with a cup of water that would mean one less cup of Coffee for him today. Some mornings he just couldn't stand the feel or stink of methyl alcohol.

Shivering, he gulped the coffee and pulled on pants, parka and sand boots. "Let's see the stuff," he said. "Did Benoway give you a letter or note for me?"

"Oh, sure. I almost forgot."

Hank handed over an ampoule and an onionskin. The note from the Mars Machine Tool physician said:

Dear Hellman:
Here is the T7-43 Kelsey you requested by radio message. Re your note by messenger, sorry to tell you symptoms completely unfamiliar

to me. Sounds like one of the cases any company doc would ship back to Earth as soon as possible. The T7-43 has worked wonders in heat burns here and have seen no side reactions. Please let me know how it comes out.

In haste.

A. Benoway, M. D.

Tony grunted and beckoned Hank after him as he picked up his physician's bag and went out into the bitter morning cold.

"Did you say you *walked* from Pittco?" he asked Hank, suddenly waking up.

"Sure," said the youngster genially. "It's good exercise. Look, I don't want to get out of line, but I couldn't help noticing that you're building up kind of a bay window yourself. Now it's my experience that those things are easier *not* to put on than to take off—"

"Shh," said Tony as they stopped at the Radcliff shack. They slipped in and Tony filled a needle with the new Kelsey drug. "Stay in the background until I get this over with and motion you in, Hank."

He awakened the girl.

"Here's the new stuff, Joan," he said. "Ready?"

She smiled weakly and nodded. He shot the stuff into her arm and said: "Here's your reward for not yelling." Hank duly stepped forward; switching on a light in her eyes that did Tony's heart good.

\*     \*     \*

BREAKFAST was fried green Mars beans and "coffee"—bearable, perhaps, under ideal conditions, but completely inedible in the gloomy atmosphere around the big table this morning. Tony gulped down the hot liquid, and determinedly pushed away his beans, ignoring the pointed looks of more righteous colonists, who cleaned their plates stubbornly under any circumstances.

The Lab radiation checked out okay; no trouble there at least this morning. After a meticulous cleanup, he visited Nick Cantrella in the hole-in-the-wall office at the back of the Lab.

"How's it look, now you've had a night's sleep on it?" Nick demanded. "You still want to throw in the sponge? Or are you beginning to see that we can lick this damn planet if we only try?"

"I can't see it," Tony admitted. Soberly he told the other man about his visit to the Tollers. "And look at Old Man Learoyd," the doctor added. "He can't be much past 60 and that's stretching it. I know he came here when he was twenty-one; at least, that's what he says—so how old can he be? But I gave that man a physical checkup a few months back, and, Nick, he not only *looks* like an ill-preserved octogenarian, but if I didn't know otherwise, I'd stake my medical reputation on his being close to ninety."

Nick whistled. "As bad as that?"

"What do you expect? Chronic vitamin deficiencies, mineral deficiencies, not enough water, never-ending fatigue from neverending work—you pay high for trying to live off the country. More than it's worth."

Half to himself, Nick said: "Six months. We lose our commercial contacts, we pay forfeits that eat up our cash reserve—what if we just go to the buyers and tell them what happened?"

Tony started to answer, but Nick answered himself: "It won't work. They won't dare place another order with us because they'd be afraid it'd just happen all over again. And we haven't got the funds to sweat it out until they forget. Tony, *we're washed up.*"

"There's still a search."

"Hell, you know none of our people took the stuff."

"Let's have a council meeting. I want a search."

Nick, Tony, Gracey and Mimi Jonathan held one of their irregular conclaves in the doctor's hut. Gracey was fiercely opposed to a shakedown check of the homes and belongings of the colonists, swearing that it was a frame-up by Brenner and Bell. The other three out-voted him, loathing to invade the pitifully small area of privacy left to Sun Lake people, but not daring to leave a possibility uninvestigated.

"I suppose," grunted Gracey, "that when you find there isn't any marcaine in our trunks, you'll tear the Lab apart looking for it."

"If we have to, we may," said Tony, poker-faced, but sickened at the memory of what isolation from the life giving flow of materials from Earth had done to the Tollers. "I've had some nasty jobs before this." He thought of how he had lanced the swollen ego of Mrs. Bayles, the neurotic, and how she must hate him for it—an ugly thought.

By mid-morning, Mimi had the shakedown under way. Tony settled himself in the radio shack, firing message after message to

Commission headquarters at Marsport, trying to get through to Lt. Nealey. The operator at Pittco who relayed from Marsport telefaxed the same reply to the first four messages:

"UNAVAILABLE WILL RELAY MESSAGE END CORPORAL MORRISON COMMISSION MESSAGE CENTER."

On the fifth try, Nealey still had not been reached—but Bell had.

This time the reply was: "LIEUTENANT NEALEY UNAVAILABLE MY ORDERS. UNDER NO CIRCUMSTANCES GROUND TRACING DEVICE M-27 LENT FOR PRIVATE USE. REMINDER LIMITED MARS MESSAGE FACILITIES TAXED YOUR FRIVOLOUS REQUESTS. REQUIRE CEASE IMMEDIATELY END HAMILTON BELL, COMMISSIONER P.A.C."

Gladys Porosky, the operator on duty, piped indignantly: "He can't do that, can he, Doctor Tony? The relay league's a private arrangement between the colonies, isn't it?"

Tony shrugged helplessly, knowing that Gladys was right and that Bell's petulant arrogance was a long stretch of his administrative powers—but due process was far away on Earth, for those who had the time and taste for litigation and the cash reserves to stick it out.

Gracey joined him in the hut long enough to say bitterly, "Come and see the loot we accumulated."

Tony went out to stare unhappily at the petty contraband turned up by the humiliating search: some comic books smuggled in from Marsport, heaven knew how, by a couple of the youngsters; some dirty pictures in the trunk of a young, unmarried chemist; an unauthorized .32 pistol in the mattress of a notably nervous woman colonist; a few bottles and boxes of patent medicine on which the doctor frowned; a minute quantity of real Earthside coffee kept to be brewed and drunk in selfish solitude.

By mid-afternoon this much was certain—any marcaine hidden in the Colony was not in a private home.

The Lab would have to be searched next.

*　　*　　*

IT WAS like going into a new world, to escape from the doomed, determined optimism of the search squad and council members, back to the cheerful radiance that inhabited the hospital. Tony stood in the doorway, studying the family group across the room—father and mother thoroughly absorbed in each other and in the tiny occupant of the white-painted wicker basket that served as hospital bassinet.

It was still hard to believe the delivery had gone so well. Tony wondered again, as he had so often in the proceeding months, what could possibly have gone wrong with all the previous attempts, before they came to Mars.

There had been frequent conceptions; six known miscarriages, and an unknown number of first-month failures. A series of expert's back on Earth had searched for the reason, and confessed failure. There was nothing wrong with Polly organically, and microscopic examinations failed to show any deficiency in her or in Jim. With that history, Tony had been prepared, right up to the last minute, for trouble that never materialized. It was still hard to believe that their success, his and Polly's, could have been so easily achieved.

"He's awake again." Polly hadn't quite made up her mind whether to be proud or worried. "He slept for a little while after you left," she explained, "but then he started crying and woke himself up. You should have seen how mad he was—his face was so red."

"He's quiet enough now." Tony went over and stared down thoughtfully at the small circle of face, half-obscured by the oxygen mask. Certainly there was no sign of ill health. The baby was a glowing pink color, and his still-wrinkled limbs were flailing the air with astonishing energy. But a newborn baby should sleep; this one shouldn't be awake so much.

"It's possible he's hungry," the doctor decided. "Hasn't he cried at all since he woke up?"

"Oh, a little, every now and then, but if you turn him over, he stops."

Tony went over and scrubbed his hands in the alcohol basin, then came back and surveyed the baby again. "I think we'll try a feeding," he decided. "I've been waiting for him to yell for it, but let's see. Maybe that's what he wants."

"But—" Jim flushed and stopped.

HIS wife broke into, delighted laughter. "He means my milk isn't in yet," Polly said to the doctor; and then to Jim, "Silly. He has to learn how to nurse first. He doesn't need any *food* yet. And the other stuff is there—what do you call it?"

"Colostrum," Tony told her. He removed the baby from the crib, checked the mask to make sure it was firmly in place, then lowered the infant to his mother's waiting arms.

"Just be sure," he warned her, "that the mask doesn't slip off his nose. There's enough area around his mouth exposed so he can feed and breathe at the same time."

THE baby nuzzled against her for a moment, then spluttered furiously, turned a rich crimson and spewed back a mouthful of thin fluid. Hastily Dr. Tony removed the infant, patted and held him until the choking fit stopped and restored him to his basket.

Polly and Jim were both talking at once.

"Hold on," said the doctor. "It's not the end of the world. Lots of babies don't know how to feed properly at first. He'll probably learn by the time your milk comes. Anyhow, he'll learn when he needs it. Babies don't stay hungry. It's like the oxy mask—he breathes through his nose instead of his mouth because the air is better. We don't have to cover up his mouth to make him do it. When he needs some food he'll learn what his mouth is for—fast."

"But, Doc, are you sure there's nothing wrong with him? Are you *sure*?"

"Jim, in my business, I'm never sure of anything," Tony said mildly. "Only I've never yet seen a baby that didn't find some way to eat when it wanted food. If your pride and joy won't take the breast, we'll get Anna to whip up some bottles for him. It's as simple as that."

Or not so simple—

George and Harriet Bergen's eight-month-old Loretta, conceived on Earth but born at Sun Lake, was still feeding from the breast. Loretta would be weaned not to milk but to the standard Colony diet plus vitamin concentrates when the time came. It was what the older children ate; they had forgotten what milk tasted like.

There were milch-goats, of course, and some day there would be milk for everybody in the Colony to drink. But to make that possible, it was necessary now to allocate all the milk produced by the herd to the nourishment of more goats, to build up the stock.

It was hard enough to keep the herd growing even with best of care. Yaks, at first, had seemed like a better bet for acclimatization to the Martian atmosphere, but they were too big to ship full-grown, and so far no young animals had survived the trip. So the Colony had brought over three pairs of tough kids, and bred them as rapidly as possible. Half the newborn kids still died, but the surviving half needed every bit of milk there was. Still, if necessary, a kid would have to be sacrificed, and the milk diverted to the baby.

Tony pulled himself out of the useless speculation with a start of dismay. There was no sense planning too far ahead now; Bell might solve this problem for them, too.

"Anything else you want to know before you go home?" he asked. "Have any trouble with the mask?"

"Anna checked us out on that," Jim told him. "It seems to be simple enough."

"Where is she? In the living room?" Tony started toward the door.

"She went home," Polly put in. "She said she had a headache, and when Jim came in she showed us about the mask again, and then went..."

"Hi, Tony. Can I see you a minute?" Marian Cantrella stuck her head through the outside door to the hospital. Tony turned and went out with her.

"IS SHE ready to go?" Marian wanted to know.

"Since this morning, really. But the damn search—how's their place? Did anybody get it back in order?"

"I just came from there," Marian nodded. "We've got it all fixed up and the new room's all done. The walls are still a little damp. Does that matter?"

"It'll dry overnight," Tony reflected. "They can keep the baby in the room with them till then."

"Polly must be dying to get home," Marian broke in.

"I guess she is. Okay," he decided. "But it'll have to be right away. In another hour, it'll be too cold for the baby to go out."

"Right." She started away, and Tony was about to open the door when she turned back. "Oh, I almost forgot. Is it all right for Hank to take Joan out to watch? I was talking to her before, and she felt so left out of everything..."

"I guess so." He thought it over and added, "Only if she's carried, though. Maybe Hank can fix up a tote truck from the lab for her to ride on. I don't want her to use up what strength she has."

"I'll fix it," Marian promised. "I think it would mean a lot to her." Her golden curls shook brightly around her head as she ran off down the street.

Tony went back into the hospital. "Guess it's time to get you folks out of here," he told the Kandros. "Place is too cluttered up. I might need this space for someone who's *sick*."

Polly smiled up at him from the chair where she had been sitting for the last hour. "I don't know what I can wear," she worried happily. "The things I came in would fall right off me, and I can't very well go out this way. Jim, you better..."

"Jim," Tony interrupted, "you better get some sense into that wife of yours. You'll go *just* the way you are," he told Polly, "and you'll get right into bed when you get there too. You've been up long enough for one day."

"*Just* the way I am?" Polly laughed, poking her bare toes out from under her bathrobe.

WHILE Jim helped her with her sandboots and parka, Tony wrapped the baby for his first trip outdoors. They were ready quickly, but Marian had been even quicker. When they opened the front door, a crowd of familiar faces confronted them. It seemed as if all of Sun Lake City Colony's eleven dozen residents had crowded into the street in front of the doctor's house. They were determined, apparently, that whatever happened next week, the Kandros' homecoming would not be spoiled today.

"I suppose you all want to see the baby? All right," Tony told them, "but remember, he's still too young for much social life. I don't want you to crowd around. If you'll all spread out down the street from here to the Kandros' place, everybody can get a look."

Together, Tony and Jim eased Polly into the rubber-tired hand-truck that did double duty as a hospital stretcher. They placed the baby in her arms, and adjusted the small portable tank for the oxy mask at her feet. Then they started slowly down the long curved street, stopping every few yards along the way for someone who wanted to shake Jim's hand, pat Polly on the shoulder, and peer curiously at the few square inches of the baby's face that were exposed to the weather.

The doctor fretted at the continual delays; he didn't want Polly or the baby to stay out too long. But after the first few times, he found he could speed things up by saying meaningfully, "Let's let them get *home* now." As the small party progressed down the street, they collected a trailing crowd. Everyone was determined to be in on the big surprise.

Polly and Jim didn't let them down either. The moment of dazed surprise when they saw the still-wet walls of the new room jutting out from their house was all that could be asked. Equally satisfying were the expressions on their faces when they opened their door and looked in at the array of gifts.

Some of the new plastic furniture was not in evidence—it was still curing in the electronic furnace. But the crib was finished, and it stood in the center of the room, its gleaming transparent sides proudly displaying the blankets and baby-clothes, diapers, sheets, and towels piled up inside. On the table, jars and dishes stood side by side with new plastic safety pins and an assortment—somewhat premature—of baby toys.

Tony gave them time to take it all in, then insisted that the door be closed and Polly and the baby be allowed to settle down. While he was unwrapping the baby, he heard them in whispered consultation, and a moment later the door opened again. Jim left it very slightly ajar behind him as he stepped out, so they could hear what went on.

"WAIT a minute, folks," Tony heard him call. A slight hesitation, and then Jim's voice again. "Polly and I—well, we want to thank you, and I don't know just how to go about it. I can't really say I'm surprised, because it's exactly the kind of thing a man might know you folks would do. Polly and I, when we came here—well, we'd never had much to do with politics or anything like that. We joined up because we wanted to get away, mostly.

"We—I guess you all know how long we've been waiting for this kid. When he didn't come, back there on Earth, we felt like we had no roots anywheres, and we just—wanted to get away, that's all. When we signed up we figured it sounded good. A bunch of people all out to help each other and work together, and the way the Statute says, extend the frontiers of man by mutual endeavor. It made us feel more like we belonged, more like a *family*, than just working for some Mars Company would have been.

"It wasn't until after we got here that we began to find out what it was all about, and I guess you know we liked it. Building up this place, everybody working together—it just couldn't ever get done that way back on Earth.

"And then this other thing happened, and the doc said it looked like it was going to work out all right this time.

"We started thinking then, and this is what I've been working up to. Maybe it's silly, but we figure it's something about Mars that made it work, or something about the Colony. And now the baby's here, I hope none of you will mind, but we'd like to name him Sun Lake City Colony Kandro…"

Jim stopped abruptly, and for a too-long moment there was only the grim silence of the crowd, the same bitter thought in every mind.

Then he went on: "Maybe you folks think that's not a very good idea right now. I don't know. If you don't like it, we won't do it. But the way we feel, Polly and me—well, we know things look bad now, but they're going to have an awful hard time, the Planetary Affairs Commission or anybody else, getting *us* off Mars."

"You're damned well right, Jim," shouted Nick Cantrella. He faced the crowd with his fist's hanging alertly. "Anybody think the kid shouldn't be called Sun Lake City Colony Kandro?"

The harsh silence broke in a roar of confidence that lifted Tony's chin, even though he knew there was no justification for it.

## CHAPTER EIGHT

INSIDE, the baby was wailing lustily again. From her position on the couch, Polly raised a commanding arm.

"Turn him over, Jim. He'll probably stop crying if you put him on his tummy."

Tony watched while the new father slid his hand under his son's back with an exquisite caution that belied his proud air of assurance. Turning to hide his smile, the doctor began piling hospital equipment on the hand-truck to take back with him when he went.

"Look! Tony, look! Look at Sunny!"

"Sunny, is it?" The doctor turned around slowly. "So he's lost all his dignity already. I was wondering how you were going to get around that tongue twister of a name… Well, what do you know?"

HE WATCHED the baby struggle briefly, then rear back and lift his head upright. He had to admit there was cause for the pride in

Polly's voice when a baby not yet two days old could do that.

"Well," the doctor teased, "he's Sun Lake City Colony Kandro, after all. You ask anybody in town if that doesn't make a difference. I won't be surprised if he walks next week, and starts doing long division the first of the month. Who knows, he might learn how to eat pretty soon."

He realized abruptly, he'd made a mistake. Neither parent was ready to joke about that.

"Doc," Jim asked hesitantly, "you're pretty sure there's nothing *wrong?*"

"I told you before," Tony said shortly, "I'm not sure of a blessed thing. If you can see any single reason to believe there's anything wrong with that baby, I wish you'd tell me, because I can't, but this is Mars. I can't make promises, and I'll make damned few flat statements. You can go along with me and trust me, or—" There was no alternative, and his brief irritation was already worn out. "You can *not* trust me and go along with me. We have to feel our way that's all. Now," he said briskly, "you're all checked out on the mask? No trouble with it?"

"No, it's all right. I'm sorry, Doc—"

"Got enough tanks?" Tony interrupted.

"You gave us enough to go from here to Jupiter," Polly put in. "Listen, Tony, please don't think we—"

"What I think," Tony told her, "is that you're good parents, naturally concerned about your child, and that I had no business blowing off. Now let's forget it."

"No," Jim said firmly. "I think you ought to know how we—I mean there's no question in anyone's mind about trusting you. Hell, how do I go about saying this? What I want to tell you is—"

"He wants to say," said Polly from the bed, "that we're both very grateful for what you've done. It's a happiness we thought we'd never know."

"That's it," said Jim.

"He's your baby," said Tony. "Do a good job with him." he pushed the hand-truck to the door, and waited for Jim to come and help him ease it through. "Oh, by the way," he added, smiling, "I'll fill out the birth certificate tonight, now that I know the name, if you'll come over and..."

"Doc!"

IT WAS Hank Radcliff, running down the street breathless and distraught.

"Doc, come quick—Joan's dying!"

Tony grabbed his black bag and raced down the street with Hank plowing along beside him.

"What happened?"

"When I took her out in the tote truck," Hank panted, "before she could walk to the street, she toppled right over—"

"*Walk?* You let her *walk?*"

"But she told me you said it was all right!" The youngster seemed close to tears.

"Joan told you that?" They slowed in front of the Radcliff hut. Tony wiped the anger off his face and went in.

Joan was on the bunk in a parka; the doctor stripped it off and applied his stethoscope. He had adrenaline into her heart in thirty seconds and then sat, grim-faced, at the edge of the bunk, not taking the black disk from her chest.

"Get that coffee," he snapped at Hank without turning. "The stuff they found in the shakedown."

Hank raced out.

After long minutes, Tony exhaled heavily and put away the stethoscope. She'd pulled through once more.

The girl lifted her parchmentlike eyelids and looked at him dully. "I feel better now," she whispered. "I guess I fainted."

"You don't have to talk." Tony sat again on the edge of the bed.

She was silent for a minute, lying back with her eyes closed. He picked up her bird's claw of a hand; the pulse was racing now.

"Doctor Tony?" she asked.

"I'm right here. Don't try to talk. Go to sleep."

"Is Hank here?"

"He'll be back in a minute."

"I want to tell you something, Doctor Tony. It wasn't his fault. I didn't tell him the truth. I told him you said it was all right for me to walk."

"You knew better than that."

"Yes. Yes, I did. I know you'll have to send me back to Earth—"

"Never mind about that, Joan."

"I do, Doctor Tony. Not for me; for Hank. That's why I did it.

I'd go back for the Colony because it isn't fair of me to take up all your time, but what about Hank? If I went back, he'd have to go back, too. He couldn't stay here in the Colony if I were on Earth—alive."

"What are you talking about?" demanded the doctor, though he knew with terrible certainty what she meant—what she had tried to do. "Of course he's going back with you. He loves you. Don't you love him?"

She smiled a little and said softly, without urgency, "Yes, I love him." And then, again hysterically: "But this is what he's wanted all his life. He doesn't feel the way I do about the Colony, the wonderful way we're all working together for everybody. With him it's Mars, ever since he was a little boy. He's in the Colony and he works hard and everybody likes him, but it would be enough for him to be a prospector like old Learoyd. Ever since he was a little boy he used to dream about it. You know how he's always going out into the desert—

"Tell him he doesn't have to go back with me. Tell him I'll be all right. Talk to the shareholders. Make them let him stay. It would break his heart to send him back."

TONY didn't dare excite her by telling her that they might all be sent back, that the Colony was a failure. Even if they pulled through by a miracle, Hank couldn't stay.

They called it the "M or M" rule—"married or marriageable." Far from the lunacies of the jam-packed Earth, they had meant to build with children and allowed no place for new immigrant women past childbearing—or for Hank in love with a woman returned to Earth. It didn't matter now, he thought.

Wearily, he lied. "They wouldn't make him go back if he didn't want to. But he'd want to go himself."

She sighed and closed her eyes. It seemed a long time before he was sure she was asleep.

Hank was waiting in the living room with the coffee.

"She'll be all right for a while," Tony told him. "She's asleep now, I think." He looked at the open doorway and added, "Come outside a minute."

Sitting on the tote truck he said, "Give her one cup of coffee each day as long as it lasts, after any meal. It'll make her feel better. God, I wish I knew what else we could do. That stuff from Benoway didn't have any effect. I'm sorry I sent you all the way out there."

"That's all right, Doc. There was a chance. And I like seeing the country."

"You certainly do. You should have been one of the pork-and-beaners."

"Hell, Doc, I like it fine here in the Colony."

Liked it, yes. It was on Mars. *Tell him or not?* wondered Tony. *Young man, your wife tried to commit suicide so you would be free to stay on this planet. And what do you think of that?*

The hell with it. What he didn't know wouldn't hurt him, upset him, make him feel guilty—

"Doc, do you think we *will* have to go back?" Hank's voice was more than strained, it was desperate.

Tony stared. "It looks that way right now, Hank. But we have three weeks. Something—anything—may happen. I'm not giving up hope."

But the young man's face was tortured as Tony left him.

*   *   *

JOAN RADCLIFF had wanted death and been cheated of it by adrenaline. Sunny Kandro wanted life, which meant his mother's breast, but some savage irony was cheating him, too. Newly born, five pounds of reflexes depending on the key suckling reflex that somehow was scrambled.

Sunny lay awake without crying, didn't seem to need sleep, could lift his head—all right, put that down to lighter gravity, even though the Bergens' little Loretta hadn't done it. Sunny had a wonderful color, a powerful nursing instinct—but he choked and gagged at the breast. Without fuel the machine of reflexes would run down and stop...

It didn't make sense to Tony. He had guiltily half-lied to the Kandros when he told them many babies didn't know how to nurse at first. That was the truth; the lie was that *this baby knew how,* but choked all the same. A feeding problem, they would have blandly called it on Earth, where there still were millions of cows, sterile hospitals, relays of trained nurses for intravenous nourishment regimes. Here a feeding problem was a feeding *problem.*

Anyone of the wealthier industrial colonies would automatically have taken Earth-import powdered milk from its stores, but Sun Lake couldn't afford it, didn't have any. And what was more, Sun Lake wouldn't get powdered milk if Commissioner Bell made good on his threat...

If Sunny died, it would be worse than the unnamed little boy the Connollys had lost, and he had left a scar on the doctor's mind that time would never heal. Tony could still see the agonized blue face and the butterfly gasping for air—a preemie, but he never should have cleared Mrs. Connolly, and seven months gone, until they'd had oxygen cylinders and masks and a tent for emergencies.

The Connollys had shipped back to Earth on the next rocket after the tragedy.

The father had cursed him insanely, damned him for a killer because he hadn't foreseen the need of oxy gear for their baby two months before it was due. OxEn they had, but OxEn made no change in the lungs of a baby. He'd given it intravenously, orally, in every solvent he could lay his hands on during the desperate hours before the improvised mask fed the last trickle of oxygen from their single tank into the lungs of the infant.

Tony forced his face into a smile as he passed a couple—Flexner and his girl Verna. Behind the smile he was thinking that it would be harder to bear a muter reproach from the patient Kandros than Connolly's raging curses.

Tony dragged the loaded handtruck into the middle of his living room, and left it there. He could put the stuff away later; it was getting late now, and he had yet to make his afternoon radiation inspection at the Lab. There was a package on the table; he took time to pick it up and read: "For Doctor Tony from Jim and Polly Kandro—with much thanks."

For a moment he held it, weighing it in his hand. No, he decided, he'd open it later, when there was time to relax and appreciate the sentiment that lay behind it. The gift itself would be—would *have* to be—meaningless.

There was no way for any colonist to purchase or procure anything at all from the outside. Except for the very few personal treasures that were somehow squeezed into the rigid weight limit on baggage when they came out, all plastic chairs and sinks, blankets, and windows were uniformly functional and durable. But they *were* uniform, and they were also scarce. Each household contained the same irreducible minimum; Lab space and work hours were too precious to be used for the production of local consumption items.

TONY closed his door behind him, and set out for the Lab once more. *Dull, monotonous, primitive, uncomfortable*, he raged inwardly. *Every home, inside and out, just the same.*

Why had they come to Mars? For a better, saner way of life, to retrieve some of the dignity of men, to escape from the complexities and inequities and fear pressures of Earth. And what were they doing? Building a new life, with hard work and suffering, on the precise pattern of the old. There wasn't a person in the Colony who wouldn't do better back on Earth.

He found the Lab in an uproar. All work had stopped, so the grim hunt for the marcaine could go on. Nick had already begun an inventory.

"Make this an extra-good check, Doc." Tony was told in the office before he started out. "We'll be handling a lot of stuff that hasn't been used in a long time. And getting into all the corners, too."

"Are the checkout tubes racked yet?" Tony asked.

"Right. We issued new ones to the men on the inspection squad."

"I'll do them first," the doctor decided, and went into the cleanup room where the wall racks were already lined with the tubes for that day. Usually they were checked in the following morning's inspection; but today the plant had closed down early for all practical purposes.

The tubes checked clean all down the line.

Tony selected a fresh tube from the opposite wall and went on out through the shipping room to the workrooms. He didn't need armor for the afternoon inspection. The technicians had been in there working, and if their tubes were all clean there couldn't be any deadly hot stuff. The purpose of the late day check was to catch reactions that were just starting up, and that might make trouble overnight. In the morning it was different. Anything that had been chaining for twelve or more hours could be vicious.

Back in the office, when he was finished, Tony reported a clean check through. "What" he asked, "are you going to do about the shipment crates?"

"Leave them till last," Mimi Jonathan told him. "If anything turns up in the workrooms or storage bins, we'll have to open up the shipment crates one at a time. Doc, do you think...?"

She stopped, looked down a moment and then back at Tony, with a wry smile. "That's silly, isn't it? I don't know why I expect you to know more about it than I do. Oh, listen—they want you to stick around and monitor if they do have to open the crates. I'll let you know when it gets that far."

"Okay." Tony smiled back at her. "Try to give me more than five minutes notice, will you? I wish we had either a full-time radiological man or another doctor."

"How about Harve?" she suggested. "Could he fill in for you? We didn't want to assign him without your okay—he hasn't done any monitoring on his own yet, has he?"

"No," Tony said thoughtfully. "Not yet. But this won't be anything more than standing by with a counter and keeping his eyes open. I don't see why not; he knows the routine as well as I do by now. I'd leave it up to him," the doctor decided. "If he feels ready to take it on, it'll be a big help to me."

"I'll ask him," Mimi promised.

\*     \*     \*

THIS afternoon the familiar splendors of the Martian scene evoked no glowing certainties in Tony's mind. He walked back from the Lab in the early twilight, his eyes fixed on the far hills, his thought roaming bitterly beyond, to the other side of the range.

Tony had been to the new town, just once, to help out when a too hastily built furnace exploded. The injuries had been more than Pittco's green young doctor could handle all at once. The doctor's inexperience, like the faulty furnace, was typical. The whole place was temporary, until it showed a profit for Pittco. When it did, solid structures would replace the jerrybuilt shacks; an efficient company administration would put an end to the anarchic social organization.

But for now the town was just a sprawling collection of ramshackle buildings, constructed of a dozen different inadequate materials, whatever was available in Marsport when a new house was needed. There was no thought of the future on the other side of the hill, no worry about permanence, no eye to consequence.

If the camp went bust, the population would move on to one of the newer locations—and move again when that collapsed. If, on the other hand, the town survived, the population would move on anyhow. A new crop of workers would be imported from Earth, a tamer, quieter crew, to do routine work in an organized company town, at considerably lower pay. And the boomtown adventurers would go, to find higher wages and a freer life somewhere else.

They struck no roots there, and they wanted none. Of all the widely scattered human settlements on Mars, the Sun Lake Colony alone believed that man could and would some day flourish naturally on the alien soil.

Tony Hellman had a religion: it was the earnest hope that that day would come before he died, that he would live to see them cut the cord with Earth. Training and instinct both cried out against the new danger of abortion to the embryo civilization.

Tony was a good doctor; in Springfield or Jackson City or Hartford—anywhere on Earth—he could have written his own ticket. Instead, he had chosen to throw in his lot with a batch of wide-eyed idealists; had, indeed, jumped at the chance.

IT WAS largely Tony's eagerness to emigrate that was responsible for the Colony's "M-or-M" ruling. The Sun Lake Society couldn't afford to turn Dr. Hellman down; they knew just how slim was the possibility of getting another doctor as good. So, after much deliberation, the by-laws were carefully revised, and the words "or marriageable" inserted after the word "married" in the list of qualifications.

The modification had resulted in a flood of new and highly desirable members. Skilled workers were inclined to be more footloose and adventurous before they were married, before they had settled into responsible, well-paid jobs on Earth. Bea Juarez, pilot of the Colony's ship, *Lazy Girl*, was one of the new acquisitions; so was Harvey Stillman, the chief radioman.

Anna Willendorf was another member who had come in after the revised "M-or-M" ruling, one whose skill was almost as much appreciated as Tony's, for a different reason. Plastics, produced in the Lab, could be, and were, used for almost every item of furniture or furnishings in the Colony; but for some chemical processes, glassware was still a must. And now that giant machines existed on Earth to turn out almost every conceivable glass utensil, glass blowers were far between, good ones almost nonexistent. Without Anna's highly specialized talent, the Colony would have had to pay fabulous prices for the transport of bulkily packaged glassware from Earth.

Anna was one of the very few unmarried members of the Colony who refused to participate in the communal meals. Laziness, or embarrassment, or both, served to drag in the others, like Tony, who might have preferred to remain aloof. Anna simply ignored the questions and remarks.

ON RARE occasions, however, she relented to the extent of "inviting" the doctor to dine with her—combining their rations, and preparing a meal for him in her own one-room hut. Then, for an hour, she would play hostess to him, an hour that restored, for both of them, the longed-for feeling of gracious, civilized living.

"One for all and all for one." "Mutual endeavor." "Collective self-sufficiency." The whole thing, Tony thought angrily, was an anachronism; more than that, an impossibility. No sane man could believe in it—unless he came from Earth and had nothing to see to believe in.

For tonight, at least, he was free of it. Anna was at the door when he reached it, holding it open for him. She watched him set down his bag as though he were unloading the troubles of the Universe.

"You need a drink," she decided.

"Who's kidding whom?" He grinned sourly at her. "Some nice, refreshing, vitamin-packed, Grade-A, synthesized orange juice, maybe?"

"I see you haven't been home yet."

She disappeared behind the drape that hid her kitchen section. Not many of them bothered to separate the kitchen from the living room; perhaps, Tony thought, that was what gave her room such a special look. A moment later, she was out again, with two long-stemmed fragile glasses in her hands.

SHE handed one to Tony, and awe and wonder crossed his face as he sipped. He looked his question at her over the rim of the glass.

"I shouldn't have spoiled your surprise, really." She smiled at him. "The Kandros. They wouldn't prepare anything for the baby, but they must have ordered these from Earth when Polly was just—let's see—three months along, to have had them here in time."

"Real wine," Tony marveled, and sipped again. "*Aged* wine. How did they get it? How could they afford—?"

"They couldn't, of course," she reminded him, "but they have relatives on Earth. You know they're not the only ones who left some cash behind, 'just in case'?"

The doctor looked up sharply, and found a faint smile flickering on her lips. "How did you know?" he demanded. "Where do you find out these things?"

"What do they call it—feminine intuition?" She shrugged and moved toward the kitchen again. "Which also tells me that supper will be a desiccated mess if I don't serve it right now."

She had set the table as usual in front of the big window. Tony took his place and looked out through the eerie twilight across the endless expanse of *Lacus Solis*. The ocean bed was like vast black velvet now, studded with a million tiny, glinting jewels.

The doctor stared out until Anna returned with a steaming dish. He regarded her soberly and was planning a dutiful compliment when she burst into laughter and set the dish down. "Jim's face," she explained hastily. "It just crossed my mind. He's so proud of the wife and child—"

He was irked by a note of insincerity and supposed for a moment—neurotically, he knew; commonest thing in the world—that she had been laughing at him.

"Nothing so funny," he said stiffly.

"I'm sorry. Serve the greens?"

Dinner performed its usual magic. Tony *had* been really hungry. Tilting his chair against the wall, with his empty pipe in his mouth, he found that things were getting back into proportion.

"Anyhow," he said, "we still have time." They had been talking about Bell's threat of quarantine. Through the daylight hours it had seemed at least the end of the world. Now, with a pleasantly noticeable buzz from the wine in his head and a palatable meal digesting, above all, with some privacy and clear space and time around him, Tony couldn't recapture the sharp alarm of the threat.

ANNA, very seriously, demanded, "Do you think Bell can run us out?"

He waved a little too expansively. "Prob'ly not. Any number of other possibilities. Somebody at Pittco might have taken the stuff; they're close enough. Nope—" He hauled up. "Ed Nealey wouldn't make a mistake like that. He was working the Bloodhound and there's a boy who'll do any job the right way. Don't worry about it, though. It's two weeks to rocket landing, another week to Shipment Day—something'll turn up. We'll send O'Donnell to Marsport. If there's a legal angle he'll find it. Maybe he can scare Bell into backing down. Bell's supposed to be a small-timer. He wouldn't want any real trouble."

Anna got up abruptly and filled his empty glass.

"Hey, you take some, too," Tony insisted.

She made a show of draining the last few drops into her own glass; the rims touched and they drank.

"You're a strange girl, Anna," said Tony. "Hell, I didn't mean exactly that—I mean you're not like the other women here. Joan. Bea. Polly. Verna."

"No," she said. "Not very much like Bea."

Tony didn't know whether she was angry or amused and decided he didn't care. "I don't know why I don't marry you."

"Two reasons," Anna smiled. "One, you're not sure you want to. Two, you're not at all sure I do."

The sudden banging on the door was like an explosion in the quiet room. Harve Stillman didn't wait for anyone to answer; he burst in. He was white-faced and shaken.

"Doc!"

Tony jumped up and reached for his bag. "What is it? Joan? The baby? An accident at the Lab?"

"Flash from Marsport. The rocket's coming in." The radioman stopped to catch his breath. "They're inside radio range now. Estimated time of arrival, 4:00 A.M."

"Tomorrow?" Anna gasped. Harve nodded and Tony put down his bag with mechanical precision in the center of the table.

Tomorrow! Three weeks had been little enough time to find the marcaine and the thief and get rid of Bell's strangling cordon. Now, with the rocket in ahead of schedule, two of those weeks were yanked out from under them.

## CHAPTER NINE

TONY got four hours sleep before Tad Campbell came banging on his door at 3:15 A. M. The boy's enthusiasm was more than Tony could face; it would be easier to carry his own equipment than to answer questions while he was dressing. He sent Tad to wait at the plane and put some "coffee" on to brew, then did a last quick check of his portable health lab, making sure that there was nothing overlooked in the hasty preparations after the news about the Earth ship.

Gulping down the hot brew, he reviewed the instructions he had given Anna: feedings for Sunny Kandro; bacitracin for Dorothy; ointment and dressings for Joan, another injection if she needed it; and under no circumstances sedative for Mrs. Beyles.

He couldn't think of anything predictable he had failed to provide for. He folded the lab to make a large carrying case and lugged his burden up the gentle slope that led to the landing field where *Lazy Girl*, the Colony's transport plane, waited.

Bea Juarez was warming the icy motors with a blowtorch. *Lazy Girl's* motors were absurdly small; their shafts spun on zero-friction air bearings. Air-bearings dated from the guided missiles of 1950, but their expensively precise machining ruled them out for Earth. Shipping space to Mars was high enough to override the high manufacturing cost. Air-bearing motors were small and light; therefore virtually everything on Mars that turned or slid, turned and slid on molecules of gas instead of oily films.

The bearings improved the appearance not only of machinery but also of mechanics. Bea looked tired, cold, and unhappy; but she lacked the grease-smeared dinginess that would have marked her on Earth. The girl nodded to him, ran a hand over the moisture condensing on the metallic surface, and applied the torch to a new spot.

She shook her head doubtfully. "Don't blame me if she falls apart in mid-air after we take off, I put her together with spit overnight, Tony. She was scattered all over the field for a hundred-hour check. You'd think they'd let you know..." she grumbled, then broke off and grinned. "What the hell, if we blow up halfway between here and there, we don't have to worry about marcaine anymore. Climb aboard, Doc." She snapped off the torch. "Hey, Tad! The doc needs a hand with his contraption."

TONY felt a twinge of conscience as Tad hopped out of the plane and ran to take the big box. It must have been a blow to the boy, to be deprived of carrying the heavy equipment from the hospital.

"How's it going?" Tony asked genially, "You seem to be getting along fine without your tail bone."

"Okay," the boy grunted.

He eased the box into the cabin, pulled it out of the way, and reached down a condescending hand to help Tony. "It don't seem to matter," he added, when the doctor was inside. "You'd never know it wasn't there."

Tad was the recent victim of an unhappily humorous accident. Butted in the seat by an angry goat, he'd had his coccyx severely fractured, and the doctor had had to remove the caudal vertebrae. It probably qualified, Tony thought, as another of those history making occasions—the Colony's first spinal, if you want to stretch the term, operation. Historic or not, it was a permanent bond between the boy and the doctor—the only one who had been able to take it seriously.

Tony padded a couple of spare parkas into a comfortable couch on the cabin floor and stretched out. The plane had no seats. Coming back, they'd sit on the bare floor, and the parkas would have another use. The ship was unheated and the newcomers weren't likely to have warm clothes unpacked.

*Lazy Girl* was short on comfort and speed cannibalized on Mars from the scrapped remains of obsolete models discarded by wealthier colonies. Tony, who didn't fly himself, had been told that she handled easily and flew an immense payload without complaining.

Tad had built himself a luxurious nest of parkas. He pulled the last one up around his shivering shoulders, leaned back, and examined the interior of the plane with a good imitation of a practiced appraisal.

"Nice job," he pronounced finally. "You don't get them like this back on Earth."

"You sure don't," Bea agreed ironically from the pilot's seat. "Hold on to your hat. Here we go…"

Say what you like about Mars, about the Colony, about the poor old relic of a plane, Tony thought, when you took a look at the kids you began to understand what it was all about. A year ago, Tad had been a thoroughly obnoxious brat. But how could he be anything else on Earth?

THEY were all that way. You got born into a hate-thy-neighbor, envy-thy-neighbor, murder-thy-neighbor culture. In your infancy your overworked and underfed mother's breast was always withdrawn too soon and you were filled again and again, day after day, with blind and squalling rage. You were a toddler and you snatched at another one's bit of candy; you were hungry and you hated him; you fought him. You learned big boys' games—Killakraut, Wackawop, Nigger inna Graveyard, Chinks an' Good Guys, Stermation Camp, Loot the City. The odds were you were hungry, always hungry.

Naked dictatorship and leader worship, oligarchy and dollar-worship; sometimes one was worse, sometimes the other. The forms didn't matter; the facts did. Too many mouths, not enough topsoil. Middle classes with their relatively stable, relatively sane families were growing smaller and being ground out of existence as still more black dirt washed into the ocean and still more hungry mouths were born and prices went higher and higher—how long, in God's name; could it go on? How long before it blew up, and not figuratively speaking either?

The Panamerican World Federation, first with the most, refused to tolerate the production of mass-destruction weapons anywhere else in the world. Long calloused to foreign mutterings, the Western colossus would at irregular intervals fire off a guided missile on the advice of one of its swarm of intelligence agents. In Tartary or France or Zanzibar. Then, an innocent-looking structure would go up in a smoke mushroom. But they never stopped trying, and some day Tartary or France or Zanzibar would launch a missile of its own and it would mean nothing less than the end of the world in fire and plague as the rocket trails laced continents together and the bombers rained botulisn, radiocobalt and flasks of tritium with bikinis in their cores.

THE damned, poverty-ridden, swarming Earth. Short of food, short of soil, short of water, short of metals—short of everything except vicious, universal resentments and aggressions bred by the other shortages.

That's what they were running from, the new arrivals he was going to meet today. He hoped there wouldn't be any more communicable disease carriers to quarantine at Marsport and fire back on the return trip without even a look around. There were supposed to be six medical examinations between the first application filed at the Sun Lake Society office in New York, and embarcation. But things must have got appreciably worse on Earth since—he started a little at the thought—"since his time." It seemed that now anybody could be reached. They used to say everybody had his price. Maybe it was true.

He'd never had a chance to turn down a really big bribe, so he I couldn't say. But if six boards of doctors could all be fixed, everybody's price must have taken a drastic slump.

Tad, sound asleep, rolled onto his stomach and humped up his behind, scene of the history-making operation, in a brief reversion to infancy.

"How come the rocket's getting in early?" Bea called back. "I didn't even have time to ask Harve about it last night, with the *Girl* spread out all over the field."

"Something about the throat liner. They have a new remote control servicing apparatus on Earth," Tony said. "Gets the liner out and cleaned and in faster. We save two weeks on each trip, and get an extra trip—what is it?—every two years?"

"Year and a half," Bea corrected. She was silent a moment, then snorted, *"Rockets."*

"At least," Tony deadpanned, "rockets give you a smooth ride. Fat chance of getting any sleep in this pile…"

"The *Girl* never gave you a rough trip in your life," she interrupted angrily. She pulled on the stick and swung the *Girl* into a downwind.

The doctor drowsily studied her, silhouetted against the stars through the windshield. She was attached to the old crate—ought to find herself a husband. It had looked like her and Flexner for a while, but then the chemist had paired off with Verna Blau. As the motor warmed up, Bea unzipped her parka and shrugged out of it. Definitely, Tony decided, the best shape in Sun Lake. Trim, fined-down, athletic, but no doubt at all, from this angle that the figure was feminine—even under the bulky sweater she still wore.

HE LAY back on his improvised couch and reflected on how pleasant it would be to stand behind her and run his hands down over her shoulders—infinitely pleasant just to stand behind her while she flew the ship. Pleasant but impractical. Play hell with her Estimated Time of Arrival at Marsport, for one thing, and, to take a longer view, he probably would end up by marrying her—her and *Lazy Girl*: the two went together.

Tony stirred uncomfortably. While he was thinking idly goatish thoughts about Bea, Anna had turned up in his mind, with a halfsmile on her face. It was typical, he thought, puzzled; Anna never intruded until the moment you wanted her…*if* you wanted her, he added unhappily, giving the verb a new meaning. Anna's smile was a tingling mystery; her dark eyes were wells of warmth in which a man could lose himself; but after all these months, he wasn't sure of their color. And even when she crept into his mind, it was only from the neck up that he visualized her.

That wasn't the way he saw Bea. Tony shook himself, stretched out and let his eyes linger on the girl in the pilot's seat until he fell asleep.

\*   \*   \*

THE sun was up when Bea eased the freighter in among more planes than they had ever seen before on Arrival Day. They recognized the elegant staff-carrier from Sun Lake's neighbor, Pittco Three, but didn't know the other twelve that were parked.

"Swell ride, Bea," said the doctor. "Now what is *this* dress parade all about...? Oh, sure. Douglas Graham is going to gunth Mars. These should be the bigshots from the commercial colonies."

"I hate these damned superficial gunthers," Bea said fiercely. "Is he going to bother Sun Lake?"

"Nick thinks he might zip through at the end of his tour, if he has time." He hopped to the ground, Tad following with the boxed lab. "You've got the shopping list, Bea?" the doctor asked. "I have to go over to the Ad Building. Don't think I'll have time for anything else. Can you get all the stuff?"

"Sure," she said easily. "We're not buying much this time."

Tony ignored the bitter significance of the remark. "We'll see you later, then. I hope this red-carpet business for Graham doesn't slow things up too much. I'd like to get back before lunch."

Tad was fidgeting next to him, waiting for a chance to break in.

A year ago, the boy had spent two days in Marsport, when he arrived with his family and the other founding members of the Colony. Then he had nothing more than a pitying sneer for the village of 600 people; now it was a place of wonder.

"Dr. Tony," he asked eagerly, "can we go to the Arcade?"

"We can go *through* it," Tony decided.

The Arcade was Aladdin's cave to Tad. To the Planetary Affairs Commission, which rented out booth space in the ramshackle building, it was a source of revenue. To Tony it was the stronghold of the irrepressible small retailer, who found his way even to Mars with articles he could buy cheap and sell dear…a reminder of the extent to which Mars was already taking over the social and economic patterns of Earth.

Booths at the Arcade did not display radiation counters, hand tools, welders, rope, radio, aluminum I-beams, airplane parts or half-tracks. Those you bought at the P.A.C. Stores, which were reliable, conservative and dull.

At the Arcade there was one booth, which sold nothing but coffee in the cup: MARTIAN $2.00; EARTHSIDE $15.00 (WITH SUGAR $25.00). Tony knew the privateer who ran this concession might be ruined by another arrival aboard today's racket, landing in paper-light clothes with his garment and personal luggage allowance taken up by bricks of Earthside coffee and sugar, burning to undercut the highwayman who had beaten him to the happy hunting grounds of Mars.

At another booth the most beautiful collie, boxer and English shepherd pups were for sale at the astounding price of only twenty dollars each. The catch was that the proprietor of this booth was the only merchant on Mars with a stock of dog food.

At another booth Tad's jaw dropped with perplexity. "Dr. Tony, what are those?" he asked.

"Underwear, Tad. For women."

"But don't they get *cold* in those things?"

"Well, they would if they went out and worked like our women. But—well, for instance in Pittco, over the Rimrock Hills from us, there are some ladies who only work indoors, where it's heated."

"*All* heated? Not just beam heat on the beds and things?"

"I'm afraid I don't really know. Say… Look at those boots there—aren't they something?"

"Boy…" The boots were mirror-shiny zipper jobs. "What I wouldn't give for a pair of *those*. Put 'em on when new kids come in, and then watch them try to walk around in Earth sandals, and get a load of that sand."

Here on Mars, the price put the boots infinitely far out of reach for a boy like Tad, even if Sun Lake's policies did not prevent the purchase of such an item. Some supervisor in an industrial colony, Tony thought, would eventually acquire them as illusion of escape from the sands of Mars.

And that reminded him. He turned to Tad.

"By the way, what do you know about kids going barefoot around the colony? When did that start?"

"Barefoot?" Tad looked outraged. "What do you think we are—dopes?"

"I think," Tony answered drily, "that anybody who'd go strolling around the Rimrock caves without boots on is about as much of a jackass as he can be."

"In the *caves?*" This time Tony thought he detected a note of more honest horror. All the kids went barefoot sometimes in the experimental fields; everybody knew about it and pretended not to. The kids were pretty careful about not stepping on marked planted rows, and the fields had been processed to remove native poison-salts from the soil.

"Listen, Dr. Tony," Tad said earnestly, "if any of the kids are doing that, I'll put a stop to it. They ought to know better. *You* remember that time you had to fix my hand, before the—uh—other thing, when I just thought I'd pick up a piece of rock and it practically sliced my finger off. They shouldn't be walking barefoot around there."

"I remember." Tony smiled. "'Sliced your finger off is a slight exaggeration, but I wouldn't like to have to handle a mess of feet like that. If you know who's doing it, you tell them I said to cut it out...or they may not be walking at all after a while."

"I'll let them know." Tad walked along silently, ignoring the bright displays as they passed, and Tony seized the chance to direct their footsteps out of the Arcade. "Dr. Tony," the boy said finally, "you didn't mean for me to tell you who it was in case I knew, did you?"

"Lord, no!" The doctor *had* been hoping to find out. But he realized now what an error he'd almost made.

A year ago, Tad had been as miserable a little snitch and talebearer as Earth could produce, "I just want it stopped, that's all."

"Okay, then." Tad's face relaxed into a friendly grin. "It will be."

*We've got to keep going*, the doctor thought. For himself, for the other adults, it didn't matter so much. But for the kids...

\* \* \*

TONY had absolutely no respect for Nowton, the P.A.C. medical officer, because Nowton was stupid. Fortunately Nowton was so stupid that he didn't realize this and greeted the Sun Lake medic joyfully.

"Hear you been up to tricks, boy. Why didn't you come to me instead? I got ways to get marcaine."

"Glad to hear it, and I'll bet you do. While we were stealing that marcaine, we also had a baby. Got a form?"

"Corporal!" yelled Nowton. "Birth form!" A noncom produced the piece of official paper and Tony filled it in, checking weight and other data with notes in his pocket.

"That hot pilot of yours still around?" asked Nowton.

"Bea Juarez? Sure. Interested? Just tell her that her plane's a disgusting old wreck and you'll get her a new one. She always falls for that line."

"No kidding?"

"Who'd kid you, Nowton? Say, is Ed Nealey anywhere?"

"In the signal room. Where's Juarez, did you say?"

"I'll see you, Nowton." Tony hurried off.

HE FOUND the lieutenant reading a medical journal, which had passed through his own hands months earlier, on its way around the joint subscription club of which both men were members. The club made it possible for them, in common with twenty-odd fellow-members on Mars, to keep up with technical and scientific publications without paying ruinous amounts in interplanetary postage.

"Hello, Ed."

Nealey put out his hand. "I didn't know whether you'd still be talking to me, Tony."

"Hell, you don't give the orders. You have to play it the way Bell calls it. Ed, off the record—you're pretty sure it was one of our people?"

"All I'm sure of, it wasn't a phony. To qualify with the Bloodhound on Earth, we had to follow made trails—where they dragged bags of aniseed over the spoor. You can tell the difference. This one faded and wobbled like the real thing. And we lost it not more than a couple of miles out of your place, headed straight your way. Tony, have you *searched*?"

"Some. We're not done yet." The doctor lowered his voice. "What's the matter with Commissioner Bell, Ed? Does he have anything special against us?"

The lieutenant jerked his chin a little at a Pfc sitting with earphones on his head, reading a comic book, and led the doctor into the corridor.

"God, what a post," he said. "Tony, all I know is that Bell's a lost soul outside the Insurantist Party's inner circle. He had fifteen years of being looked up to as the Grand Old Man of the Mexicaliforniarizonan Insurantists, and now he's been booted to Mars. He'd do anything, I believe, to get back into the party. And don't forget that Brenner's been a heavy contributor to the Insurantist campaign funds during the last three elections. You know I'm professional military and I'm not supposed to and don't want to have anything to do with politics—"

Commissioner Bell came stumping down the corridor. "Lieutenant Nealey," he interrupted.

Nealey came to as casual an attitude of attention as his years of drilling would allow.

"Surely you have better things to do with your time than palavering with persons suspected of harboring criminals."

"Dr. Hellman is my friend, sir."

"Very interesting. I suggest you go on about your duties and pick your friends more discriminatingly."

"Whatever you say, *sir*." With slow deliberation, the lieutenant turned and shook Tony's hand. "I'm on duty now," he said tightly. "I'll see you around. So long, kid." he put his hand on Tad's shoulder, wheeled about smartly, and turned back into the signal room.

"Come on, Tad," said the doctor. "We're all done here. We might as well get out to the rocket field."

## CHAPTER TEN

THEY were approaching the rocket field and what was, for Mars, an immense crowd—some five hundred people behind a broad white deadline marked on the tamped dirt of the field. It was an odd-looking crowd because it was not jammed into the smallest possible space, body to body, Earth-fashion. The people stood separately, like forest trees, with a good square meter around each of them. It was a Mars crowd, made up of people with lots of room, Tony stopped well away from the fringe of the group.

"This looks like a good spot," he decided. "Put the box down there; we can start setting things up."

"Doctor Hellman—hello!" A tall man, fully dressed in Earthside business clothes, strolled over. Tony had seen him only once before, when he had appeared at the Lab with Bell to make his monstrous accusation of theft. But Hugo Brenner was not an easy man to forget.

"Hello," Tony said shortly, and turned back to his box.

"Thought you might be here today." Brenner ignored the doctor's movement away from him, and went on smoothly. "I want to tell you how sorry I am about what happened. Frankly, if I'd known the trail would lead to your place, I might have thought twice before I called copper—but you understand, it's not the first time. I've let it go before. This time they took so much I couldn't very well overlook it."

"I understand perfectly," Tony assured him. "We disapprove of theft at Sun Lake too."

"Well, I'm glad to hear you don't take it personally, Doctor. As a matter of fact, I'm almost glad it happened. I've heard a lot about you and the kind of job you've been doing over there. I wish we could have met under more pleasant circum—"

"It's very kind of you to say so," Tony interrupted, deliberately misunderstanding. "I didn't think a man in your position would be much impressed by what we're doing at Sun Lake."

Brenner smiled. "I think Sun Lake is a very interesting experiment," he said in a monotone that clearly expressed his lack of interest. "What I had in mind…"

"Of course, Mr. Brenner." Whatever the drug man had to say to him personally, the doctor did not wish to hear it. "We realize your only interest is in the recovery of your stolen goods. We're doing our best to find the thief…*if* he really is a member of our Colony, that is."

"Please, Doctor, don't put words in my mouth. Naturally I'm interested in recovering my goods, but I'm not worried about it. I'm quite sure your people will turn up the guilty party." Again his voice carried a flat lack of conviction.

"Commissioner Bell has seen to it that we turn up *a* guilty party," Tony retorted.

"I think the Commissioner was unnecessarily harsh." Hugo Brenner shrugged it off. "If it had been up to me…well, that's Bell's job; I suppose he has to handle it his own way. Let's quit beating around the bush, Doctor. I came over here to offer you a job, not to talk…"

"No."

"Suppose you listen to my offer first."

"*No.*"

"All right, then. Name your own terms. I'll meet your price. I need a doctor. A good one."

"I don't want to work for you at any price."

Brenner's mouth turned up at the corners. Obviously he enjoyed the game, and equally obviously he thought he was going to win.

"LET me mention a figure." He moved closer. "One million dollars a year."

Well, thought the doctor, now he had a clearer idea of what his own price was; now he knew it wasn't a million dollars. Ten times what he made in a peak year on Earth. He looked full into Brenner's smirking face, and knew something else: he hadn't been so clear through boiling mad in a long time; and he was fed up with diplomacy. Deliberately, he raised his voice: "Didn't you hear me before, Brenner? Or didn't you understand?"

He found it was gratifying to notice people turning his way, edging in to listen.

"Let me make myself absolutely clear," he went on loudly. "I don't want to work for you. I don't like the business you're in. I know what you need a doctor for, and so does everyone else on Mars. If your boys over at Hop Heaven can't keep their noses out of your marcaine, that's not my worry. I don't want to be resident physician in a narcotics factory. Stay away from me."

The smirk had left Brenner's face; it was ugly, contorted, and much too close. Tony realized, too late, that Brenner's fist was even closer. Abruptly, he stopped feeling like a hero and began to feel like a fool.

Then, quite suddenly, Brenner's fist was no longer approaching, and Brenner was flat on the ground. Tony tried to figure out what had happened. It didn't make sense. He became aware of a ring of grinning congratulatory faces surrounding him, and of Tad next to him, giggling gleefully. He called to the boy curtly, turned on his heel, and walked back the few steps to his portable lab.

Nobody helped Brenner to his feet. He must have got up by himself, because when Tony looked back, out of the corner of his eye, Brenner was gone.

A short man bustled up. "I heard that, Dr. Hellman. I didn't see you hit him, but I heard you tell him off." He pumped Tony's hand delightedly.

"Hello, Chabrier." That makes two of us, Tony thought—I didn't see myself hit him either. "Look, I know it's no use asking you not to talk about it, but go easy, will you? Don't blow it up too much when you tell it."

"It needs no amplification. You slap his face in challenge. He reaches for a weapon. You knock him unconscious with a single blow. You tell him: 'Hugo Brenner, there is not gold enough—'"

"Knock off, will you?" begged the doctor. "He wanted me to work over at his place by Syrtis Major—Brenner Pharmaceuticals Corporation, whatever he calls it. You know all his people get a marcaine craving from the stuff that leaks out of his lousy machinery. He wanted me there to keep giving his boys cures. I said no and he offered me a lot of money and I got sore. I shot off my mouth. He started to sock me and—"

And what? Tony still hadn't figured that out. He turned back to the box, still only half set up.

Chabrier said thoughtfully: "So you know that much, eh? Then you know it's nothing new, this business of missing marcaine?"

TONY abruptly turned back to him, no longer uninterested. "Brenner said something about previous thefts. What's it all about?"

"Only what you said yourself." Chabrier shrugged. "What did he offer you? Three hundred thousand? Four?" He paused, and when Tony made no reply, went on: "You can get better than that. It would be cheaper than junking his plant and building a new one."

"I know I can get better than that," the doctor said impassively. "What do you know about the missing marcaine, Chabrier?"

"NOTHING all of Marsport doesn't know. Was it in the neighborhood of half a million? That would be much less than the freight rates for new machines. He's used to freight being only a small part of his overhead. He ships a concentrated product." Chabrier chuckled happily. "How it must hurt when he thinks of importing plate and tubes and even, God forbid, *castings*. I tell you, a man doesn't *know* what freight can mean until he's handled liquor. Bulk is bad. Even just running the bulk liquor into the glass-lined tanks of the

rocket ships is bad. It means that Mars ships water to Earth. *Actually!*
But the foolish laws say we cannot dehydrate, let the water be added
on Earth, and still label it Mars liquor."

"Please," said Tony wryly. "Please, Chabrier..."

The man shrugged. "So we take a *little* of the water out—fifty
percent, say. Water is water, they pour it in on Earth, nobody knows,
nobody cares. Bulk shipment is still bad, very bad. But *bottles.* Dr.
Hellman, there is no known way of dehydrating a glass bottle. We
ship them in, we fill them, we ship them back. They break, people
steal them here and aboard ship, and at the Earth rocket port. All so
the label can say 'Bottled on Mars.'"

"Muffle your sobs, Chabrier. I happen to know that people pay
for Mars liquor and pay a great deal for bottled-on-Mars. At least,
you're legal, and I understand you make good stuff."

"I drink it myself," said Chabrier righteously.

"To save the freight on Earthside rye?" Tony grinned, then asked
seriously, "Listen, Chabrier, if you know anything about this marcaine
business that we don't, for God's sake, spill it. We...I don't have to
tell you how hard this thing is hitting us out at Sun Lake. *What* does
all of Marsport know?"

"Was it perhaps seven-fifty?" the other man asked blandly.

Fair exchange, Tony decided. "A million," he said.

"*So?* This I do not understand. Why so much for a doctor, if he is
to have a new plant?" Chabrier shook his head, shrugged, and went
on more briskly: "I have told you already, if you understand: Brenner
needs a new plant. His machines are no good. They leak. His men
inhale the micron dust, they get the craving, and they start to steal the
product. Soon they are no good for the work, and he sends them
back to Earth. You see today how many new men he brings in? Then
one day there is more marcaine missing. He..."

"One minute, Chabrier." Tony turned and signaled Tad to take a
break, then moved off a few steps, and motioned to the other man to
follow him. "You think it's a frame-up?" he demanded in a low,
intense voice.

"You would have me speak against our Commissioner Bell?"
Chabrier asked with only the faintest trace of sarcasm showing. "Such
a thing I will not do, but I beg of you to consider, if Sun Lake Colony
should be bankrupt, their Laboratory must be sold at auction by the
Commissioner, and such a plant would suit Mr. Brenner very well

indeed. They say here in Marsport the machinery in this Laboratory is adaptable to many kinds of production. They say it is good, tight, well-built equipment, it will not leak. Till now it seemed quite clear." The little man shook his head doubtfully. "Now I do not know. A plant? Yes. A doctor? Yes. But *both*...and he offered a million? This I do *not* understand, unless he plans to work both plants. There is a rumor, which has some currency today..."

THE deep bass booming of the warning horn cut him off. People began edging away from the center of the field, terminating conversations, rejoining their own groups.

"You will excuse me now? I must go," Chabrier said, when the horn died down enough to permit conversation again. "I have my place reserved, but they will not hold it..."

"Place?" Tony, still trying to catch up with the implications of the other man's news, didn't follow the quick shift. "What for? Oh, are you after Douglas Graham, too?"

"Of course. I understand he is...let us say, a drinker. If I can reach him before any of these other vultures...who knows? Maybe a whole chapter on Mars liquor." He seized Tony's hand in a quick grasp of friendship. "Good luck, Doctor Hellman," he said, and dashed off, running ludicrously on his short legs to rejoin his own party before the landing.

Tony searched the sky; the rocket was not yet in sight. He got back to work, swiftly now, setting up his equipment. Chabrier had mentioned a rumor. Never mind, there was enough to think about.

The whole thing planned beforehand, to ruin Sun Lake. *Maybe.* Chabrier was notorious as a gossip and petty troublemaker. A frame-up. *Maybe.* And how could they find out? Who was responsible? Who was innocent? Nealey, Nowton; Bell and Brenner; Chabrier with his fluid chatter and his shrewd little eyes. Nealey at least was a decent, competent man... *Maybe.* But how could you tell? How could you single them out?

Parasites, he thought bitterly, the cheerful Chabrier as much as the arrogant Brenner. Mars liquor brought fantastic prices because it was distilled from mashes of Martian plants containing carbohydrates, instead of being distilled from mashes of Earth plants containing carbohydrates. And the friendly, plump little man got plumper on the profits culled from Earth's neurotic needs. It wasn't really much of an improvement on Brenner's marcaine business. A minor difference in moral values, but all of them were parasites as long as they didn't devote their time to the terrible problem of freeing Mars from the shadow of Earth's dominance.

And what about our Lab? Unquestionably, it was better to concentrate radioactive methylene blue for the treatment of cancerous kidneys than it was to concentrate alkaloids for Earthside gow-heads, but that, too, was only a difference in moral values. Parasites, all...

"The rocket," yelled Tad.

## CHAPTER ELEVEN

IT LOOKED like a bit of the sun at first; that was its braking blasts seen from under. The monster settled swiftly, roaring and flaring in a teasing mathematical progression of successively shorter blasts more closely spaced. When you could see its silvery bulk in profile it was going *pop-pop-pop-pop-pop*, like a machine gun. It settled with a dying splutter and stood on the field some two hundred meters from the crowd like a remembered skyscraper.

Trucks raced out to meet it. Inside, the doctor knew, crewmen were walking around capstans that fitted over and unscrewed ten-kilogram hex-nuts. The trucks slowed and crawled between the fins on which the rocket stood, directly under its exhaust nozzle. Drivers cut and filled to precise positions; then platforms jacked up from the crane trucks to receive the rim of the rocket's throat. Men climbed the jacks to fasten them.

The captain must have radioed from inside the ship; the last of the first hex-nuts was off. Motor away. Slowly the platforms descended, taking the reaction engine with them. The crane trucks crawled off, two ants sharing an enormous burden.

The crew inside was busy again, dismantling fuel tanks, while the trucks moved to the inspection and repair shed off the field. A boom lifted off the motor, and the drivers scuttled back to receive the first installment of the fuel tanks, the second, the third and the last.

"Now do the people come out?" asked Tad.

"If the rocket hasn't got any more plumbing, they do," Tony told him. "Yes—here we go." Down between the fins descended a simple elevator, the cargo hoist letting down a swaying railed platform on a cable. It was jammed with people. The waiting port officer waved them toward the Administration Building. The crowd, which had overflowed gently past the broad white line on the field, drifted that way, too.

"Stanchions! Get stanchions out!" the port officer yelled. Two field workers broke out posts and a rope that railed off the crowd from the successive hoist-loads of people herded into the Administration Building for processing. There was a big murmur at the third load—*Graham*. The doctor was too far back to get a good look at the great man.

The loudspeaker on top of the building began to talk in a brassy rasp:

"Brenner Pharmaceuticals. Baroda, Schwartz, Hopkins, W. Smith, Avery for Brenner Pharmaceuticals," it said. Brenner ducked under the rope to meet five men issuing from the building. He led them off the field, talking earnestly and with gestures.

"Pittco. Miss Kearns for Pittco Three."

A pretty girl stepped through the door and looked about helplessly. A squat woman strode through the crowd, took the girl by the arm and led her off.

Radiominerals Corporation got six replacements; Distillery Mars got a chemist and two laborers; Metro Films got a cameraman who would stay and a pair of actors who would be filmed against authentic backgrounds and leave next week with the prints. A squad of soldiers headed by a corporal appeared and some of the field workers let out a cheer; they were next for rotation. Brenner got two more men; Kelly's Coffee Bar got Mrs. Kelly, bulging with bricks of coffee and sugar.

"Sun Lake City Colony," said the loudspeaker. "W. Jenkins, A. Jenkins, R. Jenkins, L. Jenkins, for Sun Lake."

"Watch the box," Tony called to Tad as he strode off.

HE PICKED up the identification and authorization slips waiting for him at the front desk inside, and examined them curiously. Good, he thought, a family with kids. The loudspeaker was now running continuously. Two more for Chabrier, three engineers for Pittco Headquarters in Marsport.

A uniformed stewardess came up to him.

"Dr. Hellman? From Sun Lake?" Her voice was professionally melodious. He nodded. "These are Mr. and Mrs. Jenkins." she turned to the family group behind her. "And Bobby and Louise Jenkins," she added, smiling.

The kids were about seven and four years old respectively. Tony smiled down at them, shook hands with their parents, and presented his authorizations to the stewardess.

"—Prentiss, Skelly and Zaretsky for Sun Lake," the loudspeaker called.

"Excuse me, I'll be right back," Tony said and headed back to the desk.

They gave him more authorization slips. He riffled through the papers quickly as he headed back to find the Jenkinses and wait for the newcomers. All different names. Only one family, the rest singles. Too bad.

He hunted through his pockets and found two packets of peanuts, mutated beyond recognition into chewy objects with a flavor something like grape pop.

By the time Bobby and Lou had overcome their shyness enough to accept the gifts, another stewardess was bringing up the rest of the group destined for Sun Lake.

"Dr. Hellman?" Her voice was as much like the first stewardess' as her uniform, but according to ancient custom this one was blonde and the other brunette. "Miss Skelly, Miss Dantuono, Mr. Graham, Mr. Prentiss, Mr. Bond, Mr. Zaretsky," she said and vanished.

Tony nodded and shook hands all around.

"Let's get out of here," he said. "It's quieter outside and I have to give you all a physical checkup, so—"

"Again?" one of the men groaned. "We just had one on board."

"I think I've had a million different shots since I started all this," the other girl put in. What was her name? Dantuono? "Do we get more needles?"

"I'm afraid so. We have to be careful, you know." Some day he would meet a rocket, and nobody—but nobody—would make that particular remark. Or perhaps that was too much to hope for. "Let's get out of here," Tony said again. He offered his hands to the children, and they started moving.

BY THE time they reached Tad and the box that held the portable health lab, the crowd was already thinning out.

"We'll get right to it," the doctor addressed his group. "I'm sorry I can't examine you indoors under more comfortable circumstances, but

I have to make a quick check before we can even let you on board the ship. It won't take long if we start right away."

"Doesn't the port have facilities for this sort of thing?" someone asked.

"Sure. They've got a beautiful setup right inside the Ad Building. Anybody can use it. Sun Lake can't afford the price."

He called them up one at a time, starting with the Jenkinses, parents and then children, so the kids wouldn't have too much time to get apprehensive about the needles. His trained reflexes went through the business of blood and sputum tests, eye-ear-nose-and-throat, fluoroscopy, and nervous-and-mental, while he concentrated on getting acquainted.

Names began to attach themselves to faces. He finished with the two single girls, and started on the men. The big, red-faced one was Zaretsky; skinny little bookkeeper-type was Prentiss. The talkative one was Graham.

"First name?" Tony was filling in the reports while the samples went through analysis.

"Douglas."

"Drop-in or shares?"

"Drop-in, I guess. On Earth we call it the working press."

"Press?" Tony looked up sharply. "*The* Douglas Graham?"

"The *This Is* man. Didn't you know I was coming out?" Tony hesitated, and Graham asked quickly, "Your place *is* open to the press, isn't it?"

"Oh, sure. We just—well, frankly, we didn't think you'd bother with us. Certainly didn't think you'd come to us first. We'd have rolled out the red carpet." He grinned and pointed to the array of planes at the other end of the field; for the first time, he became aware of the curious and envious stares their small group was receiving from passersby. "Everybody else did. I guess we were about the only outfit on Mars that didn't at least *hope* to bring you back home today." He turned his attention to the checkup form. "Age?"

"Thirty-two."

"FROM appearance and general condition, Tony would have given the journalist ten more years; it was a shock to find that they were both the same age. He finished without further comment and went on to the next and last, a lanky blond youth named Bond. By the time he was done, the analyses and reaction tests were complete.

The doctor checked them over carefully. "You're all right," he announced to the group at large. "We can get started now."

It was a slow trip. None of the newcomers were accustomed to the low gravity; they were wearing heavy training boots acquired on board the rocket. And all of them were determined to see everything that was to be seen in Marsport before they took off. Tony led them across the spaceport field, and down the main street of Marsport, a mighty boulevard whose total length was something under five hundred yards, the distance from the spaceport to the landing strip.

He answered eager questions about the ownership and management of the hotels and office building that lined the block adjacent to the spaceport. These were mostly privately owned and privately built, constructed of glass brick. The native product had a sparkling multicolored sheen that created a fine illusion of wealth and high fashion—even when you knew that no building made of the stuff could possibly stand more than ten years: the same slightly different chemical content of Martian potash that produced the lustrous coloration of the bricks made them particularly susceptible to the damaging effects of wind and sand. Glass brick construction was, by far, more costly than the rammed-earth buildings at Sun Lake, or the scrap-shanties that characterized the Pittco camp across the Rimrock Hills from the Colony; but it was still much less expensive than the Earth-import steel and alumalloy used wherever strength and durability were important.

THE Administration Building of the Planetary Affairs Commission, which occupied one entire side of the center block, was sheathed in a muted green alumalloy; the P.A.C. Stores and official P.A.C. hotel, across the street, were respectively dull rose and dove gray. The doctor pointed out each building in turn to his wide-eyed group. The writer was as eager as any of the others, and asked as many questions. Tony was surprised; he had anticipated a bored sophistication.

Graham responded equally unpredictably to the series of interruptions they met with en route. Chabrier was first, even before they had left the spaceport. He dashed up to pump Tony's hand and babble that he was delighted to see him again, and how well Tony looked despite his drab sojourn in the so-dull Sun Lake where *nothing* ever happened.

"But this is Mr. Graham, isn't it?" he exclaimed in delight.

"Yeah," said the writer dryly.

"How fortunate. Distillery Mars, my concern, small but interesting, happens to be preparing a new run of Mars liquor, 120 proof—we should be so honored if you could make a point of sampling our little effort, shall we say this afternoon? I have *comfortable*—" a sidelong glance at Tony—"transportation here."

"Maybe later."

"To a connoisseur of your eminence, of course, we should think it a privilege to offer you an honor-arium—"

"Maybe later, maybe not," grunted the writer.

Chabrier only shrugged and smiled; the gunther could say no wrong. "You will perhaps be pleased to accept a small sample of the product of Mars Distillery?" The little man held up a gaudily wrapped package. He pressed the gift into Graham's indifferent grasp, wrung Tony's hand warmly, said heartily, "We will look forward to see you soon," and departed.

Halliday of Mars Machine Tool was next. His manner was more that of a man inviting a guest to his country club, but he *did* mention that MMT would, of course, expect to provide for a writer's necessary expenses. Graham cut off Halliday's bluff assurances as curtly as he had stopped Chabrier's outpourings. It was like that all the way.

Everybody who was anybody on Mars was in town that day, and each of them managed to happen on the Sun Lake crowd somewhere along the road from the spaceport to the landing strip.

THOSE who met Tony at any time in the past were all determined to stop him for a chat; then they noticed Graham, and extended a coincidental but warm invitation. Those who were unacquainted with Sun Lake's doctor were forced to be more direct, and the bribe was sometimes even more marked than Chabrier's or Halliday's offers.

Graham was cold and even nasty to them. But once he took Tony's arm and said: "Wait. I see an old friend." Commissioner Bell was up ahead, striding toward the Administration Building.

"Him?" asked Tony.

"Yeah. Hey, Commish!"

Bell stopped as if he had been shot. He turned slowly toward Graham, and stood his ground as the writer approached. When he spoke, there was cold hatred in his voice. "Just the company I'd expect you to keep, Graham. Stay out of trouble. I'm the man in charge here, and don't think I'm afraid of you."

"You weren't the last time," said Graham. "That was your big mistake—Commish."

Bell walked away without another word.

"You shot his blood pressure up about 20 millimeters," said Tony. "What's it all about?"

"I claim a little credit for sending Bell to Mars, Doc. I caught him with his fingers in the till up to his shoulder, at a time when his political fences were down, if you don't mind a mixed metaphor. I couldn't get him jailed, but I'll bet up here he sometimes wishes I had."

A wild hope flared in Tony. The *This Is* man was, sporadically, known as a crusader. Perhaps Graham's annoyance at the crude plays for attention meant that an appeal could be made on the basis of decency and fair play.

\* \* \*

BY THE time they reached the plane, Tad was already on the spot with the portable health lab stowed away, and Bea was warming up the motors.

"Hi!" She stuck her head out of the cockpit to grin at Tony. "Got everybody? Tad, hand out parkas to these people. Tony, they tell me you're a hero—had it out with big, bad Brenner in real style." She didn't quite say: "I never thought you had it in you."

"Things get around, don't they? Bea, this is Douglas Graham. He's coming out to have a look at Sun Lake for a book he's doing. This is Bea Juarez," he told the writer. "She's our pilot."

Graham surveyed Bea. "I hope everything in the Colony looks as good."

"We'll be extra careful to show you only the best," she retorted. "Hey, Tad, get that mink-lined parka, will you? We've got a guest to impress."

Tony was delighted. If everyone else in the Colony could take the Great Man in stride so easily, he would be pleased and very much surprised.

Tad came running up with a parka. "What kind did you say you wanted? This is the only one left, except Dr. Tony's."

The three adults burst into laughter, and Tad retreated, red-faced.

Graham called him back. "I'm going to need that thing if the temperature in the cockpit doesn't go up."

"You're going to need it anyhow," Tony assured him. "There's a lot to be said for *Lazy Girl* here, but she's not one hundred percent airtight."

"I get the idea," the journalist assured him. "You people don't throw heat around, do you?"

"Not heat or anything else," replied Tony. "You'll see, if you can stick it out."

"What the hell, I was a war correspondent in Asia."

"This isn't a war. There isn't anything exciting to make up for the discomfort—except, say, when a baby gets born—"

"No? I take it there was something going on just a little while ago. What were you saying about the doctor being a hero?" he called forward to Bea.

She shrugged. "All I know is what I hear on the grapevine."

Tony heaved a mental sigh of relief—too soon.

"I was there." Tad had stuck right by them. "This man Mr. Brenner came over and asked Dr. Tony to come work for him, and he wouldn't, and he tried to get him with a whole lot of money, but he still wouldn't, and—"

"HOLD on," Graham interrupted. "First thing you have to learn if you're going to be a reporter is to get your pronouns straight. This Brenner was doing the offering, and Doc was refusing; that right?"

"Sure. That was what I was saying—"

"Look, Tad, we were only kidding about impressing Mr. Graham," Tony said quickly. "You don't have to make a hero out of me. I just had a disagreement with someone," he said to Graham, "and they're trying to make a good story out of it."

"That's what I'm after," Graham came back, "a good story. Tell me everything that happened, Tad."

The boy looked doubtfully from the doctor to the guest and back again.

"All right." Tony gave in. "But let's not make a 15-round fight out of it, Tad. Tell it just the way it happened, if you've got to tell it."

"Just *exactly*?"

"Yes," the doctor said firmly, "just the way it happened."

"Okay." Tad was far from disappointed. If anything, he was gleeful. "So this Mr. Brenner wanted Dr. Tony to come work at his place, curing people from *drugs*, and he wouldn't, and Mr. Brenner kept pestering him till he got mad, and he said he didn't like him and wouldn't work for him no matter what—I mean, Dr. Tony said that to Mr. Brenner—and Mr. Brenner got *real* mad, and started to swing at him, and—"

"Well, don't stop *now*," Graham said. "Who won?"

"Well...then Mr. Brenner started swinging and—I stuck my foot out and tripped him, and Mr. Chabrier came over right away and said how wonderful it was the way Dr. Tony had socked Mr. Brenner, and I guess that's what everybody thought." He looked up at Tony's astonished face, and finished defensively, "Well, you *said* to tell it just the way it happened."

## CHAPTER TWELVE

TONY fastened the hood of his parka more tightly around his head, as the chill air of flight crept into the cabin. Graham, beside him, was full of flip comment and curiosity, to which ordinary decency, let alone special diplomacy, demanded reply. But Tony shifted position and let his eyelids drop closed.

There was no mental eye to close and so thrust out the revised memory of the ridiculous incident with Brenner, nor any mental ear that could turn off the resounding echo of Bea Juarez' hilarity.

*You knew all along you never hit Brenner, didn't you?* he asked himself angrily. *You could have figured it out for yourself—if you wanted to. All right, then, don't think about that.*

The new colonists...he ought to do something about them, something to dispel the tense, apprehensive silence in the cabin. A speech of welcome, something like that.

Thank them for coming? Welcome them to Sun Lake? With the threat that hung over them all, new members and old, any speech like that would be ridiculous. Later in the day, they would be asked to sign final papers, turning over, once and for all, the funds they had already placed in the hands of the trustees on Earth, and receiving their full shares in the Colony. Before then they would learn the worst; they would be told about the accusation that might doom the Colony. But how could he tell them now, before they had ever seen Sun Lake, before they had glimpsed the spellbinding stretches of *Lacus Solis*, or had a chance to understand the promise implicit in the Lab's shining walls, in Joe Gracey's neatly laid out experimental fields?

And in front of the gunther, too, how much could he say, how much did he dare to say? Graham could wreck their hopes with a word—or solve their problems as easily, if he chose. Graham had exposed the Commissioner's corruptness once; he wasn't always just a gunther; he was a part-time crusader. Possibly, he would understand Sun Lake's desperate necessity...possibly?

"Oh, by the way," the writer was saying. "I've been wondering what kind of a checkup you have on these people for security."

"Security?" For a minute the word didn't make sense; Tony realized suddenly that he hadn't even heard the word for a year; not, at least, with that sinister, special meaning.

"Don't you investigate the newcomers' backgrounds?"

"The Sun Lake Society—the recruiting office—checks on their employment records and their schooling to see that we don't get any romantic phonies masquerading as engineers and agronomists. That and plenty of health checks are all we need. The office wouldn't have time for more, anyway. It handles all the Earthside paperwork on our imports and exports, advertises, interviews, writes letters to the papers when that damn fool free-love story pops up again—" He gave Graham a look.

"All right," laughed the writer. "I'll make a mental note: Sun Lake doesn't believe in sex."

TONY was ruefully aware that a comeback was expected of him, but he substituted a feebly appreciative smile and leaned back, tiredly letting his eyelids drop again, in an effort to simulate sleep.

Through slitted eyes, he studied the new arrivals. They were crouched on the cabin floor, bundled into their parkas, talking only occasionally. Even Tad, at the far end of the cabin with the Jenkins' children, was low-voiced and restrained. Tony could see him pulling miraculous Martian treasures from his pockets for display, then pouncing on the few Earth items the new children had to show in return, cautiously pulled forth from supposedly empty pockets, and held for view in a half-cupped hand.

Near them, Bessie Jenkins, the mother of the two youngsters sat half watching them, half talking to the mousier of the two single girls...Dantuono? Rose Dantuono that was it. Anita Skelly, her vivid red hair concealed under the hood of her parka, was carrying on a conversation in monosyllables with Bob Prentiss; they seemed to be communicating a good deal more by hand pressure than by word of mouth. A shipboard romance, Tony wondered, or had they known each other back on Earth?

He shifted his gaze to the other side of the cabin, where the remaining three men sat: Arnold Jenkins, the lanky Bond, and young Zaretsky. They were lined up in a silent row, leaning against the bulkhead, evidencing none of the interested enthusiasm one might have expected. His own depression, the doctor realized, was affecting everyone.

What could he say to them? Here they were, newly escaped from Earth, from a madhouse with a time bomb in the basement. It had cost each one of them more than he could estimate, in courage, in money, in work, to make the escape—and what could he promise them now?

With luck, with the help from Graham, with all the breaks, the best they could look forward to was the everyday life of the Colony: working like dogs, living like ants, because it was the only way to pull free of the doomed world from which they had fled. At worst, and the worst was imminent—back on the same rocket, or the next, or the one after that, back with all the others, destitute. Back to Earth, with no money, no job, no place to live, and no hope at all.

"Tony."

It was Graham again. "Yes?"

"It just occurred to me. Do you people charge for guest privileges? I'll be happy to shell out anything you think is reasonable. Sun Lake looks like a good story to me, and I want to stay on top of it."

"It hasn't come up before," Tony told him. "That means we'll have to vote on it. Personally, I'd vote for charging you."

"That's the idea. If I roast you in the book, you can say I was sore because you soaked me. If I give you a good report, you can prove it wasn't bought and paid for. Right."

"You're too shrewd for us Martian peasants, Graham. I was only thinking that we could use the money."

"Doc," Bea yelled back into the cabin. "Radio."

TONY got up and leaned over into the cockpit to accept the earphones Bea passed him.

"I can only spark a message back," she told him. "We didn't load the voice transmitter this trip."

He nodded. Through the phones a self-consciously important teenage voice was saying: "Sun Lake to *Lazy Girl*, Dr. Hellman. Sun Lake to *Lazy Girl*, Dr. Hellman. Sun Lake—"

"*Lazy Girl* to Sun Lake, I read you, Hellman," he said and Bea's hand sputtered it out on the key.

"Sun Lake to *Lazy Girl*, I read you—uh—seventy-two at Pittco, can *Lazy Girl* sixteen Pittco, over."

"Dr. Tony to Jimmy Holloway," he dictated, "cut out the numbers game, Jimmy, and tell me what you want, over."

The teen-age voice was hurt. "Sun Lake to *Lazy Girl*, medical emergency at Pittco Camp, can *Lazy Girl* change course and land at Pittco, over."

"*Lazy Girl* to Sun Lake, wilco, Jimmy, but where's O'Reilly, over."

"Sun Lake to *Lazy Girl* I don't know, Dr. Tony. They messaged us that O'Reilly wasn't due back from Marsport all day, over."

"*Lazy Girl* to Sun Lake, we'll take care of it, Jimmy, out." He passed the phone back to Bea. "Somebody's sick or hurt at Pittco. Drop me off there and I'll get back on one of their half-tracks."

"Right." Bea pulled out her map table.

The doctor went to the rear of the cabin where Tad had stowed the portable lab. He came back with a box of OxEn pills, and stood in the doorway between the cabin and the cockpit, facing the assembled group.

"These are the same pills you took on board the rocket this morning," he told them. "I don't think I have to warn you always to keep a few with you. Wherever you go, whatever you do, as long as you're on Mars don't forget that it's literally as much as your life is worth if you don't take one of these *every twenty-four hours*." They all knew that, of course; but there was no harm in impressing them with it again.

There was more he should say, but he didn't know what. He chose the next best alternative and sat down.

"What's cooking?" demanded Graham.

"Somebody sick or something at the Pittco outfit across the hills from our place. Their doctor's still in Marsport."

"Mind if I stick with you? I'd like to have a look at the place anyhow—when they're not ready for me."

Tony considered a moment, and decided he liked the idea. "Sure, come along."

"I'd kind of like to see that girl who was for Pittco."

"You met her on the rocket?"

"I met her, all right, but she gave me a faster freeze than your girl pilot here. What is she anyhow—a lady engineer? All brains and no bounce?"

"Not exactly," Tony said. "I guess she figured she was on vacation. She's a new recruit for the company brothel. Those are the only women they've got at Pittco."

"Well, I'll be damned…" Graham was silent a moment, then added thoughtfully, "No *wonder* she wasn't interested."

\* \* \*

*LAZY GIRL* touched down at Pittco near noon. The doctor and writer were met by Hackenberg, the mine boss, who drove out in a jeep as Bea zoomed her ship off over the hills to home.

"I think you're too late, Doc," he said.

"We'll see. Hack Hackenberg, Douglas Graham." They climbed in and the jeep rolled past the smokestacks of the refining plant, toward the huts of the settlement.

"Hell of a thing," grumbled Hackenberg. "Nobody's here. Madame Rose, Doc O'Reilly, Mr. Reynolds, all off at Marsport. God knows when they're coming back. Douglas Graham, did you say? You're the reporter Mr. Reynolds was going to bring back? How'd you happen to come in with the doc?"

"I'm the reporter," Graham said, "but it's the first I knew about coming here with Reynolds. Did he tell you that?"

"Maybe he just said he hoped you would. I don't know. I got my hands full as it is. I got a contract to be mine boss; everybody takes off and Big Ginny gets her chest busted up, the girls go nuts, and I take the rap. What a life."

"Was there a brawl?" asked the doctor.

"Nobody told me—they yanked me out of plant. They found Big Ginny over by the hills. She was all messed up—you know what I mean, Doc. They thought she was raped. Rape Big Ginny, for God's sake! It ain't reasonable."

"They *moved* her?"

"They took her back to Rose's. I tell them and tell them to leave 'em lay, just get 'em warm, give plasma, and wait for a doctor. It don't do any good. First thing they think of whenever anybody gets smashed up is he don't look neat enough, so they yank him around to lie nice and straight and they yank him up so they can get a pillow under his head and then they haul him like a sack of meal to a bed. I hope to hell I never have a cave-in here with these dummies. Back in Jo'burg it happened to me: A timber fell and broke my leg nice and clean. By the time all my friends were through taking care of me and getting me comfortable, it was a compound complicated fracture with bone splinters from my ankles on up."

The jeep stopped in front of a large house, solidly constructed of the expensive native glass brick. Unlike most of the jerrybuilt shacks that housed the temporary workers in the camp, it was one of the few buildings put up by the Company itself, and few expenses had been spared.

The door opened hesitantly, and a girl peered out, then opened it all the way. "Hello, Hack. Is this the doctor?"

She was dressed in neither the standard tunic of most Marswomen nor the gaudy clothes of her sisterhood on Earth; instead she wore tailored house-pajamas of Earthside synvelvet. She might have been any business woman or middle-class housewife answering her door back on Earth.

"Hello, Mary." Hackenberg turned to Tony. "Doc Hellman, this is Mary Simms. She's in charge when Rose is out. Mary, this is Douglas Graham, the famous gunther." He stressed the last word only slightly. "You've heard of him?"

"Oh, yes." She was distantly polite. "How do you do, Doctor? Won't you come in?"

"I'll have to take off now." Hackenberg shook Graham's hand vigorously. "Glad to have met you. I'll pick you up later, Doc." He waved and headed back for the jeep. Tony and Graham followed Mary Simms indoors and pulled off their parkas.

THE whole house *was* heated, the doctor noticed.

The girl led them through a large and rather formal parlor and into a smaller sitting room. She crossed the small room, and opened a door on the far side.

"In here, *Doctor*," she said. Tony stepped into the small bedroom, and heard Graham right behind him.

"How about me?" demanded the writer.

The girl's voice was icy. "Professional courtesy, I suppose; we *are* in the same business, aren't we? By all means, come in."

The doctor turned his smile in the other direction. A huge blonde lay on the bed between fresh sheets. She was in coma, or...

"Out," Tony said firmly, and closed the door on both of them.

He lifted the sheet and swore under his breath. Big Ginny had been washed and dressed in a rosebud-trimmed pink nylon nightgown. Few people with internal injuries could survive such first aid. He opened his bag and began the examination.

He stepped into the parlor. Mary rose from her chair to question him, but Tony forestalled her. "She's dead." He added in a puzzled voice, "Her chest was beaten in. Who found her?"

"Two of the men. Shall I get them?"

"Please. And—was there anything they found nearby?"

"Yes. I'll bring it." The girl went out.

"How about the rape?" Graham asked.

"She wasn't," Tony said.

He dropped into a chair and tried to think it out. The woman had been pregnant, and there were signs of a fresh try at abortion—the "rape." Was the father known? Had they tried to abort it? Had there been a scene and a fatal beating out there by the hills? How did you know who was the father of a child conceived in a place like this? And who else would have any reason for the violence?

Mary Simms came in and said, "I passed the word for the men." She moved coolly so that her body was between Graham and the doctor, and handed over something wrapped in a handkerchief. "They found this."

"Did you know she was six months pregnant?"

"Big Ginny?" she asked, amazed.

"Why not?"

"Why, I've seen her medical card, and she's been here two years. She was married a couple of times on Earth—" The girl was flustered.

"Well?"

"Well, it surprised me, that's all."

95

He went into the small bedroom and unwrapped the object she had given him. It was a stained scrap of stout copper wire, about twenty-five centimeters long. That confirmed his diagnosis: attempted self-abortion, clumsy and dangerous because of the woman's bulk and probably hazy knowledge of anatomy. But the innumerable blows on her chest and back didn't make sense...

BACK in the parlor, two men in miners' leathers were waiting. The writer was questioning them idly about living conditions in the camp.

"I'm Dr. Hellman from Sun Lake," Tony said. "I want to ask you about finding Big Ginny."

"Hell, Doc," said one of the miners, "we just walked over that way and there she was. I said to Sam, 'It's Big Ginny! Jeez!' and he said, 'Some cheapskate musta hit her on the head,' and we tried to bring her around, but she wouldn't come to, so we made her comfortable and we went and told Mary and then we went back on shift."

"That's all there is to it," said the other miner. "But it wasn't one of our boys. You ask me, it was one of those Communist crackpots from over your place, all the time reading—it drives you nuts, did you know that? How is the old bag, Doc? Is she yelling for her money?"

"She's dead," the doctor said shortly. "Thanks for the information."

"You ask me," the miner repeated stoutly, "it's one of those Communists did it."

"Can you beat that?" the other one said softly. "What kind of guy would kill a dame like that?" They went out soberly.

"Those guys were a little too innocent," said Graham suddenly. "Didn't you think so?"

"I know what that's about," said Mary Simms. "They didn't mention why they happened to be out strolling on the desert. They're gowheads. They were picking up some marcaine. They have a deal worked out with one of the people from Brenner's Hop Heaven. He steals the stuff from Brenner and leaves it under a rock for Sam and Oscar. They leave money."

"I knew something was sour about them," said Graham broodingly. "What do we do now, Tony?"

"I'm going to write a note to Dr. O'Reilly and see if I can get Hackenberg to drive us to Sun Lake." He sat down and took out his notebook and pen, found a blank page, and carefully recorded what he had seen, without adding any of his conclusions.

He signed his name, folded and handed the sheet to Mary Simms. "When you give the doctor this," he said, "please tell him I was sorry I couldn't stay to see him. We're having big times over at our place. Ten new colonists." He smiled. "Nine immigrants and a new baby."

"Boy or girl?" she asked, with sudden interest. "How is it—all right? Was it hard?"

"A boy. Condition fair. Normal delivery."

"That's nice," she said, with a musing smile. Then she was all business again. "Thank you for coming, Doctor. I can make some coffee for you while you're waiting for Mr. Hackenberg. We have real coffee, you know."

"I didn't know," he told her. "I'll take two cups."

\*     \*     \*

DR. TONY filled Hackenberg in on the jeep ride to Sun Lake. The mine boss profanely said nothing like that had ever happened before and he'd get the nogood swamper that did it and swing him from the gantry if he had to beat up every leatherhead in camp. He told some grisly stories about how he had administered rough justice to native coal miners in Johannesburg.

"Course," he admitted, "you can't do that to Panamericans."

It's a good thing, thought Dr. Tony, that there wasn't any Martian animal life. An intelligent race capable of being sweated would really have got the works from Hackenberg, who could justify abominable cruelty to his brothers on the grounds that they'd been born in a different hemisphere of his own planet. God only knew what he would think justified by an extra eye or a set of tentacles.

Hackenberg took the wide swing through the gap in the hills and highballed the dozen miles to Sun Lake City. He came to a cowboy stop in front of the Lab and declined their hospitality.

"I have to get back before the big shots," he said. "Thanks, Doc. I'll see you around."

# CHAPTER THIRTEEN

THE big main hall of the Lab was jammed with people, standing in earnest groups, strolling around, all talking at once. As the door slammed behind the doctor and the writer, the hubbub quieted, and seventy-odd pairs of eyes turned on the newcomers.

"Quite a delegation," Graham commented. "For me?"

"I don't know," Tony confessed. He searched the room, and saw Harve Stillman break away from a small group and head their way.

"Hi, Tony, did you bring a friend?"

He turned to find Mimi Jonathan at his elbow.

"Oh, Mimi, this is Douglas Graham. Did Bea tell you he was coming? Graham, Mimi Jonathan. Mi—Mrs. Jonathan is the Lab Administrator, in charge of making the wheels go round. And this is Harve Stillman. Harve used to be…"

"…a newspaperman himself," Graham finished.

"Nope," Harve grinned. "A radioteletype repairman with the J. P."

"What a switch." Graham smiled back and shook the other man's hand.

Tony turned from them to ask Mimi urgently: "How's it going? Did you finish up with the Lab search yet?"

"Afraid so. It's the same as the huts. Nothing turned up," she said harshly. "We'll have to check the shipping crates."

"Lord," breathed Tony.

"Maybe it won't be so bad," Stillman ventured. "I've just given this crowd a briefing on handling hot stuff. Mimi seems to think we can clear it up in a day or two if we all pitch in."

"Provided," Mimi added, "we all work just a little harder than possible. I'm sorry you had to come to us at such a busy time, Mr. Graham. I hope you won't mind if we don't fuss over you too much. You're welcome to wander around and ask all the questions you want. Everyone will be glad to help you."

"It will be a welcome change," he assured her.

TONY waited very impatiently through a few more minutes of

polite talk. As soon as Harve engaged the writer's attention again, the doctor turned back to Mimi. "What's the plan?" he asked.

"Five crews to get out about a kilometer into the desert, a half-kilometer apart. Everybody else brings them crates one at a time, they open and search, repack before the next one comes in. No contamination from crates standing open. Through all this you and Harve run back and forth checking the handling crews and the tote crews to see that they don't get danger doses and remove and treat them if they do. We figure four days to finish the job."

"Harve, do you think you're good enough to monitor the unpacking sites?" Tony asked. "Contamination from the native radioactives would be as bad as getting our own radiophosphorus into our radiomethyline blue."

"I didn't want to go out and try it on my own. Do you think I can swing it?"

"Sure. Go pick us five of the coolest spots on Mars."

The technician headed for the racked counters.

"Doc, can you let me in on that cryptic business?" demanded Graham.

"In a minute," said Tony, his eyes wandering over the crowd. "Excuse me." He had spotted Anna and was starting her way when she turned, saw him and approached.

"We tried another feeding with the Kandro baby," she began without a preamble, "but he didn't take to it—choked it up again like yesterday."

Tony took out his pipe and bit abstractedly on the scarred stem. "No difference? No change at all?"

"Not that I could see. Tony, what's *wrong* with that baby?"

The doctor shook his head unhappily. "I don't know," he admitted.

There was something damnably wrong with the Kandro baby, something he couldn't quite figure. There was a clue somewhere in the vividly remembered picture of the gasping, red-faced infant, choking and spluttering on a mouthful of milk. Should he have tried water instead of normal feeding to get those scrambled reflexes into order?

"Doc—" said Graham.

"I'll be with you in a minute."

Anna went on serenely: "No trouble with Joan. I gave her her regular shot and changed the bandages when Tad told me you'd be late. She seemed fairly comfortable."

"Good. Miscellaneous complaints?"

"Kroll in engineering had a headache. And there's Mrs. Beyles. Her husband came and asked if there was anything I could do—they had a quarrel and he thought she went into a fit. It was a temper tantrum; I know you said not to give her anything, but John was so upset I gave her sedation to quiet her." She turned to Graham. "Sorry to have to drag out our hospital horrors. I'm sure you understand."

"Oh," said Tony, "I'm sorry. Douglas Graham, Anna Willendorf. Excuse me a minute, will you?" Mimi was tapping her foot, waiting for an opening. He told her: "I better get the afternoon safety done right now, and I'm damned if I'm going to do it with the whole Colony lurching around the Lab. Get 'em out of here so I can go to work, will you? Graham, I can answer questions while I go through the Lab looking for over-level radiation. If you want to come along, you're welcome."

He led the writer out of the office into the dressing room, as Mimi began to break up the knots of non-Lab personnel who had shown up to thrash out the search plan and learn their own parts in it.

\* \* \*

TONY helped Graham into the suit of protective armor. He didn't usually bother with it himself on the afternoon inspection, when other people were all over the Lab, unprotected. In the morning it was different; the elaborate precautions of the outer-door locker were necessary when a hot spot had, possibly, had time to chain overnight. But while work was actually going on, nothing very hot could develop without being noticed. The late check was primarily for the purpose of insuring the absence of the hot spots that could develop overnight.

The doctor started his meandering course through the Lab, with Graham in tow.

"I'm making the second of our twice-a-day safety checks for excess radioactivity. It happens that we've got to unpack all our material scheduled for export, examine it and repack it in a hurry if we want to get it aboard the outgoing rocket in time to get credit to pay our bills."

"Just routine, I suppose?" asked Graham blandly.

"I think you gathered that it certainly isn't. The fact is, your friend, Commissioner Bell, has accused us of harboring a thief and his loot— a hundred kilos of marcaine. We've searched everybody and everything so far except the export crates; now we've got to search them."

"Why not tell the old windbag to go blow?"

"If we don't turn up the marcaine, he can seal us up for six months to conduct an inch-by-inch search."

"What's so dreadful about that?" Graham asked.

"We're geared to two ships in six months now instead of one ship a year. If we missed two shipments, both incoming and outgoing, we'd be ruined."

GRAHAM grunted thoughtfully, and Tony waited—and waited— the grunt was all. He'd been half-hoping the writer would volunteer to help—perhaps by picking up his anti-Bell crusade or by promising to see his powerful friends, or by exposing the sorry mess to the public. But Graham, apparently forgetting the Bell business entirely, pitched the doctor a ferocious series of questions that threatened to stretch out the inspection endlessly:

"What's in this box? Why isn't this conveyor shielded? Where's the stock room? What do you do here? Is it technical or trade school stuff? Where did this soil come from? What did you pay for it? Tile on this floor, concrete on that—why? Who's in charge here? How many hours does he work? That many? Why? How many hours does *he* work?"

As Tony paraded solemnly back and forth with the counter, checking off items on his report, he pressed a little on the writer.

"This crate here," he said, "is a typical sale. Radiophosphorus for cancer research. It goes to the Leukemia Foundation in San Francisco. It's a traceless pure—better than nine-nines. We're in business because we can supply that kind of thing. On Earth they'd have to first make the traceless-pure phosphorus and then expose it to a reactor or a particle accelerator, and the extra step there usually means it gets contaminated and has to be refined again. Here we just produce phosphorus by the standard methods and it *is* radioactive because the whole planet's got it. Not enough to present a health problem any more than cosmic rays on Earth do, but damned convenient for Sun Lake."

"Some crate," commented the writer.

"Lead, air gaps, built-in counter with a loud alarm. It's the law. Normally, we have five percent of our manpower working in the shipping department. Now we have to unpack and recrate all this stuff in less than four days."

"You people should have a lobby," suggested Graham. "If something like that was handicapping Pittco, they'd get rid of it quick. Are we just about through?"

"Just about," said Tony flatly. So much for that, he thought; at least he'd given the writer an eyeful of the safety precautions they observed, and made him sweat a little under the heavy suit at the same time.

In the cleanup room they stripped and showered, with Graham chortling suddenly: "O'Mally was a prophet. My first city editor—he said when I got rich I'd install hot and cold running Scotch in my bathroom."

"Sorry we only have cold, and don't drink this stuff unless you want to go blind. It's methyl."

"Can't be worse than the stuff I used to guzzle in Philly," Graham said blandly, but he stepped out quickly enough and followed the doctor's advice about a lanolin rubdown afterward.

"Dinner time now," said Tony, buttoning on his tunic. "Mess hall's here in the Lab. Only building big enough."

"Synthetics?" asked Graham.

"No, that's not the Sun Lake idea. We want to get on an agricultural cycle as fast as we can. Sun Lake has to be able to live on vegetables that grow naturally, without any fertilization except our own waste products. Naturally we're strong on beans, kudzu, yams, goobers—any of the nitrogen-fixing plants that contain some natural protein. You'll see."

GRAHAM saw, he tasted, he expectorated. Into the shocked silence of the half-dozen at the table, he muttered an embarrassed apology and manfully choked down almost half of his vegetable plate—Mars beans, barley, stewed greens and another kind of stewed greens.

To Tony he muttered when conversation had sprung up again: "But why do they taste like a hospital smells? Do you have to disinfect them or something?"

Joe Gracey overheard it from the other side of the table. "That's my department," he said. "No, it isn't disinfectant. What you and most other people don't realize is that we with our Lab are pikers compared with the lowliest cabbage in synthesizing chemicals. We taste the chemicals in our Earth plants and we accept them as the way they ought to taste. These are unfamiliar because these are Mars plants modified so that their chemicals aren't poison to Earth animals, or Earth plants modified so that Mars soil isn't poison to them. We're still breeding on this barley, which is generating too much iodoform for me to be really happy. If I can knock one carbon out of the ring— but you don't care about that. Just be glad we didn't tryout the latest generation of our cauliflower on you instead of our test mice. The cauliflower, I'm sorry to say, generates prussic acid."

"Stick with those mice," said Graham with a greenish smile.

"Only guaranteed-Earth animals on Mars, including you," said Madge Cassidy, beside Graham. He watched her wonderingly as she finished her barley with apparent enjoyment.

"How was that again?"

"My mice. The only animals on Mars guaranteed non-mutated. We have them behind tons of concrete and lead with remote feeding. It'd be no joke if some of the natural Mars radioactivity or some of the stuff flying around the Lab mutated them so they'd gobble Mars food that was still poison to people."

"You mean I might go back to Earth and have a two-headed baby?"

"It's possible," said Madge, getting to work on variety number one of stewed greens. "Odds are somewhat higher than it happening from cosmic rays or industrial radioactivity on Earth. But mouse generations go by so fast that with them it's a risk we can't take. Some of the pork-and-beaners died very unpleasant deaths when they tried eating Mars plants as a last resort. It *was* the last resort, all right."

"But isn't *anything* on Mars good to eat?"

"A couple of items," Gracey told him. "Stuff that would probably be poisonous to any native animal life, if there was any. You find the same kind of thing on Earth—plants that don't seem to be good for anything in their native environment. My theory is that the ancestors of poison ivy and other such things aren't really Earth plants at all, but came to Earth, maybe as spores aboard meteorites. We need a broader explanation of the development of life than the current theories offer. We've grown a giant barley here, for instance, out of transplanted Earth stock, but it wouldn't be viable there. The gene was lethal on Earth. Here—"

He rattled on, to the accompaniment of Graham's nods of agreement, until Harve Stillman broke in: "Hey, there was a rumor through the radio relay today. You know about it, Mr. Graham?"

"Doug," the writer corrected.

"Okay," Harve smiled. "About marcaine—no, not about us," he added hastily. "About marcaine being forbidden in Tartary. The Cham pronounced a rescript or whatever it is, and according to the guys in Marsport that means the price goes up, and Brenner's business is doubled. Do you know anything about it, Doug?"

The newsman looked surprised. "It was all over the ship," he told them. "Everybody was talking about it. How come you don't get it till now? The radio op on board told me he spilled it in his first message to PAC"

"It's true then?" Gracey asked sharply.

"I wouldn't know. I'm only a reporter myself." He looked across to Tony. "Don't tell me Marsport wasn't buzzing with it. Brenner, knew, didn't he?"

"No," the doctor said slowly. "Didn't hear nothin' about it there." But he had heard of a rumor; who was it? Chabrier! Of course, that was Chabrier's rumor: marcaine prices going up, production will double, Brenner needs a new plant, needs a doctor, too...

Tony stood up abruptly. "Excuse me. Gracey, are you finished? Want to come along?"

The agronomist rose quickly, and the two left together. On the way to collect Nick and go over to the Jonathans', Tony explained the situation rapidly to Gracey.

"I wanted to get the Council together tonight anyhow," he finished up, "to tell you about my idiotic brawl with Brenner. I don't know what kind of jam *that's* going to land us in. But this business ties in with what Chabrier told me. Rocket to Bell and Bell to Brenner, and the rest of us can get the news whenever the Commissioner gets around to it."

"It makes a nasty picture," the agronomist agreed soberly. "Now what? Where do we go from here?"

"Damned if I know. Maybe one of the others can figure it." He knocked sharply on Nick's door.

# CHAPTER FOURTEEN

"IT DOESN'T matter," Mimi said firmly. "We still have to go through with the search."

"That's how I see it, too," Tony admitted. "We can't bring any accusations until we know our own slate is clean."

"If we could only get hold of the Bloodhound…"

"Bell refused."

"And that means no matter how carefully we search, he can still come in afterward and claim it wasn't done properly."

"Could we rent one or buy it?" Gracey wanted to know.

"Government property only," Mimi told him. "O'Donnell checked on that the other day."

"Okay, so we have to do it without the Bloodhound." Nick jumped up and paced the length of the room restlessly. "I bet I could build one if we only had a little time… Well, we have to go ahead, that's all. Where does Graham come in?"

TONY realized they were waiting for an answer from him. "I don't know. He has no use for Bell, but he doesn't exactly rise to the bait when I throw it at him either. I think we better go slow and feel him out. He didn't seem to go for the blunt approach when Chabrier and the others tried it."

"Slow?" Nick stormed. "Man, we've got *six days*. Go *slow*?"

"As fast as we can," Gracey put in. "We still have to get the search finished. I think we have to do that before we ask Graham anything. He has to have some facts to work with."

"Right," Mimi agreed. "Now let's get our plans organized. If we start at dawn, maybe we can do the whole unpacking operation tomorrow…*then* we can hit Graham. Means we'll have to leave crates open and repack them later, but I don't see any alternative now. How long is Graham staying, Tony?"

"He said maybe three days."

"Okay, then that's how we've got to do it. Maybe by tomorrow night we'll know better how to get at the guy."

They spent a busy ten minutes outlining the plan of operations, and then the three men went out, leaving the details for Mimi to settle.

Tony walked down the settlement street slowly, trying to get his thoughts in order. It had been a long day—three-fifteen in the morning when Tad woke him, and now there was still work to do.

Stopping in at the hospital to collect his bag, he found Graham kibitzing idly with Harve in his living room.

"Just waiting for you, Doc." Stillman stood up. "I have to get over to the radio shack. Tad's on the p.m. shift this week, but he fell asleep before supper, so I've got to take over tonight."

Tony surveyed his guest uncomfortably. "Anything you'd like?" he asked. "I have to go out and see a couple of patients. Won't be too long."

"Could I go along?" Graham asked. "I'd like to, if it's all right with you."

"Sure. I want you to see the baby I was talking about anyhow. My other patient is pretty sick; you may have to wait while I look in on her."

They stopped at the Radcliff's first, but Joan was asleep and she usually got so little rest that Tony decided not to disturb her. Anna had said she'd had a fairly good day. He'd see her tomorrow.

"Where is this infant?" Graham asked as they walked down the Colony street.

"Here. This is the Kandros' place. Hello, Polly," Tony said as the door opened, even before he knocked. "I brought Mr. Graham along to visit. I hope you don't mind."

"I...no, of course not. How do you do? Come in, won't you?" Her manner was absurdly formal, and her appearance was alarming. Tony wondered when she had last slept. Her eyes were over alert, her lips too tight, her neck and shoulders stiff with tension.

"How's Sunny?" He walked into the new room where the crib stood, and the others followed. He wished now that he hadn't brought Graham along.

"The same," Polly told him. "I just tried. You see?"

THE baby in its basket was sputtering feebly, its face flushed bright red. *We're going to lose that youngster*, thought the doctor grimly, *unless I start intravenous feeding, and soon.*

"Tell me something, please, Doctor," she burst out, ignoring the reporter's presence. "Could it be my fault? I'm anxious—I know that.

Could that be why Sunny doesn't eat right?"

Tony considered. "Yes, to a degree, but it couldn't account for *all* the trouble. Are you really so tense? What's it all about?"

"You know how it was with us," she said evasively. "We tried so many times on Earth. And then here we thought at first it'd be like all the other times, but, Tony, do you think—is Mars dangerous?"

He saw she'd changed her mind in mid-confession and substituted the inane question for whatever she had started to ask. He intended to get to the bottom of it.

Over the woman's shoulder, he looked meaningfully at Graham. The reporter grimaced, shrugged, and obligingly drifted back to the living room.

Tony lowered his voice and told the woman: "Of course Mars is dangerous. It's dangerous now; it was dangerous before you had Sunny. I'm a little surprised at you, Polly. Some women think that having a baby ought to change the world into a pink spun-candy heaven. It doesn't. You've had Sunny; he's a small animal and you love him and he needs your care, but Mars is still what it always was. The terrain's rugged and some of the people aren't what they ought to be. But…"

"Tell me about the murder," she said flatly.

"Oh, is *that* what you're jumpy about? I saw worse every night I rode the meat wag—rode the ambulance at Massachusetts General. What's that got to do with Sunny?"

"I don't know. I'm afraid. Tell me about it, Doctor, please."

He wondered what vague notion of terror she had got stuck in her head—and wondered whether it would come out.

"You're the doctor," he said, shrugging. "The girl who got killed was named Big Ginny, as you may have heard. If you'd been on the wagon with me in Boston, you'd know there's nothing unusual about it. Women like that often get beaten up, sometimes beaten to death by their customers. The customers are usually drunk, sometimes full of dope; they get the idea that they're being cheated and they slug the girl. Another call for the wagon."

"I heard," she said, "that she was beaten to death with a lot of light blows. No man would do that. And I heard that Nick Cantrella saw footprints out by the caves—naked footprints. He thought they were children's."

"Whose do you think they were?" he asked, though he had a sickly feeling that he knew what she'd say.

POLLY moaned, "It was *brownies*. I told you I saw one and you didn't believe me. Now they've killed this woman and they're leaving footprints around and you still don't believe me. You think I'm crazy. You all think I'm crazy. They want my baby and you won't listen to me!"

Tony thought he knew what was going on in her head and he didn't like it. She had seen the attention of the Colony shift from her baby to the marcaine search, and was determined to bring it back, even if it had to be by a ridiculous ruse. She'd heard all the foolish stories about the mythical brownies; she'd had a vivid anxiety dream—which, he reminded himself, she had finally admitted was only a dream—and now she was collecting "evidence" to build herself up as the interesting victim of a malignant persecution.

"We've been over all this before," he told her wearily. "You agreed that you didn't really see anything. And you agreed that there couldn't be any brownies because no animal life has ever been found on Mars—no brownies, and nothing brownies could evolve from. Now..."

"Doctor," she broke in, "I've got to show you something." She reached into the baby's basket and drew out something that glinted darkly in her hand.

"Good Lord, what are you doing with a gun?" the doctor demanded.

There was no more conflict on her face or hesitancy in her voice. "You can say I'm crazy, Tony, but I'm afraid. I think there could be such things as brownies. And I'm going to be ready for them if they come." She looked at the little weapon tensely and then put it back under the pad in the crib.

Tony promptly drew it out. "Now listen, Polly, if you want to believe in brownies or ghosts or Santa Claus, that's your business. But you certainly should know better than to leave the gun near him. I'm going to give you a sedative, Polly, and maybe after a good—"

"No," she said. "No sedative. I'll be all right. But can I keep the gun?"

She wiped her eyes and, with an effort, laid her twitching hands quietly in her lap.

"If you know how to use it and keep the safety on and put it some place besides under Sunny's mattress, I don't see why not. But all the brownies you'll ever shoot with it you could stick in your eye and never notice."

"Like the old lady, maybe I don't believe in ghosts but I'm terribly afraid of them?" She tried to laugh and Tony managed a smile with her.

"Nothing wrong with blowing your top once in a while. Nothing at all. Women ought to bawl oftener."

She grinned weakly and said:

"Maybe Sunny's going to eat better now."

"I hope so. I'll see you tomorrow, Polly."

\*     \*     \*

As THEY walked down the street in a strained, embarrassed silence, Graham looked as if he wanted to ask something. He finally did: "By the way, Tony, do you know where I'm supposed to sleep? Or where I'd find my bag? It was on the plane."

"Might as well stay with me. And your baggage ought to be at the Campbells. Tad Campbell was that young sprout who deflated my fight with Brenner."

The baggage, a sizable B-4 bag on which Graham must have paid a ruinous overweight charge, was at the Campbells. After picking it up, the writer followed the doctor to his hospital-hut.

Tony snapped a heat beam on the two plastic chairs—standard furnishings of a Sun Lake living room—and took off his sand boots with a grunt. Graham rooted through his baggage, picked up Chabrier's gaudy package and hefted it thoughtfully, then shook his head and dove in again. He came up grinning, with another bottle.

"How about it, Doc?" he asked. "This is Earthside."

"It's been a long time," Tony sighed. "I'll get a couple of glasses."

The stuff went down like silken fire. It had been a very long time.

"What's about brownies?" the writer asked suddenly. "I couldn't help hearing part of that when I went out of the room."

Tony shook his head. "*Brownies.* As if we didn't have enough trouble here, without inventing Martian monsters..."

"Well, what *about* them? All I've ever heard is that deep purple scene in Granata's interplanetary show. It's silly stuff, but nobody's handled it yet at all except Granata. Maybe I could use something; it's a beautiful story if there's anything at all to back it up. Does anybody claim a connection between fairy book brownies and the Martian variety?"

"Two ways. First of all, Mars brownies are just as much a fairy story as the Earthside kind. Second, somebody once suggested that the ones in the story books were the space traveling ancestors of the present-day hallucinations."

"Could be," the gunther reflected. "Could be…"

"Could be a lot of rot," Tony said without heat. "Space travel requires at an absolute minimum the presence of animal life—or at least mobile, intelligent life. Show me so much as one perambulating vegetable on Mars, let alone a native animal life form. Then it's likely I'll think about brownies some more."

"How about a declining race?" Graham speculated. "Suppose they *were* space travelers, on a high level of civilization—they might have killed off all lesser life-forms. You see it happening some on Earth, and back there it's just a matter of living space. We don't have the problem the Martians had to face, of dwindling water and oxygen supplies. Probably got them in the end, and destroyed their civilization…except," he added, "for the ones who got to Earth. I understand from authoritative sources that the last expedition to Earth was led by a guy named Oberon." Graham chuckled and drank, then asked seriously: "Has anybody ever *seen* one, except Granata?"

"Hundreds of people," Tony said drily. "Ask anyone of the old prospectors who come into town hauling dirt. They've all seen 'em, lived with 'em; some even claim to have been at baby-feasts. You'll get all the stories you want out of any of the old geezers."

"What are brownies supposed to look like?" the writer insisted.

TONY sighed and surrendered, recognizing the same intense manner Graham had displayed in the Lab. The man was a reporter, after all. It was his business to ask questions. Tony gave him what he wanted, with additions, explanations, and embellishments.

Brownies: an intelligent life form, either animal or mobile vegetable. About a meter and a half in height; big ears; skinny arms. Supposed to be the naked remnants of a once-proud Martian civilization. (Except that there were no other remnants to support the theory.) In the habit of kidnapping human children (except that there was no specific authenticated case of a baby's disappearance) and eating them (except that that seemed too pat and inevitable an idea-association with the kidnapping—the sort of additional embellishment that no good liar could resist).

"It's an old prospectors' yarn," Tony wound up. "The homesteaders picked it up to frighten kids into sticking close to home. There are hundreds of people on Mars today who'll tell you they've seen brownies. But not only is there no native animal life of any kind on Mars today—so far as we can tell, there *never* has been. No ruins, no old cities, no signs of civilization, and not so much as one single desiccated dried-out scrap of anything resembling an animal fossil."

"That's strictly negative evidence," Graham pointed out. He emptied his glass, and poured another drink for both of them. "Cigaret?"

Tony shook his head. "I gave up smoking long ago. We all quit sooner or later. Too much trouble to keep tobacco burning." He reached out to pick up his empty pipe from the table beside him, and he clenched the stem comfortably between his teeth.

Graham repeated: "Strictly negative evidence. But on the other side you have footprints, for instance, and eyewitness stories."

"If you're talking about the cataract-covered eyes of old Marsmen," Tony retorted, "don't call it evidence."

"It wouldn't be," Graham agreed, "except that there are so many of them. I'm beginning to think there's a story in it after all."

"You mean you believe it?" the doctor demanded.

"Do I *look* crazy? I said it was a story."

"So you came 150 million kilometers on a rocket, and then four more hours across Mars in a beatup old rattletrap of a plane," the doctor said bitterly. "You eat food that tastes like hospital disinfectant, and live in a mud hut, all so you can go back home and write a nice piece of fiction about brownies—a piece you could have dashed off without ever leaving Earth?"

"Not exactly," the gunther said mildly. "I was only thinking of using the brownies for one chapter. Local color, tales and legends—that kind of thing."

"You could get plenty of stories back on Earth," Tony went on bitterly. "Stories worth writing. How about Paul Rosen's story? There's a real one for you."

"Rosen?" Graham leaned forward, interested again. "Seems to me I've heard the name before. Who was he?"

"Not was. Is. He's still alive; a cripple nobody knows."

"TELL me about Rosen." The writer filled their glasses again.

"I'll tell you about Mars; it's the same story. You came to write a book about Mars, didn't you? Well, Mars—this Mars, without oxygen masks—is Rosen's work. Rosen's lungs. And you never heard of him...Rosen was the medical doctor aboard the relief ship, the one that found what was left of the first colony. He had a notion about the oxygen differential, was convinced that it wasn't responsible for the failure. He was wrong, of course, but he was right, too. To prove his point he took off his mask and found he didn't need it.

"His assistant tried it, and nearly died of anoxemia. That proved some people could take Mars straight and others couldn't. When the ship got back Rosen went to the biochem boys with his lungs. They told him a few c.c.'s wouldn't be enough to work with, so he volunteered for an operation. Most of his lung tissue was removed. He was crippled for life, but they tracked down the enzyme that made the difference, and worked out a test."

"That I remember," said Graham, continuing to fill the glasses almost rhythmically. "Half the guys I met in Asia claimed they enlisted because they weren't Marsworthy and life wasn't worth living if they couldn't go to Mars."

"THAT was the beginning of it," Tony said. "The ones who passed the test began to come over. Thousand dollars a day prospecting, and always the chance of finding bonanzas. At first they were pork-and-beaners, but the Mars vegetation they brought back took us one step closer to fitting into the Martian ecology. The biochem boys came up with a one-shot hormone treatment to stimulate secretion of an enzyme from the lining of the pylorus. It's present in most people without the shot, but not enough to break down the Martian equivalent of carbohydrates into simple sugars, which the human body can handle. You asked me before what all the shots you got on board the rocket ship were for. That's one of them. It means you can handle the Mars plants, which don't contain compounds poisonous to Earth animals.

"The other shots you got were to protect you against all the rest of the things that killed off the first pork-and-beaners-fungi, ultra-violet damage to the eyes, dehydration, viruses. For every shot you got, half a dozen of the first explorers and prospectors were killed or crippled to find the cause and cure.

"Five years ago came the payoff. The biochem boys got what they'd been looking for ever since they first sliced up Rosen's trick lungs. They synthesized the enzyme, your little pink OxEn pill, and that did it. That's when the Sun Lake Society was founded; and the new rocket fuel two years ago made Sun Lake a reality. With OxEn and four trips a year, we can make out until we find a way to get along without Earth.

"Sun Lake is Mars, Graham. Sun Lake's all's gonna be left when you crazy bastards back on Earth blow yourselves up. The other colonists here aren't Mars; they're part of Earth. When Earth goes, they go. Sun Lake's all's gonna be left..."

"Coupla catches," said Graham, trying to make a glass stay put so he could fill it. "Commish Bell and his eviction notice. And you still need OxEn. Can you make that inna Lab?"

"Not yet," Tony brooded. He had forgotten the lovely optimism that could be poured out of a bottle. "Guess I had 'nough to drink. I have a hell of a day ahead of me."

## CHAPTER FIFTEEN

A HELL of a day it was. It started, for one thing, with a hangover. Tony heaved himself out of bed, glad to find Graham still asleep. He didn't want any cheerful conversation just yet. He prescribed, dispensed, and self-administered some aspirin, used an extra cup of water for a second cup of "coffee," finally decided he was strong enough to face the reek of methyl alcohol, and got washed.

Mimi Jonathan was in charge at the Lab when he got there. Law or no law, he raced through the A.M. Lab check to get ahead on the awful job of monitoring the unpacking operation. He rode out on a bike to the five spots Stillman had selected for the inspection crews and found them reasonably low in radioactivity.

Sheets of plastic had been laid down for flooring and tent walls were going up, with little tunnels through which the crates could be passed without the handlers bringing in all the dust of Mars on their feet. Blowers were rigged to change the air between each inspection, and radiologically clean overalls would be passed in at the same time.

A little after dawn, the careful frenzy was in full swing. A crew in the shipping room eased out crates and passed them to wrappers who covered them with plastic sheeting and heat-sealed them. Aboard skids, the crates were manhandled up the slight slope from the "canal" bed to the tents in the desert, unwrapped, passed in, opened, searched, checked for chemical and radiological contamination, sealed and passed out again. Back at the Lab, they would be wrapped in lead sheets pending recrating and stored separately in every workroom that could be spared.

Mimi was everywhere, ordering a speedup on the heat-sealing, or a slowdown on the bucket-brigade manhandling, routing crates to the station that would soonest be free, demanding more plastic sheeting, drafting a woman to wash more coveralls when a stand of them toppled over. The few Lab processes that couldn't be left alone were tended under the direction of Sam Flexner, by people from agro and administration, and by specialized workers like Anna Willendorf.

Tony and Harve Stillman moved constantly up and down the line, back to the Lab and out to the desert, checking persons, places and materials. Before noon Tony had the bitter job of telling Mimi: "We've got to abandon the Number Two tent. It's warming up. Radioactivity's low on the site, but it's from something that chains with the plastic flooring, I don't know what. Another hour and radiation from the flooring will contaminate the crates."

The woman set her jaw and picked another crew from the line to set up a tent on another monitored site.

Somebody slipped in the Number Three tent, and Harve Stillman found some of the Leukemia Foundation's shipment of radiophosphorus had got from the inside of the crate to the outside— enough to warrant refusal by the rocket supercargo in the interests of the safety of the ship.

But never a trace of marcaine did the search crews find.

LUNCH was at noon, carried about by Colony children. Gulping cool "coffee," Tony told Harve Stillman: "You'll have to take it alone for a while. I haven't visited my patients yet. I missed Joan Radcliff altogether yesterday."

"Hell, I don't know whether I'm coming or going," grunted Stillman, then added, "I guess I can manage."

"Send for me if there's anything you really can't handle." Tony started back toward the street of huts before a new emergency could delay him.

He stopped at his own house to pick up his medical bag, and found Graham awake, at work in front of an old-fashioned portable typewriter. Another surprise from the gunther; Tony had assumed the man worked with a dictatyper. Even in the Colony they had those.

Graham looked up pleasantly and nodded. "Somebody waiting for you in the other room, Tony." He motioned with his head toward the door that led to the hospital. "You going out again?"

The doctor nodded. "I don't know when I'll get back. You can walk around and ask questions wherever you find anybody. You understand the situation here—we can't let up on this marcaine business even for the press."

"Sure." The gunther nodded, unperturbed.

"I'll get around in time to pick you up for supper anyhow," Tony promised. "Did you get any lunch?"

"I managed." Graham grinned and pointed to an open can still half full of meat, and a box of hard crackers. "Look," said the writer, "unless you've lost your Earthside tastes completely, why don't you have supper on me tonight? There's lots more where lunch came from."

"Thanks. I might take you up on that."

Tony went into the hospital, where Edgar Kroll was waiting for him.

"Sorry to bother you today, Doc," Kroll apologized. "I came over on the chance you'd be around right about now. Another one of those damned headaches; I couldn't get any work done at all this morning. Guess I'm just getting old."

"*Old*," Tony snorted. "Man, even in Sun Lake, you're not old at thirty-five. Not just because you need bifocals. You've stalled around long enough now..." And heaven only knew what boudoir taunting from young Jeanne Kroll lay behind that, Tony thought, as he reached into the dispensary cabinet. "Here's some aspirin for now. If you come around tomorrow, I think I'll have time to refract you; I just can't manage it today. Take the afternoon off if the headache doesn't go away."

HE GOT his black bag, and walked down the street with Edgar, as far as the Kandros' place. At the door, he bumped into Jim, just leaving for the Lab, after lunch.

"Glad I saw you, Doc." The new father stood hesitantly in the doorway, waiting till Kroll was out of earshot, then burst out: "Listen, Tony, I didn't want to say anything in front of Polly, but...are you sure it's going to be all right? Sunny still isn't eating. Maybe it's cancer or something. I heard of something like that with one of our neighbor's kids back in Toledo—"

Just—just exactly the sort of thing that made Tony almost blind with rage. He liked the man; Jim Kandro was his brother, his comrade in the Colony, but... With his pulse hammering, he made it clear to Jim in a few icy sentences that he had studied long, sacrificed much and worked hard to learn what he could about medicine, and that when he wanted a snap diagnosis from a layman he would ask for one. Jim and Polly could yank him out of bed at three in the morning, they could make him minister to their natural anxieties, but they could *not* make him take such an insult.

He stalked into the house, ignoring Jim's protests and apologies both, and professional habit took over him as he greeted Polly and examined the baby.

"About time for a feeding, isn't it?" he asked. "Is it going any better? Since last night, I mean? Want to try him now while I observe?"

"It's a little better, I guess." Polly smiled doubtfully and picked up the baby. She moved the plastic cup of the oxygen mask up a little over the small nose, and put Sunny to her breast.

To Tony, it was plain that the infant was frantic with hunger. *Then why didn't it nurse properly?* Instead of closing over the nipple, Sunny's mouth pushed at it one-sidedly, first to the right, then to the left, any way but the proper way. For seconds at a time the baby did suck, then would release the nipple, choking.

"He's doing a little better," said Polly. "He's doing *much* better."

"That's fine," Tony agreed feebly. "I'll be on my way, then. Be sure to call me if there's anything."

HE WALKED down the Colony street wishing a doctor could afford the luxury of shaking his head in bewilderment. Maybe it was all straightening out. But *what* could account for the infant's fantastic behavior? There's nothing so determined as a baby wanting to feed— but *something* was getting in the way of Sunny's instinct.

He hoped Polly realized that Sunny would feed sooner or later, that the choking reflex, which frustrated the sucking reflex would disappear before long. He hoped she would realize it; he hoped desperately that it would happen.

Joan Radcliff was next and this time he found her awake. She was no better and no worse; the enigmatic course of her nameless disease had leveled off. All he could do was talk a while, go through the pulse-taking and temperature-reading mumbo-jumbo, change the dressings on her sores, talk some more, and then go out.

Now Dorothy, the sinus case, and he was done with his more serious cases for today.

Tanya Beyles had a green sick card on her door, but he decided to ignore it. He was already past the house when she called his name, and he turned to find her beckoning from the opened door.

She had dressed up to beat the band—an absurdly tight tunic to show off her passable thirty-plus figure, carefully done hair and the first lipstick he remembered seeing around in months.

"I don't have much time, today, Mrs. Beyles," he said carefully. "Could it wait till tomorrow?"

"Oh, please, Doctor," she begged, and launched into a typical hypochondriac resume of symptoms, complete with medical terms inaccurately used. What it boiled down to was that a thorough examination was in order though there was nothing *nasty* wrong with her.

"Very well," he said. "If you'll come over to the hospital—next week, perhaps—when I have more time." With a chaperone, he added silently.

"Wouldn't it be just as easy here, and more private?" she ventured shyly, indicating the bedroom, where a heat lamp was already focused on the made bed.

"Dear God," he muttered; and found the professional restraint that had taken over while he was with Polly Kandro had now quite abandoned him. "Mrs. Beyles," he said, plainly and nastily, "you may not realize it, but we do have a sense of humor here, even if we don't share your ideas of fun. We've been able to laugh off your malicious gossiping and the lousy job you do in Agronomy; you do get some work done in Agro, and you don't eat too much to keep your shape. Up to now, we've been able to laugh everything off and hope you'd straighten out. But I warn you, if you start being seductive around Sun Lake—even if you start with me—you'll get shipped out so fast you won't—"

"Is that so?" she screamed. "Well, maybe you'd like to know that I can get all the love and respect I want around here and where you got the nasty idea that I'm at all interested in you I can't imagine. I've heard of doctors like you before and if you think you're going to get away with it you're very much mistaken. And don't think I don't know all about you, and that Willendorf woman. I know things people would love to hear…"

He walked off before she could say any more. God only knew what they'd do with her—deport her, he supposed, and her sad sack of a husband would have to go, too, and it would all be very messy and bad-tempered. Maybe Bell and Graham and all the others were right, regarding Sun Lakers as anywhere from mildly insane to fanatically obsessed.

Maybe anything at all, but he still had to go to see Dorothy and her sinuses. The doctor's facial muscles fell into their accustomed neutrality as he walked into the girl's bedroom and his mind automatically picked up the threads of the bacitracin story where he had left off two days before.

\* \* \*

HALF an hour later, he was back at the unpacking and search operation where he took over alone while Stillman, groggy with the strain, the responsibility and the plain hard work, took a short break. The two of them divided the job then, moving steadily up and down the lines, checking, rechecking endlessly until, as darkness closed down, they were suddenly aware that there were no more crates.

Mimi Jonathan bitterly enumerated the results of the search: "About 1,500 man-hours shot to hell, three crates contaminated beyond salvage, nine salvageable for umpty-hundred more man-hours and no marcaine. Well, nobody can say now that we didn't try." She turned to Tony. "Your move," she said.

"Graham?" The doctor stood up. "All I can do is try to get him on our side. He's friendly anyhow; he asked me to have supper with him out of his private stock of genuine synthetic Earthside protein."

"You don't sound too hopeful," Gracey ventured.

"I'm not. Did I tell you what his favorite story is so far? *Brownies*…"

"You mean he's passing up a yarn like the killing at Pittco, and he wants to write about *Brownies?*" Nick asked incredulously.

"You think he's going to step on Pittco's toes?" Tony retorted. "Not that smart boy. Okay, I might as well get back and make my try." He started across the darkening desert, and Nick fell into step beside him. "Why don't you come along?" the doctor suggested. "Maybe you could talk his language better than I do. You might get a decent meal out of it, too."

"It's a thought. A good one. Only Marian's probably got supper all ready by now. I better check in at home first. I don't know— would you say it was official Council business?"

"That's between you and your hunger," the doctor told him. "What do you want most—meat or Marian?"

"Damned if I know," Nick admitted, grinning.

"Doc!" It was Jim Kandro, running down the street toward them. "Hey, Tony. I just came from the hospital…looking all over…"

"What's up?"

"The baby. He's having convulsions."

"I'll go right over. Pick up my bag at the hospital, will you?"


JIM set off in one direction, and Tony in the other. "See you later," Nick called out to the doctor's rapidly retreating back.

At the Kandros, he found Polly, near hysterical, with a struggling infant in her arms. Sunny was obviously in acute discomfort; the veins were standing out on his fuzzy scalp, he was struggling and straining feebly, his belly was distended and his cheeks puffed out uncomfortably.

"How's he been eating?" the doctor demanded, scrubbing his hands.

"The way you saw before," said Polly. "Better and better, but just the way you saw before, wiggling and pushing so half the time he was sucking on nothing at all. He was crying and crying, so I fed him three or four times and each time he got more—"

She fell silent as Tony picked up the baby and patted and stroked it. It burped loudly. The alarming red color faded and the tense limbs relaxed. With a whimper Sunny collapsed on the doctor's shoulder and fell asleep before he was back in his crib.

"But you said—" Polly gasped.

"I guess Sunny didn't hear me," Tony said.

"Here you are, Doc." Jim came in and looked from Polly's empty arms to the quiescent baby in the crib. "I guess you didn't need the bag. What was it?"

"Colic," Tony grinned. "Good, old-fashioned, Earthside colic."

"But you told me..." Jim turned accusingly on his wife.

"And I told Polly," Tony put in quickly. "It doesn't usually happen. Babies don't have to be burped on Mars—most of them that is. The mask feeds richer air into a Mars baby's nose so he just naturally breathes through his nose *all* the time and doesn't swallow air and get colic when he feeds: But I guess Sunny had his heart set on a bellyache. Was he crying when he fed, Polly?"

"Why, yes, a little bit. Not really crying, a kind of whimper every now and then."

"That could explain it. Alright, now you know it isn't serious. Just be sure to bubble him after feeding. Thank the Lord he's nursing. That young man of yours gave us all a bad time, but I think we're out of the woods now."

Sunny was going to be all right; for the first time, Tony really believed it.

Somehow that changed the whole dismal picture.

*   *   *

TONY entered his own house and found Graham still sitting in front of his typewriter, not writing now, but reading through a pile of onionskin pages.

"Hi. I was waiting for you." The journalist looked pleased with himself. "I'll fix us some sandwiches if you'll do something about that coffee of yours. When you make it, it's almost drinkable."

There was a knock on the door.

"Come in," Tony called out.

"Oh, am I busting in on something?" Nick asked innocently.

"No, of course not. Glad to see you. Doug, this is Nick Cantrella. I don't know if you met him before. He's in charge of maintenance and equipment in the Lab, and a member of our Council. Nick, you know who Doug Graham is."

"Uh-huh. My rival. My wife's only true love."

"And you should see his wife," Tony added.

"This gets more and more interesting. You're not married to that lady pilot by any chance?" Graham extended a greasy hand. "No? Too bad. Join us? We're eating *meat*."

"Don't mind if I do. How's the baby, Tony? Anything really wrong?"

"Yes and no. Colic. Good old colic," the doctor gloated. "It shouldn't happen, but, by God, it's something I know how to cope with; I think the kid's going to be all right. Coffee's ready. Where's the food?"

They munched sandwiches, and had "coffee," which Graham pronounced a very slight improvement over his own efforts. The two Sun Lakers were more than happy with it; it was sweetened with gratings from a brick of sugar produced by the gunther from his wonder-packed luggage. The same suitcase turned out to hold another bottle of Earthside liquor, and Graham poured drinks all around.

"It's a celebration," the writer insisted, when Tony, remembering his hangover, would have demurred. "I got a week's work done today. Whole first chapter—complete draft of the trip out and impressions of Marsport." He fanned out a sheaf of pages covered with single-spaced typing, and corked the bottle.

Nick took a long deep swallow, settled back blissfully on the bunk where he was sitting. "Marcaine," he said at last. "That could explain it."

"What?"

"I've been sitting here imagining I was eating meat and drinking whiskey. Can you beat that?" He sipped more slowly this time, savoring the drink, and said determinedly to Graham, "You're just about up to Sun Lake in your notes then?"

"That's right," Graham said. In the silence that followed, he asked brightly: "Say, aren't you the guy who saw the brownie tracks."

"Brownie tracks? Who, me? You're sure you weren't thinking of unicorns?"

"Do unicorns leave little footprints?"

"Oh, that. Yeah, I saw something out around the caves in the Rimrock Hills. That's where the kids take the goats to graze."

"Are they allowed to go barefoot around there?" Graham asked.

"Allowed?" Nick exploded. "You haven't been ten years old for quite a long time, have you? How much attention do you think they pay?"

QUITE a bit, Tony thought, remembering his talk with Tad, but he didn't bring it up. Out loud he said: "I've got a theory about that. I've been thinking about it since last night, Doug. Maybe you can use it in your book." It wasn't smart, maybe, to keep riding the writer about it, but he'd had enough of brownies for awhile. "I'll tell you what I think. I think some kids who weren't supposed to do it went exploring in a cave, and one of them got lost. Then the rest wouldn't admit what happened, and all the search party could find was kid-sized footprints. So we have 'brownies.' And a couple of dozen retired prospectors back on Earth are coining money telling lies about them," he finished, more sharply than he meant to.

"I guess that squelches me," Graham laughed boisterously, picked up his papers, and stood up. "I better be getting along. Have to find out about getting this stuff radioed out." He started for the door, and almost collided with Anna coming in.

"Oh, I'm sorry. I forgot you had company, Tony. They kept me busy all day out at the Lab, and I thought maybe I could get some work done here this evening, but..." She smiled apologetically at Tony and Nick, then turned to Graham. "Were you going out?"

"Shouldn't I?"

"Of course not," said Tony. "Not when Anna's just come in. Stick around, and you'll see something."

"What does she do?" Graham asked. "Song and dance routine? Prestidigitation?"

Nick said from his perch on the wall bunk: "Graham, if you had an ounce of Earthside chivalry in your bloodstream, you'd uncork that bottle and offer the lady a drink."

"You're right. I'll even offer you one." Tony got another glass and the writer poured. Then he turned to Anna, and asked again, "Well, what *do* you do?"

"I'm a glassblower, that's all. Tony likes to watch it, and he couldn't possibly understand that other people might not enjoy it as much."

"Oh. You do your work over here?"

"Yes," the doctor said testily. "Anna is also my assistant, if you recall—neither one is a full-time job, so she keeps her equipment here, and combines the two."

For a few minutes, the four of them sat talking inconsequentially, the three Sun Lakers answering Graham's endless variety of questions.

Finally, Anna got up.

"If I'm going to get any work done, I better get started." She opened the cupboards and began pulling out equipment.

Graham stood up too. "Well..." He picked up his sheaf of papers.

"Tony!"

ALL three men focused their attention on Anna, who stood facing them, her arms full of assorted junk.

"Tony," she said bluntly. "Have you told Mr. Graham about our problem here? Don't you think he might be able to help?"

"Well..." Graham sat down again, and suddenly grinned. "Tell me, what can I do for dear old Sun Lake?"

"You can save our necks," Nick told him soberly. "At least I think you can, if you want to. You're going back on the rocket," he explained, "and that rocket won't have our shipment on it, because—actually because—we *didn't* steal some marcaine we're accused of stealing. It's not here, so we couldn't find it, and that means Bell will throw a cordon around us on Shipment Day. You know Bell from way back. You could raise such a stink about what he's doing to us—if you wanted to—that there'd be orders recalling him to Earth on the next rocket that comes in. You're big enough to do it. And we don't know any other way."

"You're very flattering," the writer said, "and also too damn brief. I already know that much. Suppose you fill me in on some of the details."

"Bell tramped in three days ago," the doctor began carefully, and went through the story, step by step, not omitting the information he had picked up in Marsport, and reminding Graham at the same time about the Cham's new regulations against marcaine.

"Brenner wants to get his hands on the Sun Lake Lab," Tony wound up. "You got Bell kicked out of a good job once for crooked dealing. You could do it again. Unless Bell's got religion, and I see no sign of it, Brenner could easily hire him to kick us off Mars and then see that Brenner Pharmaceutical got the assets of the busted Sun Lake Colony—including the Lab—in a rigged auction."

The writer pondered, and then told them slowly: "I think I can do something about it. It's a good story, anyhow. The least I can do is try."

Nick let out a wild: "Wa-hoo!" and Tony slumped with relief. He looked back to Anna's workbench, smiling—but she was gone.

"Now that that's settled," said Graham, "I want a favor myself."

"Up to but not including my beautiful blonde wife," promised Nick fervently.

"If it was women, I'd want that lady airplane pilot. But it isn't women. I still want to get this stuff filed to Marsport by your radio. I'm going to have a crowded schedule before takeoff and every minute I dip off in advance, like getting this stuff typed and microfilmed, will help."

"Sure, pal. Sure." Nick stood up and shook the writer's hand earnestly. "I'll take you to the radio shack myself and give you the blanchest carte you ever saw."

## CHAPTER SIXTEEN

*It's a li'l* Mars *baby,*
*It's a li'l* Mars *baby,*
*It's a li'l* Mars *baby,*
*Li'l Mars* baby
*All—our—own!*

IT WAS midnight, and Polly sang her song very softly, so as not to awaken Jim. Her hand, on the baby's back, caressed the tiny, clearly defined muscles, rigid now with concentration of effort. Her eyes filled with wonder as she watched Sunny nuzzle awkwardly, but successfully, against her breast.

He was eating. He was swallowing the milk, and not choking on it or spitting it back.

With a touch of awe at the thought that she was the only mother on Mars who had the privilege, she laid the baby over her shoulder and gently patted. Sunny bubbled and subsided. She laid him in the basket and sat watching him raptly. Jim rolled over and muttered, so she decided not to sing her song again. She was hungry, anyway. She touched her lips to the baby's forehead, straightened his mathematically straight blanket and went to the little pantry cupboard in the living room.

A dish of left over navy beans would settle her for two or three more hours of sleep. She found a spoon and began to eat, happily.

She cleaned the dish and licked the spoon, put them away and started back for bed.

She was halfway to the bedroom door when it happened.

EVERYTHING went slower and slower and came to a stop. She was frozen to the floor, giggling—and she was also somewhere else, watching herself giggle. The reddish walls turned the most beautiful apple-green, her favorite color, and put forth vines and branches. They were apple tree branches, and they began to bear apples that were baby's heads—severed baby's heads, dripping rich delicious juice. The babies sang her song in a cheeping chorus, and she saw and heard herself giggle and sing with them, and pluck the heads from the branches, open her mouth—

"*Jim!*" she shrieked and it all collapsed.

Her husband stood in the doorway, looked at her and leaped to catch her.

"Get Dr. Tony," she gasped after she had vomited and he had carried her to a chair. "I think I'm going crazy. There were these— get Dr. Tony, please, Jim."

The thought of being left alone horrified her, but she clutched the chair arms, afraid to close her eyes while he was gone. She counted to more than a hundred, lost track and was starting again when Jim and the doctor burst in.

"Polly, what is it? What happened?"

"I don't know, Doctor, *I don't know.* It's all over now, but I don't know if it's going to come back. I *saw* things. I think...Tony, I think I'm crazy."

"You threw up," he reminded her. "Did you eat anything?"

"I was hungry after I nursed Sunny. I ate some beans—cold beans. And then it was horrible. It was like a nightmare, only I was watching myself..."

"This happened right after you ate the beans?" he demanded. "You didn't eat the beans earlier?"

"No, it was right after. I fed Sunny, and then I ate, and then it happened. I was frozen to the floor and I watched myself. I was going to do something horrible. I was going to..." She couldn't say it; she remembered it too clearly.

"That's too quick for food poisoning," the doctor said. "You froze, you say. And you watched yourself. And there were

125

hallucinations."

"Yes, like the worst nightmare in the world, yet I was awake."

"Stay with her, Jim. I've got to get something. Can you clean up in here?"

Jim clenched his wife's hand in his big, red fist and then began to mop.

Tony came back with a black box they all knew—the electroencephalograph.

"Look here, Tony," growled Kandro. "If you're thinking that Polly's a drug addict, you're crazy."

Tony ignored him and strapped the electrodes to the woman's head. Three times he took traces, and they were identical. Positive brain waves.

"You were full of marcaine," he told her flatly. "Where did you get it?"

"Well, I *never*—" and "God damn it all, Doc—" the couple began simultaneously.

Tony relaxed. "I don't need a lie-detector," he said. "It must have been put on the beans. Lord knows how or why."

Polly asked incredulously: "You mean people go through that for *pleasure*?"

"You had the reaction of a well-balanced person. It's the neurotic who enjoys the stuff."

Polly shook her head dazedly.

"But what are we going to *do*?" demanded Jim.

"First thing is to get some bottles and nipples and goat's milk for you. Breast-feeding is out for at least the next week, Polly. There'd be marcaine in your milk. You don't want to wean Sunny now?"

"Oh, *no*!"

Tony smiled. "We'll have to get a breast pump made, too, to keep your supply going. But that can wait till morning."

"But—" protested Jim.

The doctor swung around to face him. "All right, what do you suggest we do?"

Jim thought and said hopelessly: "I don't know."

"NEITHER do I. I'm a doctor, not a detective. All I can do is write a formula for the baby, and get people moving right now turning out the stuff you need."

He stepped into the nursery for a moment to peer at Sunny, in the crib—a beautiful, healthy child. Tony wondered for a moment whether Polly's earlier fantasy about a menacing brownie had also been caused by her food being doped. There had been no nausea that time, but it might have been a smaller dose.

Time enough later to figure all that out; Sunny would be hungry again in a few hours.

"Jim," he directed, "you better beat it over to Anna Willendorf's and tell her we'll need bottles right away. And get some milk while you're out. If you move fast, we'll have time to boil it and make the first formula before Sunny wakes up again."

"Milk?" Jim said, dazed.

"Milk. From one of the goats. Don't you know how?"

"I've milked cows," Kandro said. "Couldn't be much different."

"One other thing," Tony called to Jim, who was already at the door. "Nipples. Get Bob Carmichael for that. I think he can figure out some way...make sure he checks with Anna on the size."

"Right." Jim closed the door behind him.

*   *   *

THEY had the milk boiling on the alky stove when Anna arrived with the first bottle. "The others are still cooling," she explained. "I'll go back for them later, but I thought you'd need one right away." She handed it over, went to look down at the calmly sleeping baby, and asked Polly, "What can I do?"

"I don't know. Nothing, I guess. The doctor's showing me how to make formula and I suppose that's all there is. It was awfully nice of you to get up to make the bottles. I feel terrible about making so much trouble, but I just..." She trailed off helplessly.

"It wasn't your fault," Anna told her, then asked the doctor: "Do you want me to take over with the formula?"

"There's no need to," Tony told her. "For that matter, you can go back to bed if you want to. There shouldn't be any more trouble tonight."

"I have to go back and get the other bottles later anyhow," she protested. She took over at the stove, showing Polly the simple procedures of sterilization and measuring involved in the baby's formula.

Jim came back from a second trip to the Lab in time to boil up one of the new nipples, and fill a bottle before Sunny woke. Polly, still shaken, but determined to behave normally, picked the baby up and changed him, warmed the bottle herself under Anna's watchful eye, and settled herself on a chair with baby and bottle.

"You want to make sure the neck of the bottle is full of milk," Tony told her. "Aside from that, there's nothing difficult about it. Don't try to force his position. Let him wriggle around just as if he was at the breast." He watched while she nudged the new plastic nipple into his mouth. "That's right. Fine. I think he's going to take it all right."

Sunny sucked hungrily, wriggled, pushed his mouth sidewise, and then to the other side, sucking all the time. Milk spilled out the side of his mouth as he sucked without swallowing, and turned his reddening face from side to side, squirming desperately.

Tony, suddenly frightened took a step forward. He could see the trouble clearly enough, but from above, looking down at the baby's face, Polly couldn't possibly see what was happening.

Sunny was trying to make use of the peculiar sidewise suckling he had developed at his mother's breast, but he couldn't wedge his small mouth around the comparatively firm plastic of the new nipple. Tony opened his mouth to speak; in a minute the baby would...

*"Stop it! O-o-h-h stop it! You're choking—"*

Polly's hand, holding the bottle, shot away from the baby's mouth. Tony whirled to see Anna crumble to the floor, her mouth still open in the drawn-out shriek.

"Jim," he shouted. "Quick. Take care of her." Then he turned back again without waiting to see what Kanrdro did. He lifted the choking, convulsive infant out of Polly's limp arms, turned him upside down, and stroked the small stiff back vigorously. Within seconds, a thick curd of milk dribbled out of the baby's mouth, and the terrible gasping sounds turned into a low monotonous wailing.

TONY put the baby back in his mother's arms, and turned briefly to look at Anna. Jim had lifted her onto the wall bunk. Tony checked quickly to make sure she hadn't hurt herself.

"Just fainted," he said, puzzled, and gave Kandro instructions to restore consciousness.

Sunny's wailing was turning into a steady, vigorous hunger cry.

The doctor picked him up again, and wrapped him in one of the warm new blankets.

"Where are you taking Sunny?" asked Polly with shrill nervousness.

"To the hospital." he turned to Jim, still standing over the unconscious Anna. "Don't let her leave when she comes to, Jim. I'll be back later."

He went out, carrying the screaming baby in one arm and his black bag in the other.

The walk back to his own house was haunted. The ghost of a newborn baby went with him along the curving street, in the dark, a ghost that gasped and choked as Sunny did, twisting in agony until it died again as it had already died a thousand thousand times for Tony, only the first time was the worst, the first baby born and the first one dead in Sun Lake, and he'd had to watch it all, the ghost of a baby that died for want of air...

He went in by the hospital door. He didn't want to see Graham.

Systematically, he turned on the lights and assembled his instruments in the sterilizer, turned a heat lamp on the examination table, and stripped off the baby's clothes. This couldn't go on; there had to be an answer to Sunny's troubles, and he was going to find it now, tonight.

Tony examined the child with every instrument and technique in his repertory. He felt it, probed and thumped it, listened to its interior plumbing. He could find nothing that resembled organic trouble. And he could think of no rational explanation for a mask baby breathing through its mouth.

"It's got to be nasal," he said out loud. Three times he had used the otoscope, and three times he had found no obstruction. But—

CAREFULLY, Tony slipped the mask off Sunny's nose. He slipped it over the mouth instead, stifling its scream in mid-voice. At least, he thought grimly, the baby would *have* to breathe through the mask now if it wanted to keep on crying. The doctor began to probe delicately into one nostril, and Sunny promptly reacted with the unexpected. Impossible or not, he tried to draw a breath through his exposed nostrils, found an impediment and began to choke again.

Tony withdrew the slender probe and stared at the gasping, red-faced infant. For just a moment, a clear and frightening picture of the other baby blotted out what was before his eyes—the ghost baby that had come up the street with them. Then he looked at Sunny again and everything began to fall into place.

Sunny was the wrong color.

He should have been blue and he wasn't. He was gasping for air, he couldn't breathe; he should have been oxygen starved. *And he was flushed a bright crimson.*

It wasn't lack of oxygen, then. It was impossible. But it was the only logical answer. Tony removed the mask from the baby's face with trembling hands.

He waited.

It took Sun Lake City Colony Kandro less than thirty seconds to do what Tony knew he couldn't do—and most certainly would do. Sunny gasped sharply for a moment. Then this breathing became even, his color turned a normal healthy pink, and he resumed his monotonous hunger cry.

Sunny didn't need an oxygen mask at all to survive on Mars, nor did he need OxEn.

The fact was scientifically paralyzing…the child was adapted not to the rich air of Earth, but the deadly thin atmosphere of Mars.

## CHAPTER SEVENTEEN

"SUNNY!" Polly ran to the table where Sunny still lay crying, wrapped in his blanket again, hungry, angry, and perfectly safe. "Doctor, what did you—how can he—?"

"He's fine," Tony assured her. "Just leave him alone. He's hungry, that's all."

Polly stared, fascinated by the naked-looking baby. "How can he breathe without a *mask*?"

"I don't know," Tony said bluntly, "but I tried it and it worked. I guess he's got naturally Mars-worthy lungs. Seems to have been the only trouble he had."

"You mean—I thought Marsworthy lungs just meant you *could* breathe Mars air; people like that can breathe Earth air, too, can't they?"

Tony shrugged helplessly. He was licked and didn't care who knew it as long as Sunny was all right. For the time being, it was enough to know that the baby had been breathing through his mouth all along just because he *did* prefer Mars air. He got too much oxygen through the mask, so he didn't use his nose; a simple reversal of the theory on which the mask was based. When his source of Mars air was blocked—first by his mother's breast, and then, when he had learned to adapt to that, by the less flexible plastic nipple—he had to breathe the richer air through his nose, and he turned red, coughed, sputtered, and choked.

"I want to take him back now," said the doctor, "and try another feeding. Bet he'll eat right away." He picked up the baby, firmly refusing to surrender him to his mother, and led the way out of the hospital room and back to the Kandros' house.

Just before they left, Tony heard for the first time, consciously, the steady clicking of Graham's typewriter in the other part of the house. He realized it had been going almost continuously, and thought briefly of going inside to say hello, then decided against it. *I'll see him later on*, he thought...*I can explain everything then*. Obviously, the writer understood that an emergency was in progress, or else he was so busy himself that he didn't want to be bothered, either.

\* \* \*

JIM was thunderstruck by his maskless Sunny. Anna seemed to have recovered from her faint. She was a little pale, but otherwise normal, moving about briskly, picking up scattered blankets and baby equipment.

"I tried to make her rest," Jim explained, "but she said she felt fine."

"You take it easy, Anna," the doctor told her. "And I want to talk to you later—as soon as I'm finished with the baby."

"I'm perfectly all right," she insisted. "I can't imagine what made me do anything so foolish. I'm awfully sorry..."

"Polly, I want *you* to go to bed right away. You've had enough tonight—this morning, rather. Jim, you can handle the baby can't you? You want to change him and get him ready for his feeding?"

Jim stooped over his son at the wall bunk, his big hands fumbling a little with closures on the small garments. Tony sat down and leaned back, closing his eyes. The baby screamed steadily, demanding nourishment.

"Doc, I still don't get it. How did you figure it out?"

Patiently, without opening his eyes, Tony repeated his explanation for Jim.

"I'll take your word for it," the man said finally, "but I'll be darned if I can understand it. Okay Doc, I *guess* he's all fixed up."

Tony stood up. "Do you know how to fix a bottle? I'll show you."

"Here." Anna was at his elbow. "I thought you might want one," she said, as though apologizing, and handed it over.

"Thanks." Tony dashed a drop on his wrist—temperature just right—and passed it to Jim. "Let's try."

The big man, looking absurdly cautious, put the bottle to Sunny's mouth. Then he looked up, a tremendous grin on his face and his eyes a little wet. "How do you like that?" he said softly. The little mouth and jaw were working away busily; Sunny was feeding as though he'd been doing it for months.

They watched while he took a whole three and a half ounces, and then fell asleep, breathing quietly and regularly.

"A Mars child," said Anna gently, looking down at Sunny. "Jim, you have a real Mars child."

"Looks that way," said Kandro, beaming.

"Jim," said the doctor, "somebody ought to stay up and keep an eye on Sunny tonight, but I'm beat. And Polly's got to get some sleep. Will you do it?"

"Sure, Doc," said the father, not taking his happy eyes off the child.

"He'll probably need another feeding during the night. You know how to sterilize the bottle, and there's enough formula made up."

"Sure," said Jim. "You take care of Anna."

"I'll do that."

"Oh, Tony, I'm all right, I told you that—"

"You get your parka, Anna, and don't argue with the doctor," Tony told her. "I'm going to take you home and see if I can find out what made you pull that swoon. Come on... If you need me for anything, Jim, I'll be at Anna's or at home."

"I DO have a headache," she admitted when they reached her house. "Probably all I need is a little sleep. I haven't been living right." She tried a smile, but it didn't come off.

"None of us have," Tony reminded her. He studied her and

decided against aspirin. He selected a strong sedative and shot it into her arm. Within a minute, she relaxed in a chair and exhaled long and gratefully. "Better," she said.

"Feel like talking?"

"I—I think I ought to sleep."

"Then just give me the bare facts." He ran his fingers over her head. "No blows. Was it a hangover?"

"Yes," she said defiantly.

"Very depraved. From the one drink you had with us?"

"From—from—Oh, hell." That came from the heart, for Anna never swore.

"I've had enough mysteries for one night, Anna. Talk."

"Maybe I ought to," she said unwillingly. "Only a fool tells a lie to his doctor or the truth to his lawyer and so on." She hesitated. "I've got a trick mind. All those people who think they're psychic—they are. I am, but more. It doesn't matter, does it?"

"Go on."

"I didn't know about it myself for a long time. It's not like mind-reading; it's not that clear. I was always—oh, sensitive, but I didn't understand it at first, and then later on it seemed to get more and more pronounced. I—haven't told anyone about it before. Not anyone at all."

She looked at him appealingly. Tony reassured her, "You know you can trust me."

"All right, I began to realize what it was when I was about twenty. That's why I became, of all things, a glassblower. If you had to listen to the moods and emotions of people, you'd want a job far away from everything in a one-man department, too. That's why I came to Mars. It was too—too noisy on Earth."

"And that's why you're the best assistant I ever had, with or without an M. D. or R. N. on your name," said the doctor softly.

"You're easy to work with." she smiled. "Most of the time, it is. Sometimes, though, you get so *angry*—"

HE thought back, remembering the times she'd been there before he had called, or had left quickly when she was in the way, handed him what he needed before he actually *thought* about it.

"Please don't get upset about it, Tony. I'd hate to have to stop working with you now. I don't know what you *think*, just what you—

*feel*, I guess. There are a lot of people like that, really; you must have sensed it in me a long time back. It isn't really so very strange," she pleaded. "I'm just a little—a little more that way, that's all."

"I don't see why I should get upset about it," he tried to soothe her, and realized sickeningly that it was a useless effort. He literally could not conceal his feelings this time. He stopped trying. "You must realize how hard I try not to show I'm even angry. It is a little disconcerting to find out—I'll get used to it. Just give me time." He was thoughtful for a moment. "How does it work? Do you know?"

"Not really. I 'hear' people's feelings. And—people seem to be more aware of my moods than they are of other people's. I—well, the way I first became aware of it was when somebody tried to—assault me, back on Earth, in Chicago. I was very young then, not quite twenty. It was one of those awful deserted streets, and he ran faster than I could and caught up with me. Something sort of turned on—I don't know how to say it. I was sending instead of receiving, but sending my emotion—which, naturally, was a violent mixture of fear and disgust—each more strongly than—than people usually can. I'm afraid I'm not making myself clear."

"No wonder," he said heavily. "The language isn't built for experiences like that. Go on."

"He fell down and flopped on the sidewalk like a fish, and I ran on and got to a busy street without looking back. I read the papers, but there wasn't anything about it, so I suppose he was all right afterward."

SHE stopped talking and jumped up restlessly. For quite a while she stood staring out of her window, toward the dark reaches of *Lacus Solis*.

Finally she said in a strained voice, "Please, Tony, it's not really as bad as that sounded. I can't send all the time; I can't do it mostly." She turned back to face him, and added more naturally: "Usually, people aren't as—open—as he was. And I guess I have to be pretty worked up, too. I tried to send tonight, and I couldn't do it. I tried awfully hard. That's why I had that headache."

"Tonight?"

"I'll tell you about that in a minute. Right now, I want—well, I told you I never told anyone about this before. It's important to me, Tony, *terribly* important, to make you understand. You're the first person I ever wanted to have understand it and if you keep on being frightened or unhappy about it, I just don't know—"

She paused. "Let me tell you about it my way. I'll try to ignore whatever you feel while I'm telling it, and maybe when I'm done it will all be all right.

"When that happened in Chicago—what I told you about—I had a job in an office. There was a girl I had to work with who didn't like me. It was very unpleasant. Every day for a month I tried to turn that 'send-receive' switch and transmit a calm, happy feeling to her, but I never could make it work. No matter how hard I tried, I couldn't get anything over to her. I knew what she felt, but her emotions were closed to mine. She didn't want to feel anything from me, so she didn't. Do you understand that? It's important, because it's true; you can protect yourself from that part of it. You believe me, don't you, Tony?"

He didn't answer right away. He had to be absolutely certain in his own mind, because she would know.

It would be far worse to tell her anything that wasn't true than to say nothing.

Finally he got up and walked over to her, but he didn't dare speak.

"Tony," she said, "you're—oh, please don't be embarrassed and difficult about it, but you're so *good*. That's what I meant, you're easy to work with. Most people are petty and a lot of them are mean. The things they feel aren't nice; they're mostly bitchy. But you—even when you're angry, it's a big, honest kind of anger. You don't want to hurt people, or get even, or take advantage of them. You're honest, and generous, and *good*. And now I've said too much."

He shook his head. "No, you didn't. It's all right. It really is."

There were tears shining in her eyes. Standing over her, he reached mechanically for a tissue from his bag, tilted her head up, and wiped her eyes as if she were a child.

"Now tell me more," he said, "and don't worry about how I feel. What happened tonight? Tell me about the headache. And the fainting—was that part of it too? Of course. What an idiot I am. The baby was choking and scared, and you screamed. You screamed and said to stop it."

"Did I? I wasn't sure whether I thought it or said it. That was strange, the whole business. It was terrible, somebody who hurt awfully all over and couldn't breathe, and was going to—to burst if he couldn't, and that didn't seem to make sense—and terribly hungry, and terribly frustrated, and—I didn't know who it was, because it was so strong. Babies don't have such 'loud' feelings. I guess it was the reflex of fear of dying, except Sunny is very loud, anyhow. When he was being born—"

SHE shuddered involuntarily. "I was awfully glad you didn't think to ask me to stay in there with you. When you sent Jim out, I talked to him, and sort of—concentrated on 'listening' to him, and then, with the door closed, it was all right. Anyhow, you want to know about tonight. The baby topped it off. I don't think that would have made me faint, by itself, but I was working in there, in the same room with Douglas Graham for an hour or more, and—"

"Graham," Tony broke in. "Do you mean to say he *dared* to—"

"Why, Tony, I—I didn't know you cared."

For the first time that evening, she laughed easily. Then, without giving him time to think about how his outburst had given him away, she added: "He didn't do anything. It was—it was about what he was writing, I *think*. I know what he was feeling. He was angry and disgusted and *contemptuous*. He hurt inside himself, and he felt the way people do when they hurt somebody else. And it seemed to be all tied up with the story he was writing. It was a story about the Colony, Tony, and I got worried and frightened. If only I could be sure. See, that's the trouble. I didn't know whether to tell somebody or not, and I tried and tried to 'send' to him, but he wasn't open at all, and the only thing that happened was that I got that headache."

"Then when you came over to the Kandros'," Tony finished for her, "and the baby had all that trouble, of course you couldn't take it. Tell me more about Graham. I understand that you're not sure; tell me what you *think*, and why."

"When Jim woke me up, we went back to your place together, and Graham was working there," she said. "He asked me what the excitement was all about and I told him. He listened, kept asking questions, got every little detail out of me, and all the time he was feeling that hurt and anger. Then I started to work and he began banging away on his typewriter. And those thoughts got stronger and stronger till they made me dizzy, and then I started trying to fight back, to send—and I couldn't. That's all there was to it."

"That's all? You're sure?"

She nodded.

"And you can't be certain what it was that he was feeling that way about?"

"How could I?"

"Well, then," he said, with a sighing laugh of relief, "there's nothing at all to worry about. You made a natural enough mistake. Those feelings of his weren't directed *against* the Colony at all, Anna. Earlier tonight, after you left, Graham promised to help us. He was writing a story about the spot we're in, that's all, and I know that he felt all the things you've described, but not about us, about Bell." He sat a moment longer. "I'm sure of it, Anna. That's the only way it makes sense."

"It could be." She seemed a little dazed. "It didn't feel that way, but, of course, it could." She sighed and leaned back in her chair. "Oh, Tony, I'm so glad I told you. I didn't know *what* to do, and I was sure it was something vicious he was writing about the Colony."

"Well, you can relax now. Maybe I'll let you go to bed." He took her hands and pulled her to her feet. "We'll work it out, even if I have to take a few new experiences in stride. Believe me, we'll work it out."

She looked up at him, smiling gently: "I think so, too, Tony."


HE could have let her hands go, but he didn't. Instead, he flushed as he realized that even now she was aware of all his feelings. There were tears shining in her eyes again, and this time he couldn't reach for a tissue. He leaned down and kissed her damp eyelids; then he dropped one hand to brush away the moisture on her cheek.

A thousand thoughts raced through his mind. Earth, and Bell, and the Colony, now or forever or never. That time in the plane, thinking of Bea. Anna—Anna always there at his side, helping, understanding.

"Anna," he said. He had never liked the name. "Ansie." There had been a little girl, a very long time ago, when he was a child, and her name had been Ansie.

He released her other hand and cupped her upturned face in both of his. His head bent to hers, slowly and tenderly. There was no fierceness here, only the hint of growing passion.

When he lifted his lips from hers, he laughed and said quietly: "It saves words, doesn't it?"

"Yes." Her voice was small and husky. "Yes, it does...dear."

If his mind was "open," he might feel what she did. Cautiously and warily, he reached out to her, with his arms and with his mind. He needed no questions and no answers now.

"Ansie," he whispered again, and lifted her slender body.

## CHAPTER EIGHTEEN

TAD'S left ear itched; he let it.

"Operator on duty will not remove headphones under any circumstances until relieved—" There was a good hour before Gladys Porosky would show up to take over.

"Mars Machine Tool to Sun Lake," crackled the headset suddenly. He glanced at the clock and tapped out the message time on the log sheet in the typewriter before him.

"Sun Lake to Mars Machine Tool, I read you, G. A.," he said importantly.

"Mars Machine Tool to Sun Lake, message. Brenner Pharmaceutical to Marsport. Via Mars Machine Tool, Sun Lake, Pittco Three. Request reserve two cubic meters cushioned cargo space outgoing rocket, Signed Brenner. Repeat, two cubic meters. Ack please, G. A."

Tad said: "Sun Lake to Mars Machine Tool," and read back painstakingly from the log: "Message. Brenner Pharmaceutical to Marsport. Via Mars Machine Tool, Sun Lake, Pittco Three. Signed Brenner. Repeat, two cubic meters. Received okay. T. Campbell, Operator, End."

TAD'S fingers were flying over the typewriter keyboard. Mimi and Nick would want to know how the rocket was filling up. The trick was to delay your estimated requirements to the last possible minute and then reserve a little more than you thought you'd need. Reserve too early and you might be stuck with space you couldn't fill but had to pay for. Reserve too late and there might be no room for your stuff until the next rocket.

"Mars Machine Tool to Sun Lake, end," said the headset. Tad started to raise Pittco's operator, the intermediate point between Sun Lake and Marsport, to boot the message onto the last stage of its journey.

"Sun Lake to Pittco Three," he said into the mike. No answer. He went into "the buzz," droning: "Pittco Three, Pittco Three, Pittco

Three, Sun Lake—"

"Pittco Three to Sun Lake, I read you," came at last, mushily, through the earphones. Tad was full of twelve-year-old scorn. Half a minute to ack, and then probably with a mouthful of sandwich. "Sun Lake to Pittco Three," he said. "Message. Brenner Pharmaceutical to Marsport via Mars Machine Tool, Sun Lake, Pittco Three. Request reserve two cubic meters cushioned cargo space outgoing rocket. Signed Brenner. Repeat, two cubic meters. Ack, please. G. A."

"Pittco to Sun Lake, message received. Charlie Dyer, Operator, out."

Tad fumed at the Pittco man's sloppiness and make-it-up-as-you-go procedure. Be a fine thing if everybody did that—messages would be garbled, short stopped, rocketloading fouled up, people and cargoes miss their planes.

He tapped out on the log sheet: "Pittco Operator C. Dyer failed to follow procedure, omitted confirming repeat. T. Campbell." He omitted Dyer's irksome use of "out" instead of "end" and the other irregularities, citing only the legally important error. That was just self-protection; if there were any errors in the final message, the weak spot on the relay could be identified. But Tad was uncomfortably certain that Dyer, if the report ever got back to him, would consider him an interfering brat.

He bet Mr. Graham's last message had got respectful handling from Pittco, in spite of the pain-in-the-neck Phillips Newscode it had been couched in. They all wanted Graham. Tad had received half a dozen messages for the writer extending the hospitality of this industrial colony or that. The man had good sense to stick with Sun Lake, the boy thought approvingly. There was this jam with the rocket and the commissioner, but the Sun Lakers were unquestionably the best bunch of people on Mars.

"Pittco to Sun Lake," said Dyer's voice in the earphones.

"Sun Lake to Pittco, I read you, G. A.," snapped Tad.

"Pittco Three to Pittco One, message. Via Sun Lake, Mars Machine Tool, Brenner Pharmaceutical, Distillery Mars, Rolling Mills. Your outgoing rocket cargo space requirements estimate needed here thirty-six hours. Reminder downhold cushioned space requests minimum account new tariff schedule. Signed, Hackenburg for Reynolds. Repeat, thirty-six hours, ack please, G. A."

HUH. Dyer repeated numbers on *his* stuff, all right. Tad acked and booted the message on. The machine shop in the "canal" confluence would get it, then the drug factory in the highlands dotted with marcaine weed, then the distillery among its tended fields of wiregrass, then the open hearth furnaces and rolling mills in the red taconite range, and at last Pittco One, in the heart of the silver and copper country.

He hoped he wouldn't have to handle any of Graham's long code jobs. Orders were to cooperate fully with the writer, but even Harve Stillman, who'd taken Graham's story on his rocket trip and Marsport, had run into trouble with it. Tad loafed through the material to the coded piece by Graham and shuddered.

IT was okay, the boy supposed, for on Earth, where you didn't want somebody tapping a PTM transmission beam and getting your news story, but why did the guy have to show off on Mars where the only way out was by rocket and you couldn't get scooped?

"Marsport 18 to Pittco Three," he heard faintly in the earphones. Automatically he ran his finger down the posted list of planes. Marsport 18 was a four-engine freighter belonging to the Marsport Hauling Company.

"Pittco Three to Marsport 18, I read you, G. A."

"Marsport 18 to Pittco, our estimated time of arrival is thirteen-fifty. Thirteen-fifty. We're bringing in your mail. End."

"Pittco to Marsport 18, O. K., E. T. A. is thirteen-fifty and I'll tell Mr. Hackenburg. End."

Mail, thought Tad enviously. All Sun Lake ever got was microfilmed reports from the New York office and business letters from customers. Aunt Minnie and Cousin Adelbert's wouldn't write to you unless you wrote to them; and Sun Lake couldn't layout cash for space-mail stamps.

Tad's ear itched. One thing he missed, he admitted to himself in a burst of candor, and he'd probably have to go on missing it. The Sun Lake Society of New York couldn't spontaneously mail him the latest *Captain Crusher Comix.*

He had read to tatters Volume GCXVII, Number 27, smuggled under his sweater from Earth. And to this day he hadn't figured out how the captain had escaped from the horrible jam he'd been in on Page 64. There had been a Venusian Crawlbush on his right, a

Martian Brownie on his left, a Rigelian Paramonster drifting down from above and a Plutonian Bloodmole burrowing up from below. Well, the writers of Captain Crusher knew their business, thought Tad, though they certainly didn't know much about Mars—the *real* Mars. Their hero never seemed to need OxEn or clothing any warmer than hose and cape when on a Martian adventure. And he was always stumbling over Brownies and dead cities and lost civilizations.

Bunk, of course. Brownies, dead cities and lost civilizations would make Mars a more interesting place for a kid. But when a person grows up, other things mattered more than excitement. Things like doing a good job and knowing it. Things like learning. Getting along. Probably, Tad thought uncomfortably, getting married some day.

"Mars Machine Tool to Sun Lake. Sun Lake, Sun Lake, Sun Lake, Mars Machine Tool, Sun Lake—"

"Sun Lake to Mars Machine Tool, I read you, G. A.," Tad snapped, peeved.

The operator might have waited just a second before he went into the buzz.

"Mars Machine Tool to Sun Lake, message. Pittco One to Pittco Three. Via Rolling Mill, Distillery Mars, Brenner Pharmaceutical, Mars Machine Tool, Sun Lake, outgoing rocket cargo space requirements are: ballast, thirty-two cubic meters; braced antishift, twelve point seventy-five cubic meters; glass-lined tank, fifteen cubic meters; cushioned, one point five cubic meters. Regret advise will require steerage space one passenger. F.Y.I., millwright's helper Chuck Kelly disabled by marcaine addiction."

The repeats followed and Tad briskly receipted. He raised Pittco Three and booted the message, grinning at a muffled *"God damn it."* over the earphones as he droned out the bad news about Kelly. Steerage passenger space didn't come as high as cushioned cargo cubage; a steerage passenger was expected to grab a stanchion, hang on and take his lumps during a rough landing; but it was high enough.

SUN LAKE couldn't afford cushioned cubage, ever, and settled for braced antishift. Sometimes crates gave and split under the smashing accelerations, but the cash you had to layout for cargo protected springs, hydraulic systems and meticulous stowage by the supercargo himself wasn't there. It meant a disgruntled customer every once in a while, but the tariffs made you play it that way.

The door behind him opened and closed. "Gladys?" he asked. "You're early."

"It's me, sonny," said a man's voice—Graham's. "You mind filing a little copy for me?"

The newsman handed him a couple of onionskin pages. "Phillips Newscode," he said. "Think you can handle it?"

"I guess so," said Tad unhappily. "We're supposed to cooperate with you." Blankly he looked at the sheets and asked: "Why bother to code it, though?"

"It saves space, for one thing. You get about five words for one. 'GREENBAY,' for instance, means 'An excited crowd gathered at the scene.' 'THREEPLY' means 'In spite of his, or their, opposition.' And, for another thing, what's the point of my knowing the code if I never use it?" He grinned to show he was kidding.

Tad ignored the grin and remarked: "'I thought that was it."

He entered the time in the log and said into the mike: "Sun Lake to Pittco Three." Pittco acked.

"Sun Lake to Pittco Three, long Phillips Newscode message, Sun Lake to Marsport. Via Pittco Three. Message: Microfilm following text and hold for arrival Douglas Graham Marsport and pickup at Administration Building. GREENBAY PROGRAM SUNLAKE STOP POSTTWO ARGUABLE FUZZERS MARSEST BRIGHTEST STOP ARGUABLEST MARSING MYFACED GIN-FLOOZERS DOPEBORT FELKIL PARA UNME SUNLAKE HOCFOCUS COPLOKED ETERS EARTHED STOP SAPQUIS-FACT HOCPLAGUER ERQUICK—

GRAHAM heard the last of the story go out and saw the kid note down the acknowledgment in the log.

"Good job," the gunther said. "Thanks, fella."

Outside, the chilly night air fanned his face. It had been a dirty little trick to play on the boy. They'd give him hell when they found out, but the message had to clear and that Stillman knew a little Phillips—enough to wonder and ask questions.

Graham took a swig from his pocket flask and started down the street. He'd needed the drink, and he needed a long walk. It was surgery, he told himself, but surgery wasn't always pleasant for the surgeon. That doctor might be able to understand if he could only step back and see the thing in perspective. As it was, Tony obviously believed Mrs. Kanrdro's absurd story about somebody doping the beans.

The writer grinned sardonically. What a cesspool Mars must be if even these so-called idealists were so corrupted. Marcaine addiction by a brand-new mother, theft of a huge quantity of marcaine clearly traced to the Colony. The doctor would hate him and think him two-faced, which he was. It was part of the job. He was going to start an avalanche; a lot of people would hate him for it.

An impeccable, professional hatchet job on Sun Lake was the lever that would topple the boulder to start the avalanche. Senators would posture and declaim, bills would be written and rewritten by legislative clerks, but that would be just the dust over the rumbling, rocks.

The public relations boys of the industrials used to be newspapermen themselves, and they could pick their way through Phillips. The word would be passed like lightning. They'd learn, to their horror that it wasn't going to be a cheerful travelog quickie like his last two or three; that Graham was out for blood. The coded dispatch would be talked over and worried over in most of Mars' administration buildings tonight. They would debate whether he was going to put the blast on all the colonies. But they'd note that he pinned all the guilt so far on Sun Lake, not mentioning specifically that the abortion and the prostitution had occurred at Pittco.

So, by tomorrow morning, he'd let one of the industrials send a plane for him. He'd been playing hard to get for two days—long enough. He'd put on his jovial mask and they'd fall all over themselves dishing the dirt on each other. He'd make it a point to pass through Brenner Pharmaceutical. Quasi-legal operators like Brenner always knew who was cutting corners. And Bell—what tills did he have his hand in?

Graham knew there wasn't another newsman alive who could swing it—the first real story to come out of Mars besides press handouts from the industrials. And the planet was rotten-ripe for it.

But, mostly, he would just scare them, be the scoffing, good-humored-know-it-all, so cheerfully sinister that they'd try to buy him off with dirt about the other outfits. He'd make no open promises, no open threats, and it all would drop into his lap the way it always had.

No, not always, he grimly corrected himself. Once he'd been a green kid reporter, lucky enough to break the Bell scandal. He'd actually been sorry for the crook. There'd been a lot of changes since.

It was funny what happened to you when you got into the upper brackets.

FIRST you grabbed and grabbed. Women, a penthouse with a two-acre living room, silk shirts "built" for you instead of the nylon all the paycheck stiffs wore, "beefsteaks" broiled over bootleg charcoal made of real wood from one of Earth's few thousand acres of remaining trees.

You grabbed and grabbed, and then you got sick of grabbing. You felt empty and blank and worked like hell to make yourself think you were happy. And then, if you were lucky, you found out who you were.

Graham had found out that he—the youngest one, underfed, the one the big boys ganged up on for snitching, the one the cop called a yellow little liar, the one nobody liked, the one who always got his head knucked when they played Nigger Inna Graveyard—yes, he had power. It was the monstrous energy of Earth's swarming billions. If you could reach them, you could have them. You could slash down what was rotten and corrupt; a thieving banker, a bribed commissioner, a Mars colony.

Under the jovial mask it hurt when they called you a sensationalist, said you were unanalytical, had no philosophy, couldn't do anything but set down facts to titillate the uncritical audience. But what you could do and they couldn't was stir the billions of Earth, make them laugh, make them hopeful, make them rage—and when they raged, focus their rage to a white-hot spot that cauterized a particular bit of rottenness.

Graham stumbled and took a swig from his flask.

Who had to have a philosophy? What was wrong with exposing crackpots and crooks? The first real news story out of Mars would break up the Sun Lake Colony. Some good would go with the bad; the surgeon had no choice. That Kandro woman and her baby. The child belonged on Earth. And it would go there. The little thing would never know if not for Graham that there was anything but Mars. *I'm supposed to be hardboiled*, he thought, a little drunk and sentimental, *but I know what's right for that kid.*

"Hey," he said. Where the hell was he, anyway? Wandering in the desert, high as a kite on his expected triumph. His feet had led him down the Colony street, along the path to the airfield, past it and a few kilometers toward the Rimrock Hills. He blamed it on the Mars gravity. Your legs didn't tire here, for one thing. The radio shack light was plain behind him; dimmer and off to the left of it shone the windows of the Lab, merged in one beacon.

The radio shack light went out and then on again. A moment later, so did the light from the Lab.

"Power interruption," he said. "Or I blinked."

It happened again, first the radio shack and then the Lab. And then it happened once more.

The writer took out his flask and gulped. "Who's out there?" he yelled. "I'm Graham!"

There wasn't any answer, but something came whistling out of the darkness at him, striking his parka and falling to the ground. He fumbled for it while still trying to peer through the night for whatever had passed between him and the lights of Sun Lake.

"What do you want?" he yelled into the darkness hysterically. "I'm Graham! The writer! Who are you?"

Something whizzed at him and hit his shoulder.

"Cut that out," he shrieked, and began to run for the lights of Sun Lake. He had taken only a few steps when something caught at his leg and he floundered onto the ground. The next and last thing he felt was a paralyzing blow on the back of his head.

## CHAPTER NINETEEN

TONY woke up in time for breakfast, an achievement in itself. He'd had, at best, some hundred and fifty-minutes of sleep after a long and hard day, and that interrupted by emergency, crisis, and triumph.

He washed without noticing the stench of the alcohol. He noted the time; good thing there was no Lab inspection to do this morning. He noticed the closed bedroom door; good thing he'd so hospitably given up his own bed to Graham, considering the unexpected turn of events the night before. He threw his parka over his shoulders and stepped out into the wan sunlight, oblivious to the lingering chill; good thing he—

Good thing he could still laugh at himself, he decided. What was the old saw about all the world loving a lover? Nothing to it—it was the lover who loved the whole world. *Love, lover, loving*, he rolled the words around in his mind, trying to tell himself that nothing had really changed. All the old problems were still there, and a new one, really, taken on.

But that wasn't so. Graham had spent half the night writing his promised story. Sunny Kandro was all right at last. And Anna—Ansie—a problem? He could remember thinking, in the distant past, as long as two days ago, that such an involvement would present problems, but he couldn't for the life of him remember what they were supposed to have been.


HE went in to breakfast, not trying to conceal his exuberance, and sat down between Harve Stillman and Joe Gracey.

"What's got into you?" Harve asked.

"Something *good* happen?" Gracey demanded.

Tony nodded. "The Kandro baby," he explained, using the first thing that popped into his head. "Jim woke me up last night. Polly was—was having trouble with the baby," he hastily amended the story.

He'd have to tell Gracey about the marcaine. There *was* a problem after all, but this wasn't the place for it; a Council meeting after breakfast maybe.

"You know we've been having feeding trouble all along," he explained. "I found the trouble last night. I don't understand it, but it works. I took Sunny's mask off."

"You *what?*"

"Took his mask off; he doesn't need it. Eats fine without it, too. Trouble was, he couldn't breathe through his mouth and eat at the same time."

"Well, I'll be— How do you figure it?"

"Hey, there's a story for the gunther," Harve suggested. "'Medical Miracle on Mars,' and all that stuff. Where is he anyhow?"

"Still sleeping, I guess. The bedroom door was closed."

"Did you talk to him last night?" Gracey asked.

Tony attacked his plate of fried beans, washed them down with a gulp of "coffee," and told the other man about Graham's promise. "He was up half the night writing, too. I heard him while I was examining the baby."

"Did he show it to you?"

"Not yet. He was asleep when I got back."

Harve, pushed back his chair with a grunt of satisfaction. "I feel better already," he grinned. "First decent meal I've had in days.

What's the program for today, Doc? You going to need me on radiological work?"

"I don't think so. I'll let you know if we do, after Joe and I get together with the others. Got time for a meeting after breakfast?" he asked the agronomist, and Gracey nodded.

"Okay, I'll be in the radio shack if you want me," Harve said. "The kids took over all day yesterday. Don't like to leave them too long on their own."

"Right. But I don't think we'll need you."

That marcaine business—how in all that was holy, the doctor wondered, did anybody get marcaine on to Polly's beans? After all the searching, in the middle of the hunt, who would do it? Why? And above all, *how*?

Maybe one of the others would have an angle on it.

\*     \*     \*

"ONE thing I'm glad about," Gracey said soberly. "We *did* make a thorough search. Whatever happens from here on out, at least we've proved to our own satisfaction that nobody in Sun Lake stole the stuff."

"That's nice to know," Mimi agreed with considerably less feeling. "But frankly, I'd almost feel better if we *had* found it. I'd gladly turn the bum who took it over to Bell's tender mercies, if it was one of us. This way, we have to depend on Graham. You're *sure* he's with us?" She looked questioningly from the doctor to the electronics man.

"How sure can you get?" Nick shrugged. "He said so. Now we wait to see his story, that's all."

"I don't think we have to worry about that," Tony said briefly. He couldn't tell them any more. He was sure himself, but how could he explain without giving away Anna's secret? "Look," he went on briskly, "there's something else we *do* have to think about. I told you about Sunny Kandro, Joe. There's more to it than what I said at breakfast."

Nick and Mimi both sat forward with new interest, as Tony repeated the news about the removal of Sunny's mask. He cut off their questions. "I didn't tell you how it started, though. Jim came to get me, not for the baby, but for Polly."

A sharp rap on the door stopped him. Harve Stillman walked in.

His face was grim; he carried a familiar sheaf of onionskin pages in his hands.

"What's the matter, Harve?" Mimi demanded. "Aren't you supposed to be on shift in the radio shack?"

"That's right. I walked out."

"No relief?" she snapped. "Are you sick?"

"I'm sick, all right. And it doesn't make any difference now whether radio's manned or not." He slapped the onionskin onto the table, and threw down on top of it two sheets of closely written radio log paper. "There you are, folks, have a look. It's all down in black and white. That's the translation on the log sheets. The bastard filed it in Phillips, so Tad wouldn't know what he was sending. When I think what a sucker I was, letting him pump me about who knew newscode around here. Go on, read it."

Mimi picked up the sheets and glanced at the penciled text. Her face went white. She reached for the onionskin, glanced at it, and returned her eyes to the log sheets. In a minute she looked up again.

"Harve, there couldn't be any mistake?"

"I know the code," he said, bluntly.

"Hey," Nick protested, "could you maybe let us in on it?"

"CERTAINLY," she smiled bitterly. "This is the story written for us by D. Graham, your friend and mine. I was greeted by a frightened crowd on my arrival at Sun lake, and no wonder. After two days in this community, I am able to reply to the heads-in-the-clouds idealists who claim that on Mars lies the hope of the human race. My reply is that on Mars I immediately came face-to-face into drunkenness, prostitution, narcotics, criminal abortion, and murder. It is not for me to say whether this means that Sun Lake Colony, an apparent center of these activities should be shut down by law and its inmates deported to Earth. But I do know—"

"That's crazy," Nick broke in. "I heard him say myself—" He stood up angrily.

Tony reached out a hand to restrain him. "He didn't promise a damn thing, Nick. We just heard it that way. He said he'd do a story, that's all."

"That's enough for me," Cantrella replied. "He promised, and he's by God going to keep his promise."

"Sit *down*, Nick," Mimi interrupted. "Beating Graham up isn't going to solve anything. Harve, you get back on duty, and buzz one of the kids to go over to Tony's and collect Graham. If he's asleep, tell them to wake him up. We'll go through the rest of this while we're waiting." She eyed the sheets of paper distastefully.

Harve slammed the door behind him, and Mimi turned to the others. "I'm sorry. I should have checked with you first. Every time something goes wrong, I start giving orders as if I owned the place. Here." She handed the sheets to Joe Gracey, still sitting quietly to her left. "You look calm. You read it."

Joe took the papers and went on where she had stopped before.

"He can't do that," Nick protested furiously, when Joe finished. "That story is full of lies. The murder wasn't here. Neither was most of the other stuff. How can he—"

"He *did*," Tony pointed out. "How much convincing do you need?"

"It's carefully worded," Gracey said. "Most of it isn't lies at all, just evasions and implications."

"We've got to assume he's smart enough to write a libel-proof story." Mimi had recovered her briskness. "There's one place I think he slipped, though. Can I see those sheets of Graham's again, Joe?"

HER eyes were shining when she looked up again. "We've got him," she said. "I'm sure of it. Let's call in O'Donnell and get his opinion on it. This stuff about Polly." She read aloud: "'...the young mother of a newborn baby, unable to feed her infant because of her hopeless addiction to marcaine. This reporter was present at a midnight emergency when the Colony's doctor was called to save the child from the ministrations of its hysterical mother...' Tony, you can testify to that."

"I don't know," said the doctor, painfully. "Sure, I realize Polly's not an addict, but—that's what I was starting to tell you when Harve came in. That's what Jim got me up for last night. Polly was sick, and there's no doubt that it was a dose of marcaine that was responsible."

"*What?*"

"*Polly?*"

"But she couldn't be the one. She was—"

"How did Graham find out about it?"

Tony waited till the questions stopped, then gave them the whole story, from the time Jim Kandro roared into his house at one o'clock, in the morning, right through the removal of the mask.

"We were both asleep when Kandro came in," he explained, "and the noise woke Graham, too. I didn't see him again myself, but I heard him typing when I was in the hospital with the baby. And Ans—Anna told me she talked to him while she was making the bottles. She had no reason to hold back any information. I told her myself that he was writing a friendly story."

"Well, that fixes us, but good. Where did Polly get the stuff?" Nick demanded. "We've hunted every inch of this place looking for marcaine; how come it didn't show up?"

"I've been trying to figure that myself," Tony said. "I don't think *she* got it. Her reactions were not those of a marcaine user, and I'd swear she was as shocked as she said she was when I diagnosed it. The stuff was put there—and don't ask me who, or why, because I can't even begin to guess."

"Well, we've got our hands full," Mimi said thoughtfully. "Where do we start? It seems to me the same answer is going to settle two of our problems. Where did Polly's marcaine come from, and how are we ever going to get out of this impossible situation with Bell?"

"That's not all," Nick added grimly. "We can solve both of those, and still get booted off Mars when this story breaks."

"That's a separate matter. All I can do about that is try and talk to Graham—or prove to him that at least part of the story is libelous…"

"Come in," Mimi called, in answer to a knock outside.

Gladys Porosky pushed the door open and announced breathlessly: "We can't find him. We looked all over and he's not any place."

"Graham?" Tony jumped to his feet. "He was asleep in my bedroom; I left him there. He has to be around."

GLADYS shook her head. "We opened the door when he didn't answer, and he wasn't there. Then we scattered; all the kids have been looking. He's not at the Lab, or in the fields, and he's not in any of the houses. Nobody's seen him all morning."

"Thanks, Gladys," Mimi cut her short. "Will you try to find Jack O'Donnell for me? Ask him to come over here."

"Okay." She slammed out of the door, leaving a whirlwind of babble and excitement behind her.

"I suppose he's skipped," Tony said. "Probably messaged one of the industrial outfits in that damn code of his, and got picked up during the night. His bags are still at my place, though—I saw them this morning. That's funny."

"Very funny," Nick echoed glumly. "Ha, ha."

"What's luggage to a guy who can write like that?" Gracey asked. "He can get all the luggage he wants just by wiping out another plague spot like us."

O'Donnell came in, and they waited in tense silence while the ex-lawyer read through Harve's penciled translation. "Only possible libelous matter I see is about the marcaine-addict mother. What's all that?"

They told him, and he shook his head. "No more chance in a court of law than a snowball in hell," he said flatly.

"But I don't care *how* he worded it. The story's not true."

"How many stories are? If truth or justice made any difference in the Earth courts, I wouldn't be here. I loved the law. The way it looked in the books, that is. I guess I'll have to pass my bar examinations all over again. Mars is under the Pan State, but I suppose this constitutes interrupted residence anyway."

"Big fat chance you'll have of getting to take your bar exams after that smear," said Gracey. "I'm not kidding myself about getting to teach college again. If I can get some money together, I'm going to try commercial seaweeds."

"God help Sargasso Limited," said Nick Cantrella. "And God help Consolidated Electronic when I start my shop again in Denver. It took them three months to run me into bankruptcy last trip around, but I'll get them up four this time. They can't stand much of that kind of punishment."

"Let's not jump to conclusions," Mimi said, with the quiver back in her determinedly businesslike voice. "Let's assume Graham skipped and the story's going through. We might still be able to hang on if we can square ourselves with Bell."

"Bell and Graham have no use for each other," Tony said. "Maybe this will make Bell easier to deal with."

"That I doubt. Let's figure on the worse. Suppose we *can't* convince Bell. We'll have two possible courses of action. We can sell out fast. From what I understand of this situation, I'm sure that the Commissioner would find a legal loophole for us on the marcaine deal if we decided to sell to, for instance, Brenner. If we do that we can payoff what money we owe on Earth, book passage for our members, and, with luck, have few a dollars left over to divide between us." She smiled humorlessly. "You might even have a capital investment of five or ten dollars Nick, to start working on Con-Electron."

"Good enough," he said. "It'll give me courage—if I can still find a bar with a five-buck beer, that is."

"That," Mimi went on, "would be the smart thing to do. But there's another way. We can hang on through the cordon, hoping to prove our point. It leaves us some hope, but it leaves us penniless, even if we manage to stick out the six months. Whatever cash credit we have on hand we'll have to pay out for OxEn. Don't think Bell is going to let us have the stuff free. Meanwhile, our accounts payable keep coming due, and accumulating interest. There's a good chance that long before the six months are up we'll be forced into involuntary bankruptcy. That's how Pittco got Economy Metals last year."

"Like the cat got the canary," said Nick.

"Yes. We'd then be shipped back to Earth as distress cases, with a prior lien on our future earnings. If any."

MIMI sat down and Tony studied her handsome face as if he were seeing it for the first time. She'd been way up in the auditing department of a vast insurance company once. It would be hard on her. It would be hard on them all. But he wanted to yell and beat down doors when he thought of what it would mean to Anna, plunged back into the screaming hell of Earth's emotional "noise" that she couldn't block out.

He tried to think like a schemer, and, knowing that it wouldn't work, told himself: *You marry Anna, take Brenner's offer—it's still open; good doctors aren't that easy to come by on Mars—and you set her up in a decent home.* But the whole thing crumbled under its own weight. She wouldn't marry a doctor whose doctoring was to patch up marcaine factory hands when they sniffed too much of the stuff.

"Eh?" he asked. Somebody was talking to him.

"Sell now, or hang on?" Mimi patiently repeated.

"I want to think about it," he told her.

The others felt the same way. It wasn't a thing you could make up your mind about in a few minutes, not after the years and years of always thinking one way: Colony survival. To have to decide now which way to kill the Colony...

The meeting broke up inconclusively. There was some recrating still to be done. The Lab had to be back to production, get this rocket's shipments ready just in case. And maybe by the time those chores were done, one of them would have some notion of how to start all over again, looking for the mysterious marcaine.

Tony headed out to the Lab, racking his brains for an answer. But halfway there, he found to his chagrin that he wasn't serious at all. He was striding along freely in the clean air and light gravity, to the rhythmic mental chant: Ansie—Anna—Ann—Ansie—

## CHAPTER TWENTY

JOAN RADCLIFF lay almost peacefully, drugging herself against the pain in her limbs and head by a familiar reverie of which she never tired. She saw Sun Lake Colony at some vague time in the future, a City of God, glowing against the transfigured Martian desert, spiring into the Martian air, with angelic beings vaguely recognizable in some way as the original colonists.

Her Hank, the bold explorer, with a bare-chested, archaic, sword-girt look; Doctor Tony, calm and wise and very old, soothing ills with miraculous lotions and calming troubled minds with dignified counsel; Mimi Jonathan, revered and able, disposing of this and that with sharp, just terseness; Anna Willendorf mothering hundreds serenely; brave Jim and Polly Kandro and their wonderful child, the hope of them all.

She wasn't there herself, but it was all right because she had done something wonderful for them. They all paused and lowered their voices when they thought of her. She, the sick and despised, had in the end surprised and awed them all by doing something wonderful for them, and they paid her memory homage.

Nagging reality, never entirely silent, jeered at her that she was a useless husk draining the Colony's priceless food and water, giving nothing in return. She shifted on the bed.

Pains shot through her joints and her heart labored. *You're as good as they are*, whispered the tempter; *you're better than they are. How many of them could stand the pain and not murmur, never think of anything but the good of the Colony? But I'm not*, she raged back. *I'm not. I shouldn't have got sick. I can't work now, they have to nurse me. But you didn't drink any water until Tony made you*, said the tempter. *Wasn't that more than any of them would do? Won't they be sorry when you're dead and they find out how you suffered?*

She tried to fix her tormented mind on her Hank, but he had a sullen, accusing stare. She was tying him down; if they sent her back to Earth, he'd have to go too. They wouldn't let him stay in the Colony.

SHE wished Anna hadn't left, and swallowed the thought painfully. Anna's time belonged to the Colony and not to her. It was nasty of her to want Anna to stay with her so much. She straightened one puffy leg and felt a lance of pain shoot from toes to groin; she bared her clenched teeth but didn't let a whimper escape her.

*That was very good*, said the tempter. *None of them could do that.*

Anna had propped her up in bed before; so she could look out the window. Now she turned her head slowly and looked out.

*I see through the window*, she told herself. *I see across the Colony street to a corner of the Kandros' hut with a little of their streetside window showing. I see Polly Kandro cleaning the inside of the window, but she doesn't see me. Now she's coming out and cleaning the outside of the window. Now she turns and sees me and waves and I smile. Now she takes her cloth and goes around her hut to clean the back window and I can't see her any more.*

*And now something glides down the Colony street with Sunny Kandro in its thin brown arms.*

*And now Polly runs around her hut again, her face white as chalk, tries faintly to call me, wave to me, and falls down out of sight.*

Joan knew what she ought to do, and she tried. The intercom button had been put in so she had only to move her hand a few inches. She reached out for the button, and held her finger on it, but there was no answering click. It was a few seconds and maybe minutes, and the thing that had stolen Polly's baby was gone down the other end of the street.

The sick girl sat up agonizingly and thought: *I can do something now. They won't be able to say I was foolish, because if I wait any longer I won't be able to catch up; it will be too far away. There's nobody else to do it except Polly, and she fainted. It has to be done right away. I can't wait for them to answer and then come from the Lab.*

Joan stood up, stumped over to the canteen on the wall and tilted it for a long, long drink of cool water. It tasted good. She lurched out of the hut and stood for a moment, looking at the crumpled body of Polly.

*Poor Polly*, she thought as her heart thudded and faltered. *We must help one another.*

She shaded her eyes against the late morning sun and looked up and past the Colony street through the clear Mars air. There was a moving dot passing the airfield now, and she started after it, one step, two steps, three steps, as the City of God reformed in her mind and her eyes never left the moving dot.

EARTH would be gone, a dead thing swimming in the deeps of space, a grave example for children. See? You must not hate, you must not fear, you must always help or that will happen to us. You must be kind and like people; you mustn't make weapons because you never know where making weapons will end.

And the children would ask curiously what it was like, and their elders would tell them it was crowded and dirty, that nobody ever had enough to eat, that people poured poison into the air and pretended it didn't matter. That it wasn't like Sun Lake, their spacious, clean, sweet-smelling home, that there wouldn't have been any Sun Lake if not for the great pioneers like Joan Radcliff who suffered and died for them.

She wept convulsively at the pain in her limbs as she stumped across the desert rocks. They sliced her bare feet; but she dared not look down ahead of her for fear of losing that swimming, moving dot she followed. *Magic*, she thought. *Fix a fairy with your eye and away it cannot fly.* Her heart—she could feel it thudding ponderously as a massive new pain burned through her left shoulder and arm.

*I have done what I could*, she thought. *Hank, you are free.* She fell forward and dragged her sprawled right arm along the ground so that it pointed to the moving dot and the Rimrock Hills beyond it.

\*   \*   \*

SOMEBODY grabbed him by the arm and motioned to his helmet. Tony stared a moment, uncomprehending, then switched on the helmet radio.

"What's up?"

"Joan—Joan Radcliff!" It was one of Mimi's young assistants in the Lab office. "She picked up the intercom and buzzed it. When I answered it, it went dead."

"I'll be right out." The doctor made it on the double, in spite of the hampering suit, out of the shipping room and into the shower. He would have given a year of his own life to be able to speed up the decontamination process this one time, but he'd been near the open crates. It wouldn't help Joan if he exposed himself, and her, too, to radiation disease.

He ran the distance from the Lab to the street of houses. He was still running when he approached the Kandros' hut, and almost missed seeing Polly's limp figure in the road. Thoroughly bewildered, he picked her up and looked around for help. There was no one in sight.

A moment's indecision, and then, quickly, he carried Polly toward the Radcliff hut and deposited her gently on the wall bunk in the living room. Pulse and respiration okay; she would keep. He headed for Joan's bedroom.

The doctor wasted a scant second staring at the empty bed; to him it seemed an endless time that had gone by. He pressed the intercom button, and waited through another eternity till the Lab answered.

Whatever had happened, whatever mysterious force had removed Joan from her bed and left Polly unconscious in the street, this, he realized, must have been the ultimate agony for Joan—to lie in this bed, in dreadful haste, to press this button and wait and wait until it was too late...

"That you, Doc? What's up?"

"Trouble. Get Jim Kandro out here. To the Radcliffs. And get Anna. Send her to Kandros'. There's no one with the baby. Is Mimi there? Put her on."

"Tony?" The Lab Administrator's crisp voice was reassuring; he could leave part of the problem, at least, in her competent hands.

"There's trouble here, Mim—don't know what, but Polly's fainted and Joan's disappeared."

"I'll be right there." She hung up. Tony retreated one step toward the living room, had an afterthought, and went back to the intercom.

"Get Cantrella here, too," he told the Lab office. "Tell him to bring along the e.e.g. setup. Fast."

Polly didn't look too bad. Marcaine again? He'd know soon.

*What was going on?*

Jim Kandro burst in, panting and terrified. His wide eyes went from his wife to the doctor, and a single miserable word came from him.

*"Again?"*

"I don't know. She fainted. Take her home, then look at Sunny. Anna's on her way over to help you."

Jim left with his burden in his arms, and Tony returned to the sick girl's bedroom. There was no trace, no clue, nothing he could find. He saw the wall canteen, upended, and went toward it with excitement. A puddle of water on the floor. Incredible carelessness for Sun Lake, but it meant something. Joan hadn't been carried away; she had gone herself. She had stopped for water and left the canteen this way.

A heartbroken shout from across the street sent him running out of the house, over to the Kandros'.

The living room was empty.

In the bedroom, Polly lay alone, still unconscious. He found Kandro in the new nursery, squatting on the floor beside the baby's empty crib, rocking in misery.

## CHAPTER TWENTY-ONE

"THEY ought to get the test finished in a few minutes, but if you're ready, you might as well start now. It's a hundred to one chance against its being anything but cave dirt." Joe Gracey crumbled between skinny, sensitive fingers a bit of soil taken from the nursery floor.

"As soon as we get the transceiver," Mimi said. "Harve's bringing it over now."

Anna appeared in the doorway. "She's conscious now."

Tony went back into the bedroom. "Polly?"

Her eyelids, fluttered open and closed. Her pulse was stronger, but she wasn't really ready to talk. He had to try. Without a stimulant, if possible.

"What happened, Polly?" he asked.

"What's the use?" she said feebly. "What's the use? We tried and tried on Earth, and I just got sick, and we had Sunny here, and now they've taken him. It isn't any good."

"Who's taken him, Polly?"

"I went out to clean the windows. I cleaned the front window and then I went around to clean the back window. When I looked in Sunny was gone. That's all. They took him. They just took him."

"*Who* took him, Polly?"

"I don't know. Brownies. We tried and tried on Earth—"

THE doctor took Anna to one side. "She's too lucid," he whispered. "Do you 'hear' anything?"

"Hardly anything." Anna shook her head. "She's numb. She's more conscious than she looks. Just numb. Doesn't care."

"Shock," Tony muttered. "'There will be a reaction. She shouldn't be left alone."

"I'll stay," Anna offered.

"No, not you. We'll need you along with us."

"I'd rather not," she said.

"Ansie," he pleaded, biting back his angry disappointment.

"I shouldn't have told you," she said dully. "I should never have told anybody. All right, I'll go."

He smiled and gripped her arm. "Of course you will. You would have anyway."

"No," she said. "I wouldn't."

"Then maybe it's a good thing you told me." His voice was stern, but his hand pulled her closer to him.

Polly twisted on the bed and sobbed. Anna pulled away. "Maybe." She bit her lip, looked up at him. "Only *please* don't be angry at me. I can't stand it if you keep getting angry at me." She turned and fled.

Tony went back to the bed, erasing Anna and her problems from his mind with practiced determination. Polly was trembling uncontrollably. There was no more information to be had from her. He gave her a sedative and went out to join the others.

Harve had arrived with the transceiver in his hand. On Anna's suggestion, a rush call was sent out for Hank Radcliff to stay with Polly. He didn't know about Joan; they decided not to tell him about it.

"We need a man here with her," the doctor explained briefly. "The baby's disappeared, and we're going out now and try to track it. Polly might want to get up and follow. *You keep her in bed.*"

"Sure, Doc."

"Nick Cantrella will be over with some equipment. Tell him to test Polly."

THEY left the house, Mimi and Anna and the doctor, Jim Kandro, Harve Stillman, and Joe Gracey.

"Look at that." Gracey was bending over in the road, pointing to the barely discernible mark of a bare toe. Here in the bottom of the old "canal" bed, where the settlement was built, the land retained a trace of moisture, enough to hold an impression for a while.

Only part of a toe, but it pointed a direction.

They headed up the street, past the huts toward the landing field.

"Hey, Joe!" Someone was pounding up the hill after them, shouting.

It was one of the men from the Agro Lab.

"That test—it's from the hills, all right, most likely from inside a cave, but hill dirt. That all you wanted?"

"Right. Thanks."

"They told me you wanted the word fast," the man said curiously. "Glad I caught you."

"Glad you did," Gracey agreed mildly. "Thanks again." He turned his back on the man. "Let's go."

They topped the slight rise that marked the farthest extent of the old river bed's former inundations, and faced a featureless expanse of level desert land, broken only by *Lazy Girl*, chocked on the landing field at their left, and the hills in the distance. No other human being was in sight. It was hopeless to look for footprints here, in the constantly shifting dust.

"The hills?" Mimi said.

Tony looked at Anna; she shrugged almost imperceptibly.

"Might as well," he agreed.

They moved forward, Kandro striding ahead with his great hands knotted into bony fists, his eyes set on the hills, unaware of the ground under his feet or of the people with him. It was Harve who found the print they had known was impossible—not really a footprint, but a spot of moisture, fast evaporating, still retaining a semblance of the shape of a human foot.

A little farther on there was another; they were going the right way. Tony stopped for a minute at one of the damp spots, poked a finger curiously into the ground. Grit and salt, as he had expected.

She couldn't have lived through it. He didn't know how she got as far as she did, but even if her heart held out, she must have sweated her life away to have left those damp indicators in the thirsty soil.

Only a little farther and the ground began to be littered with the refuse of the Rimrock Hills—here and there a sliver of stone, a drift of mineral salts. Gradually, the dust gave way to sharp rock and hard-packed saltpans. And the footprints of sweat gave way to footprints of blood.

Mimi drew in her breath between her teeth at the thought of the sick girl stumbling barefoot over the slicing, razor-edged stones.

"I see her," Kandro whispered, still striding ahead.

They raced a kilometer over the jagged rock and planed-off salt crust to the girl's body. She lay prone, with her right arm flung up and pointing to the Rimrock Hills.

Tony peeled back her eyelid and reached for the pulse. He turned to his bag, and Anna—blessed Anna—was already getting out the hypodermic syringe.

"Adrenaline?"

He nodded. Swiftly and efficiently, she prepared the hypo and handed it to him. He bent over the girl busily, then sat back to wait.

He glanced at Anna and straightened up quickly. "What is it?"

Her face was withdrawn and intense, her head held back like an animal scenting the wind. She scanned the broken waste, and pointed a hesitant finger. "Out there—*it's that way*—moving a little."

Kandro was on his way before she stopped speaking.

Stillman shaded his eyes and peered. "A rock in the heat haze," he pronounced finally. "Nothing alive."

Tony saw Anna shake her head in a small involuntary disagreement.

THEY stood and waited in a tense small circle until Jim reached the spot. He looked down and they saw him hesitate, then move on with the same determined stride. Gracey lit out after him. Mimi murmured approval. There was no telling what Kandro might do in his present mood.

A barely audible noise from the ground, and Tony was on his knees beside Joan. Her eyes went wide open, shining with an inner glory that was unholy in the dirt-streaked, bloodstained dead white of her face. She smiled as a child might smile, with perfect inner composure; she was pleased with herself.

"Joan," the doctor said, "can you talk?"

"Yes, of course." But she couldn't. She only mouthed the words.

"Does it hurt any place?"

She shook her head, or started to, but when she had turned it to one side she lacked the strength to bring it back. "No." This time she forced a little air through to sound the word.

She was dying and he knew it. If it were only the heart, he might have been able to save her. But her body had been punished too much; it had given up. The water and the air that kept it alive were spent. Her body was a dead husk in which, for a moment, abetted by the little quantity of adrenaline, her heart and brain refused to die.

He had to decide. They needed what information she might have. She needed every bit of energy she had, to live out what minutes were left. The minutes didn't matter, he told himself.

He knew, even as he made up his mind, that this, like the ghost baby, would haunt him all his life. If he were wrong, if she had any chance to live, he was committing murder. But another life hung in the balance too.

"Listen to me, Joan." He put his mouth close to her face. "Just say yes or no. Did you see somebody take the Kandros' baby?"

"Yes." She smiled up at him beatifically.

"Do you know who it was?"

"Yes—no—I saw—"

"*Don't* try to talk. You saw the kidnapper clearly?"

"Yes."

"Then it was someone you don't know?"

"No—yes—"

"I'll ask it differently. Was it a stranger?"

"Yes." She looked doubtful.

"Anyone from the Colony?"

"No."

"A man?"

"No—maybe."

"A woman?"

"No."

"Someone from Pittco?"

She didn't answer. Her eyes were staring at her arm. The doctor had rolled her over, and the arm was at her side, stretched out. She let out a weird cry of fury and frustration. Tony watched and listened, puzzled, till Anna bent over.

"It's all right, Joan," she said softly. "You showed us. We saw the way it pointed. Jim is going that way now."

The girl's eyes relaxed, and once again the dreadful light of joy shone from them.

"Love me," she said distinctly. "I helped finally. Tony—"

He bent over. She was trailing off again, less breath with each word. She might have minutes left, or seconds.

"Nobody—believed—me or—them—it was—"

She stopped, gasping, and the quiet smile of content gave way to a twisted grin of amusement. "Brownie," she said, and said no more.

\*     \*     \*

TONY closed her eyes and looked up to Anna's serene face. He saw that they were alone with the body of the dead girl.

"Where—?"  He got to his feet, carefully dulling sensation, refusing to feel anything.

"Over there."  She pointed to where two figures stooped over something on the ground.  Farther off, Kandro's tall figure, still resolutely facing toward the hills, was being restrained by a smaller man—Joe Gracey?  That meant it was Mimi and Harve close by.

"They found something?"

"Somebody," she corrected, and couldn't control a small shudder.

Tony started forward.  "You better stay with Joan," he said with difficulty, hating to admit any weakness in her.  "I'll call you if—if we need you for anything."

"Thank you."  She was more honest about it than he could be.

They saw him coming twenty meters off.

"It's Graham," Mimi called.

"The lying bastard steals babies too," Harve spat out in disgust.

"He looks bad," Mimi said quietly.  "We didn't touch him.  We were waiting for you."

"Good."  The doctor bent down and felt along the torso for broken bones.  Carefully, he rolled the writer over.

Graham's puffed eyes opened.  Through broken lips with dried blood crusted on them he rasped jeeringly: "Come back to finish the job?  God damned cowards.  Sneak up on a man.  Damned cowards."

"None of our people did this to you," Tony said steadily.  His hands ran over the writer's battered head and neck.  The left clavicle was fractured, his nose was broken, his left eardrum had been ruptured by blows.

"Let's get him back to the hospital," he said. "Harve, tell the radio shack to raise Marsport.  Get Bell.  Tell him we need that Bloodhound.  Tell him I will not take no for an answer."

## CHAPTER TWENTY-TWO

IN AWKWARD silence the little procession walked along the Colony street, Kandro and Stillman together, carrying the writer, and Tony bearing the dead girl in his arms.  The news had gotten around. Lab work seemed once again to have stopped completely.

They escaped the heartsick stares of the colonists only when they entered Tony's hut-and-hospital.  He deposited Joan there, on his own bed.  It was still rumpled from Graham's brief occupancy the night before.  They settled the writer on the hospital table.  With Anna's help, he removed the torn and bloody clothing from Graham's body.

"If you don't need us for anything, Tony, I think we better get going," Mimi said.  "We ought to stop in and see Polly."

"Sure.  Go ahead—oh, wait a minute."  Jim Kandro turned from his fixed spot in the doorway to listen.

Tony beckoned to the black-haired Lab administrator to the other side of the room.

"Mimi," he said in an undertone, "you ought to know that Polly has a gun.  I'm not sure whether Jim knows it or not.  You might want it if you're going out again.  Anyhow, somebody ought to get it out of there."

She nodded.  "Where is it?"

"Used to be in the baby's crib, but I think I talked her out of that. Don't know now."

"Okay, I'll find it.  I think we better take it along.  Oh—I'll send Hank back here."

He was thoughtful.  "Anna."  She looked up.  Her face was set and miserable.  "Are you going out with the search party?" he asked, an innocent question to the others who listened, with a world of agonizing significance for Anna.

"I—isn't Nick picking the people to go?"

"I thought you might *want* to go.  If you're sticking around, you can handle Hank, can't you?"

"Oh, yes," she said eagerly.  "I'd be much more useful that way, wouldn't I?"

He shrugged and tried to figure it out: She was perfectly willing to stay here in the hospital, to expose herself to Graham's physical pain and Hank's inevitable agony. But she was afraid to go out after the baby. Why?

Later, he decided, he could talk to her. He went briskly back to the table and began his examination of Graham. The writer was a mass of bruises from his chest up; he cursed feebly when the doctor felt for fractures. Tony set the collarbone and shot him full of sedation. "Your left eardrum is ruptured," he said coldly. "An operation can correct that on Earth."

"You bust 'em, somebody else fixes 'em," Graham muttered.

"Think what you want." He pushed the wheeled table over to the high bed Polly had occupied just a few days earlier.

Graham groaned involuntarily as Tony shifted his shoulder. The doctor eased up. *What for?* he stormed at himself. *Why should I be gentle with the dirty sneak?* He glanced hastily at Anna and caught the half-smile on her face as she pulled the covers over the writer.

"I'm going in the other room, Graham," Tony said. "You can call me if you need me."

"Sure," Graham told him. "I'll call you soon as I feel ready for another beating. I love it."

TONY didn't answer. In the other room, he sat down and faced Anna intently. "Do you know whether any of our people could have done that to him?"

"They aren't haters," she said slowly. "If they were, they wouldn't be here. Someone might fly into a rage, and break his jaw, but methodical *punishment* like that—no."

"I'll tell you what it reminds me of. Big Ginny."

"She was killed."

"She was beaten up, though that wasn't what killed her."

"Does it have anything to do with Pittco?" Anna asked. "Why should they beat Graham? Why should they have beaten that woman?"

"I don't know." He managed a feeble grin. "You know that." He lowered his voice. "Can you 'hear' him?"

"He's in a lot of pain. Shock's worn off. And he hates us. God, he hates us. I'm glad he hasn't got a gun."

"He's got a by-line. That's just as good."

"Evidently that just occurred to him. Can he hear us in there? He's gloating now. It must be a fantasy about what he's going to do to us."

"Hell, we're through anyway. What difference does it make? All I want now is to find Sunny and get off this damned planet and give up trying. I'm sick of it."

"You're not even kidding yourself," she said gently. "How do you think you can fool me?"

"All *right*," he said. "So you think my heart is breaking because Sun Lake's washed up. What good is it going to do me? Anna, will I be seeing you back on Earth? I want us to stay teamed up. When I go into practice—"

The woman winced and stood up. She closed the door to the hospital. "He was listening," she said. "He let out a blast of derision that rattled my skull when he heard you talk about going into practice on Earth."

Tony pulled her down beside him, and held her quietly against his chest. "Ansie," he said once, softly, "my poor sweet Ansie." He kissed her hair, and they sat very still until Hank knocked on the door.

\* \* \*

HANK stared at his wife's body, refusing to believe what he saw.

"She didn't feel much," Tony tried to explain. "Just a bad moment, maybe, when her heart gave out. She couldn't have felt anything or she'd never have gotten so far."

"We were there at the end," Anna reminded the young man. "She was—she was very happy. She wanted to be useful more than anything else in the world. You know that, don't you? And in the end she was. She loved you very much, too. She didn't want you to be unhappy."

"What did she say?" Hank wouldn't tear his eyes from the bed. He stood and stared ceaselessly, as if another moment of looking would show him some fallacy, some error.

"Did she really say that, about loving me?"

"She said—" Anna hesitated, then went on firmly. "She said, 'Tell Hank I want him to be happy all the time.' I heard her," she answered Tony's look of surprise. It wasn't much of a lie.

"Thank you. I—" He sat on the bed beside his wife, his hand caressing the face stained with blood and dust.

Tony turned and left the room. In the hospital, Graham was asleep or unconscious again. Tony went back to his own chair in the living room.

There were so many hints, so many leads, so many parts of the picture. Somehow it all went together. He tried to concentrate, but his thoughts kept wandering into the hospital where the writer lay, beaten as Big Ginny had been beaten; into the bedroom, where Joan lay dead of—of Mars; where Anna was comforting the young man who would never realize, if he was lucky that he had killed Joan himself as surely as if he had throttled her.

The last thing she said before she died... Tony snorted. The last thing she said, with that glorious light in her eyes, and a grin of delight on her face was *"Brownie."*

And there it was.

Within a few seconds' time everything raced through his mind, all the clues, the things that fitted together—Big Ginny, and Graham's story, Sunny and the mask and Joan's dying words. Everything.

He jumped up in furious excitement.

No, not everything, he realized. Not the marcaine. That didn't fit.

He paced the length of the room, and turned to find Anna standing in the bedroom door.

"Did you call?" she asked. "What happened?"

He smiled. He went over and pushed the door closed behind her. "Ansie," he said, "you just don't know how lucky you are to have a big, strong, intelligent man like me. When are we going to get married?"

She shook her head.

*"Not* until you tell me what it's all about."

## CHAPTER TWENTY- THREE

REFUSE ENTERTAIN REQUEST THIS DATE. POLICE POWERS THIS OFFICE EXTEND ONLY TO INTERCOLONY MATTERS. PAC DOES NOT REPEAT NOT AUTHORIZE USE OF POLICE EQUIPMENT FOR INTRACOLONY AFFAIRS. HAMILTON BELL PLANETARY AFFAIRS COMMISSIONER

TONY read through the formal message sheet, then the note attached to it:

"That's the master's voice up there. The PAC radio up in Marsport told me, on the side, that the old man doesn't believe a word of your story. If the baby really is missing, he figures 'that Markie Mama did it in.' Graham really fixed us. I hope you're taking good care of him. If you get him back in shape, I won't feel so bad about taking a crack at him myself. Harve."

The doctor smiled briefly, then asked Tad Campbell, who was waiting to take his answer back to the radio shack: "Did Mimi Jonathan see this?"

"No. It just came in. Harve wants to know what answer to send."

CANTRELLA and Gracey were out with the search party too, Tony realized. That left the decision squarely up to him.

He scribbled a note: "Harve, try this one on the commish. REQUEST USE PAC FACILITIES TO TRACK VICIOUS ATTACKER OF OUR GUEST, DOUGLAS GRAHAM. That ought to get us every tin soldier on the planet, and old man Bell himself heading the parade. Graham as victim gives him an out, too; he can call it intercolony. Get hot. We need that Bloodhound. Tony."

When the boy was gone, Tony paced nervously around the living room, started to heat water for "coffee," and decided he didn't want it.

There was an almost empty bottle of liquor on the floor near the table—Graham's. The doctor reached for it and drew back. It wasn't the right time or the right bottle.

He headed for the bedroom door, and remembered that Joan's body was still occupying the bed. He peered into the hospital; Graham was still sleeping. Nothing to do but sit and wait, and think it out all over again. It checked every time—but it couldn't be right.

He hadn't told Anna yet. When you came right down to it, the whole thing was too far-fetched; he wouldn't believe it himself, if somebody else had proposed it.

But it checked all the way every time.

He got up again and hunted through his meager stack of onionskin volumes and scientific journals. Nothing there, but Joe Gracey ought to know. When the search party came back...

Maybe they'd find the baby and the kidnaper; maybe he never

would tell—or have to tell—anybody his crackpot theory. He decided to make the "coffee" after all, and wished he hadn't sent Anna and Hank back to stay with Polly, but Gladys had been frantic and frightened when she buzzed him. He couldn't expect the child to handle a hysterical woman by herself.

The doctor poured his "coffee" and drank it slowly, not letting himself go to the intercom. Polly and Hank could help each other now; it worked that way. And Anna was better for them than he would be himself. Somebody had to stay with Graham. He got up and paced restlessly into the hospital room again. The writer stirred and moaned as the door opened, but that was all.

It was more than an hour since Tad had left. Why no reply from Harve?

Tony went to the front door, opened it and peered up the street, out over the housetops to the landing field. Nothing in sight. He turned to go back in, and out of the corner of his eye saw them rounding the curve of the street.

Gracey, Mimi, Juarez, and then Kandro taking each step reluctantly, his heart back in the hills, while Nick Cantrella and Sam Flexner, one on each side, urged him forward. Tony's heart sank; there was no mistaking defeat.

*   *   *

"I'M sure," Mimi said steadily, "we heard him cry. Just for a minute. Then it was as if someone had clapped a hand over his mouth. Tony, we can't wait. We've got to get him out right away."

"What about the other caves?"

"We tried them all around," Gracey said. "Five or six on each side and a couple up above. But every one of those fissures narrows down inside the hill the same way. We couldn't get through. I don't see how the kidnapers did, either."

"How about the other side?" Tony asked. "Someone could go around with a half-track and take a look."

"We thought of it," Mimi said sharply. "Nick got Pittco on the transceiver. *Mister* Hackenburg was so sorry. *Mister* Reynolds was away, and he didn't have the authority himself to permit us to search on their ground. He was *so* sorry."

SHE stood up abruptly, and turned to the wall, not quite quickly enough. Tony saw her brush at her eyes before she turned back and said throatily: "Well, little men, what now? Where do we go from here?"

"We wait," Joe Gracey said helplessly. "We wait for Bell to answer us. We wait for Reynolds to get back. What else can we do?"

"Nothing, I guess. We left half a dozen men out there," Mimi told the doctor. "They're watching, and they have the transceiver. I guess Joe's right. We wait."

Silence, and Tony tried to find a way to say what he had to say. They couldn't just wait, not while he knew something to try. The baby might be all right, but maybe they would get there just one minute too late.

He turned to Gracey.

"Joe, what do you know about lethal genes?"

"Huh?" The agronomist looked up, dazed, shook his head, and repeated without surprise at the irrelevant question, "Lethal genes?" He stopped and considered, mentally tabulating his information. "Well, they're recessives that—"

"No, I know what they are," Tony stopped him. "I thought I heard you say something about them the other day. Didn't you say you thought you'd hit on some that were visible on Mars?"

Anna drifted in, with Hank at her heels, and they went straight through, into the room beyond where Joan still lay.

"Oh, yes," Gracey said. "Very interesting stuff. Come out to the Lab when you have the time, and I'll show you. We—"

Mimi jumped up. "*What* are you gabbling about?" she demanded. "This is an emergency. We have to find some way to rescue that baby."

"I'm sorry, Mimi." Gracey was bewildered. "What's wrong anyway? Tony asked a perfectly innocent question, and I answered him when we'd all agreed that we had nothing to do but sit around and wait. Why not use the time?"

Abruptly, Tony made up his mind. It was up to him now. And to Anna. He got up and called her from the bedroom, led her outside, into the street in front of the house, where they were out of earshot of all the others.

"Well?" She smiled up at him. "Will you stop feeling sorry for me and tell me what you're sorry about?"

"In a minute. Anna, last night when we took the mask off Sunny—when you fainted—how did it feel?"

"I told you."

"Yes, you said it was very strong, stronger than you thought a baby could—feel. But was it just stronger or was there something *different?*"

"That's hard to say. I was—well, I was all worn out and upset. It might have been different, but I don't know how. I'm not even sure it was."

She looked up at him sharply. "Why?"

"It checks," he said to himself. "Listen, Ansie, there's a job to be done. A tough job. A job nobody can do but you. It may—hurt you. I don't know. I don't even know if it will work. It's a crazy theory I've got, so crazy I don't even want to explain it to you. But if I'm right, you're the only person who can do it." He stopped. "Anna, did you hear what Joan's last word really was? She said, 'Brownie.'"

He looked down into frightened dark eyes.

"Tony, there aren't any Brownies, are there?"

"You mean do I believe there are? No, I don't. But I do think there's *something.*"

"You want me to go out there and listen?"

"Yes. But that's only part of it. I wouldn't let you go alone; if you do go. I'll be with you—if that helps any. But I want to go into the cave where they heard the baby and see what we can find."

"*No.*" The cry was torn from her. "I didn't mean that," she caught herself. "It's just—oh, Tony, I'm *afraid.*"

"We've got to find out. Ansie, we've *got to find out.*"

"The Bloodhound?" she asked desperately. "Can't you track them with the Bloodhound?"

"Bell hasn't answered us. How long can we wait?"

She stood silent for a moment, then turned her face up to his, serenely quiet now and trusting.

"All right," she said at last. "All right, Tony, if you say it has to be done."

"I'll be there with you," he promised.

*   *   *

MIMI and Joe didn't understand, and Tony didn't try to explain. He simply repeated that he had an "idea;" he wanted to go out, with

Anna, to the cave where the baby's cry had been heard.

He left careful instructions about the care of Graham if he should awake, and about Hank, Polly, and Jim, all three of whom were too upset to be left to themselves.

A ten-minute ride on the half-track and they were within the shadow of the Rimrocks. The drifting stench of Pittco's refineries on the other side began to reach them; then the ground was too rocky to go on. Tony stopped the machine and they got out. Farther up the face of the nearest hill, they could make out the figures of the five who had remained on guard.

One of them came running—Flexner, the chemist. "They said on the transceiver you were coming," he told Anna and Tony. "What's your idea? We're going nuts sitting around waiting. Ted thought he heard Sunny cry again but nobody else did."

"I just wanted to see if I could turn up anything," Tony told him "We're going into the cave."

TOGETHER they walked out of the sunlight into the seven-foot opening in the hard rock. One of the guards would have preceded them, but Anna firmly refused. A chalk mark along the wall, drawn by the others when they left the cave, was guide enough.

They followed the white line in and down some fifty meters, then fifty more along a narrowing left-hand branch, and then a hundred meters, left again and narrowing, to another fork. Both the branches were too small for an adult to squeeze through. The chalk line pointed into the right-hand cranny.

That was as far as they could go. They stood at the narrow opening, listening.

There was nothing to hear, no sound at all in the rock-walled stillness except their own breathing and the tiny rustling of their hands along rough alien stone.

They waited, Tony's eyes fixed on Anna's face. He tried to silence his thoughts as he could his voice, but doubts tore at him. He turned, finally, to the one certainty he knew, and concentrated on Anna and her alone: on his love for her, her love for him.

"I hear something," she whispered at last. "Fear—mostly fear, but eagerness, too. They are not afraid of us. I think they like us. They're afraid of—it's not clear—of people?"

She fell silent again, listening.

"People." She nodded her head emphatically. "They want to talk to us, Tony, but—I don't know..." Her brow furrowed in concentration and she sat down suddenly on the hard rock floor, as though the physical exertion of standing were more than she could bear.

"Tony, go and tell the guards to go away," she said at last.

"No," he said firmly.

"Go ahead. Please. Hurry. They are trying—" Abruptly, she stopped concentrating on the distance. "You spoiled it," she said bitterly. "You frightened them."

"How?"

"You didn't trust them. You thought they'd hurt me."

"Ansie, how can we trust them? How can I leave you here alone and send the guards away? Don't you see I can't take that risk?"

"You made me come here," she said tiredly. "You said I was the one who could do the job. I'm trying to do it. Please go now and tell the guards to leave. Tell them to get out of range—down at the bottom of the hill, maybe as far away as the half-track. Please, Tony, do as I say."

"All right." But he was still hesitant. "Anna, who are they?"

"I—" The bitterness left her face. "Brownies," she said.

"But that's not—I'm sorry. I didn't mean to feel angry and frustrated. What does the word mean?"

"They're *different*."

"Like Sunny?"

"Not exactly." She made a small useless gesture with her hands. "More—distinct. No, maybe you're right. I think they're like him, only older."

"How many are there?"

"Quite a few. Too many for me to count. One of them is doing all the—talking."

"*Talking?*" Yes, that was part of what had bothered him. "Ansie, how can you understand so clearly? You told me you can't do that. You didn't know what Graham was angry about. How do you know what they're afraid of?"

"Tony, I don't know. I *can* understand, that's all and I'm sure it's right, and I know they're not tricking us. Now please, please go and tell the guards."

He went.

## CHAPTER TWENTY-FOUR

"KEEP him away from me," Graham screamed.

Mimi raced through Tony's living room into the hospital half of the hut.

It was Hank, standing rigidly still, glaring at the writer. "You don't understand about Mars," Hank was saying in a hard monotone. "You never saw the Rimrocks when there was just enough light to tell them from the sky, or walked a hundred miles in the desert watching the colors change every minute."

"Mrs. Johnson, get him out of here. He's crazy."

Mimi took Hank by the arm. "I'm not crazy," he said. "Those boomers at Pittco, this writer here, Bell and his soldiers, Brenner and his factory, they're crazy. They're trying to cheapen Mars."

Hysteria, thought Mimi. She'd coped with enough cases of it when she'd bossed girls at desks, as far as the eye could see, on the 76th floor of the American Insurance Groups Building.

"*Radcliff*," she said.

There was a savage whip-crack in her voice.

He turned to her, startled. "I wasn't going to hurt him," he said confusedly.

Get him to cry. Break him. Until then, there's no knowing what will happen. "Your poor wife's lying in there," she said with measured nastiness, "and you find time to brawl with a sick man."

"I didn't mean anything like that," he protested.

Still unbroken. "Get into the bedroom," she said. "Sit there. That's the least you can do."

He walked heavily into the room where his wife's body lay and she heard him drop into a plastic chair.

"Thanks, Mrs. Johnson," said Graham painfully. "He was spoiling for a fight."

"Mrs. Jonathan," she corrected. "And I don't want your thanks."

She turned and rattled through drawers of medications, hoping she'd find something she could give Hank. She didn't know what to use or how much. She slapped the drawer shut and was angry with Tony and Anna for not being there when she needed them.

She stalked into the bedroom and stared at Hank without showing any pity. He was looking dully at the wall, a spot over the bed on which Joan's broken body lay. No shakes, no tears, unbroken still. But she couldn't bring herself to lash him further and precipitate the emotional crisis.

She went back into Tony's living room and threw herself into a chair. She'd hear if anything happened. Mrs. J., the terror of auditing, Old Eagle eye, and a few less complimentary things when the girls were talking between the booths in one of the 76th-floor johns. Efficiency bonuses year after year, even bad years, and that meant you *were* an old witch. She must be out of practice, or getting soft, she decided harshly, if she couldn't handle an absurdly simple little thing like this.

*We ought to have Tony train somebody besides Anna*, she thought. *There's Harve, but he only knows radio-health.* And then she remembered that it didn't matter; Sun Lake wouldn't last that long.

SHE heard a plane coming in at the landing field and wondered whose. Hank stirred in the bedroom and she tensed, but then she heard the creak of his big body slumping back into the chair. He wouldn't break. He had too much of the old Marsman in him, the tough old breed. In the old days, if she'd been assigning a pair of girls to an audit program, she wouldn't have made a match like Hank and Joan—one starry-eyed and on fire for an ideal; the other solidly and physically in love with far places for their fairness and mystery. But it had worked here and they'd had their measure of happiness before they had to taste their measure of hell.

Hank should have come earlier. He should have been one of the first, eating out of cans, mapping and mining, bearded to his waist, inarticulate, but sure about what he wanted. Joan should have come later. She should have been an immigrant after the colony had licked Mars medicine, while there still was grinding work and sacrifice enough to please the most impassioned, but not so much that a frail body would crumple under it.

But there wasn't going to be any "later," of course. It was hard to get used to that realization.

She got up and had a drink of water from the wall canteen, and then, defiantly, another, because it didn't matter now. She felt like taking on the world for Sun Lake. Joan must have felt like that. Their water supply was scanty, but it was water—not the polluted fluid of Earth, chlorinated to the last potable degree.

THE intercom in the bedroom buzzed. She walked in and picked it up, glanced at Hank, still numbly staring.

"Hello, Mimi." It was Harve. "Answer from Bell. Quote: 'R.E. ASSAULT ON DOUGLAS GRAHAM I AND DETAIL OF GUARDS WILL TAKE ACTION THIS MATTER. REQUEST USE PAC FACILITIES DENIED. HAMILTON BELL' et cetera. What do you figure he'll do—try and pin the Graham slugging on us too?"

"I don't know," she said. "It doesn't matter. What plane was that?"

"Brenner's. Snooty bastard didn't even check in with us. Just sat right down on the field."

"He might as well. He'll own it soon enough."

She heard Harve clear his throat embarrassedly. "Well, I guess that's all."

"Goodby," she agreed, hanging up. She shouldn't have said that; she was supposed to pretend that while there was life there was hope.

"Hank?" she asked gently and inquiringly.

He looked up. "I'm all right, thanks."

He wasn't, but there was nothing she could do. She looked through the door to the hospital. Graham seemed to be dozing. She sat down in the living room again.

Brenner came in without knocking. "They told me you were here, Mrs. Jonathan. I wonder if we could go to your office in the Lab. I want to talk business."

"I'm staying here," she said shortly. "If you want to talk here, I'll listen."

Brenner shrugged and sat down. "Do we have privacy?"

"There's a boy in the next room going crazy with grief over his dead wife—and over the prospect of leaving Mars. And there's a badly beaten man sleeping in the hospital quarters."

The drug manufacturer lowered his voice. "Relative privacy," he said. "Mrs. Jonathan, you have the only business head in the Colony." He opened his briefcase on the table and edged the corner of a sheaf of bills from one of its pockets. The top one was a thousand dollars. He didn't look at it, but riffled the sheaf with his thumb, slowly, like a gambler manipulating a deck of cards. They were all thousands, and there were over one hundred of them.

"It's going to be very hard on some of the colonists, I'm afraid," he said conversationally.

"You have no idea."

"It needn't be that hard on all of them." His thumb flipped the big bills. "Your colony is facing an impossible situation, Mrs. Jonathan. Let's not mince words; it's a matter of bankruptcy and forced sale. I'm in a position to offer you a chance to retreat in good order, with some money in your pockets."

"That's very kind of you, Mr. Brenner. I'm not sure I understand."

"Please," he smiled, "let's not be coy. I'm being perfectly candid with you. If it comes to a forced sale, I intend to bid as high as necessary; I need this property. But I'm not a man who believes in leaving things to chance. Why shouldn't you sell out to me now? It would save yourselves the humiliation of bankruptcy, and I believe everyone concerned would benefit financially."

"You realize I'm not in a position to close any deals, Mr. Brenner?" she asked.

"Yes, of course. You have a council in charge here, don't you? And you're a member. You could plead my case with them."

"I suppose I could."

"All right." He smiled again, and his thumb continued to riffle the pile of bills. "Then I have to plead it first with you. Why should you stay on Mars? In the hope that 'something' will turn up? Believe me, it will not. Your commercial standing will be gone. Nobody would dream of extending credit to the people who were six months behind on their deliveries. *Nothing will turn up*, Mrs. Jonathan."

"What if the stolen marcaine turns up?"

"Then, of course—" He smiled and shrugged.

MIMI read a momentary alarm in his face. For the first time since the crisis she entertained the thought that it was not a frame-up.

She pressed harder. "What if we're just waiting to hand Bell the hundred kilos and the thief?"

Brenner turned inscrutable again. "Then something else will happen. And if the Colony survives that, something else again." He quickly denied the implication of sabotage by adding: "You have a fundamentally untenable financial situation here. Insufficient reserves, foggy motives—what businessman can trust you when he knows that your Lab production workers might walk out one fine day and stay out? They aren't bound by salaries but by idealism."

"It's kept us going."

"Until now. Come, Mrs. Jonathan, I said I wanted an advocate in the Council." He thumbed out the deck of bills all the way from the pocket in the opened briefcase. "You have a business head. You know that if you *do* produce my marcaine and the thief, Mr. Graham's little story—which I read with great interest—will be another bad hump to get over. There will be more."

He meant two things: more humps, and more sheafs of thousand dollar bills for her if she took the bribe.

Mimi smiled without moving a muscle of her face. It had been a long time since she had talked this kind of talk, but she still knew how. The smile stayed inside her head; her face displayed only the most casual interest.

"Are you offering to buy the Colony, Mr. Brenner? Would you care to name a price?"

"What are you asking?" he countered.

*Oh, no*, she thought, *you're not getting away with that.*

"All right, we'll play it your way," she said. "Name *two* prices. You want to buy my services, too, don't you?"

"Whatever gives you that notion? I'm not trying to bribe you, Mrs. Jonathan." He picked up the sheaf of bills and placed them in front of her. "There's a hundred thousand here. I can bring another—say another four hundred thousand—*for a down payment*, whenever you say. My price for the Colony," he added distinctly, "is exactly five million."

"Plus your down payment?" she asked, amused.

"That's right."

"That would just about pay all our fares back to Earth. We'll smash the Lab to bits before we let you get it for any such price."

"You'll rot in prison if you do," Brenner said easily. "There is an injunction on file at Marsport signed by Commissioner Bell restraining you from any such foolishness. An act of contempt would mean imprisonment for all of you. I mean *all.*"

"No such paper has been served on us."

"The Commissioner assured me it had been served. I don't doubt his word. Not many people, including appeals judges, would doubt his word either."

MIMI didn't dare answer this display of force. She set her teeth and thought about five million—and five hundred thousand. Passage home, the respectability of having sold instead of going bankrupt, maybe the chance of another charter and another try—

"It'll have to be put into form by the Council and voted on by the entire Colony," she said painfully. "You wanted an advance. Take your money back; I'm not for sale. But I *will* plead your case if you'll make it ten million. God knows, it's a bargain. There's absolutely no depreciation on the Lab to be figured. It's better now than it ever was. Maintenance has always been top-level. Better than anything you'll ever be able to find in industry."

"Five million and five hundred thousand was my offer. I'm not the Croesus uninformed people take me for. I have my expenses on the marcaine distribution end, you know."

\* \* \*

TONY sweated out the time.

Eight minutes creeping along the chalk line in the dark—he'd left the light with Anna. Five minutes scrabbling over the boulders at the cave opening on the face of the hill. Twelve long minutes talking the guards into leaving, and a painful tortured eternity—maybe another twelve minutes reentering the cave and tracing the chalk fine by the dim light borrowed from Ted.

Tony was sweating ice by the time the radiance from Anna's light came in view. He rounded the last curve in the winding passage, and something jumped up from the floor, straightened and stood, tense and watchful as the doctor.

Anna, seated on the cold floor, laughed softly, melodiously.

She was all right. Tony relaxed a little and instantly felt—something, a gentle stroking, a tentative touch, not on his head but in it. No menace, no danger. Friendship.

The doctor stared across the cavern: leathery brown skin, barrel chest, big ears, skinny arms and legs; the height of a small man or a large boy; and—a telepath.

The friendly touch on his mind persisted through his quick distaste, his exultation, his eagerness.

"Anna," very softly, "is it all right to talk?"

"Not too loud. His ears are sensitive."

"Who is he? Are there more? *Does he have Sunny*? Ask him that, Anna—ask him."

"A Brownie," she laughed again, joyously. "You told me that. There are four more down there, inside, with Sunny."

"Is he all right?"

"Yes. They took him to help him, not to do any harm. He needed something, but I can't find out what."

The Brownie squatted again on the floor beside Anna. Tony approached slowly and sat down next to them.

He felt goose flesh and memories of old nursery book horrors, but nothing happened. He forced himself to ask Anna: "What kind of thing?"

"Something to eat, I think. Something like the first sip of water when you're thirsty, and as necessary as salt, and—*good*. Maybe like a vitamin, but it tastes wonderful."

Tony ran through a mental catalogue of biochemicals. But that was foolish; how could you tell what would taste good to anything as alien as a Brownie?

"Have you tried sign language?" he asked Anna.

"Where do you start?" she shrugged. "You'd have to build up a whole set of symbols before you could get anything across. Tony, I'm sure we can get the baby back if we just understand what it is he needs."

THE doctor reached over, hesitated, and forced himself to tap the Brownie lightly on the shoulder. When he had the creature's attention, he whispered to Anna: "Tell him we're trying to find out what it is." He pointed to his own eyes. "Show us," he said to the creature, and tried to project the thought, the image of seeing, as hard as he could.

They kept repeating it with every possible combination of thought and act. Then, suddenly, the Brownie jumped and dashed off, down the tunnel.

"Did he get the idea?" demanded Tony. "Is he coming back?"

"It's all right," smiled Anna. "He understood."

Silence in the eerie place was almost unbearable.

"Don't worry so, Tony," Anna said. "If you want to know, he almost scared the wits out of me, too. I was sitting, trying to look down the little opening, and still—talking—to the ones down there, and he came up behind me. I was concentrating on them so I didn't hear him, either way."

Tony sat back thoughtfully. It was all true then; his crazy theory was right—there were actually Brownies on Mars, a form of life so highly developed that it was telepathic, and with no lower life forms to have evolved from. He wondered if he had hit the right explanation, too, but there *was* no other explanation.

The brownie was, back, carrying something, a box. Large letters in black on the side read:

DANGER

SEALED MARCAINE CONTAINER

*Do Not Open Without Authorization*

Brenner Pharmaceutical Co.

## CHAPTER TWENTY-FIVE

TONY helped Anna dismount from the half-track, with her valuable burden in her arms. She jounced Sunny happily, and cooed down at the pink face. The doctor didn't jounce his own burden; he lifted it down even more carefully than he had helped Anna. The marcaine box was tightly wrapped in his shirt and hers. They were counting on the several layers of cloth to trap escaping dust and protect them from marcaine jags, but the doctor still wasn't taking any chances on stirring up the contents of the half-full box.

They cut across the bare land in back of the row of houses, heading toward the curved street near the Kandros.'

"Tony," Anna asked anxiously again, "*how* are we possibly going to explain it?"

"I told you I don't know." He was only a little irritable. They had the baby; they had the marcaine. "We'll have to talk to Mimi and Joe and Nick, and probably the others too. We'll see how it goes."

"No, I don't *mean* that," she stopped him. "I mean to Polly. And Jim. Jim isn't going to like it unless he hears the whole story, and I don't know if we ought to…"

"Like it or not," Tony said briskly, "Kandro'll do what I tell him to. We'll have to tell them it's marcaine; I don't dare risk mislabeling the stuff. You'll have to blow some ampoules for it, I guess, and I'll figure out some way of wetting it down and getting it into them. But you're right," he added, "if you mean we shouldn't say any more than we have to just now."

They stepped onto the packed dirt of the street and cut across to the Kandros'.

Joe Gracey was sitting alone in the living room.

"Praise God," he said quietly, and called: "*Polly! Jim!*" The couple appeared, red-eyed, at the nursery door, saw their baby, and flew to him.

"You gave him to us again, Doc," said Jim. "Thanks."

Polly was more practical: "Has he eaten? Is he well? He looks all right, but—"

"You can feed him in a minute. Now listen carefully. This young man of yours, you know, is special in some ways. He can take the Mars air and like it. It turns out that there's something else he needs—something that's good for him and bad for other people, just like the Mars air. It's marcaine."

Polly's face went white. Jim began a guffaw of unbelief that turned into a frown. He asked carefully: "How can that be, Doc? What *is* this all about? And who took him? We have a right to know."

Anna came to Tony's rescue. "You're not going to know right now," she said tartly. "If you think that's hard on you, it's just too bad. You've got your baby back; now leave the doctor alone until he's ready to tell you more."

Jim opened his mouth and shut it again. Polly asked only: "Doctor, are you sure?"

"I'm sure. And it *won't* have anything like the effect on Sunny that it had on you. But it's real marcaine, all right, and he's got to have it or die."

"Like OxEn?" asked Kandro. "It's only fair in a way..."

TONY ignored him. "I guess you're going to have to wean the baby after all, Polly," he said. "You can't keep taking marcaine for Sunny's sake. But for now, I guess you might as well nurse him. Your milk still has marcaine in it."

Kandro was still adjusting himself to the idea. "Sunny doesn't need OxEn, so he's got to take something else?"

"Yes," Tony said, "like OxEn..." He broke off, and Anna spun toward him, her eyes wide. The doctor forced his face into calm lines. "I want to have a talk with Joe now. And Nick Cantrella, Anna, will you see if you can get Nick on the intercom? Ask him to come over here right away. I've got an idea."

In the living room, he told Gracey: "You won't have to keep an eye on them any more, Joe. But watch *me*—I feel like Alexander, Napoleon, Eisenhower, and the Great Cham all rolled into one."

"You're certainly grinning like a lunatic," the agronomist agreed critically. "What's on your mind?"

"Wait a minute…did you get him?" Tony asked as Anna came in to the room.

"He's coming," she nodded. "Tony, what *is* it?"

"I'll tell you both, soon," he promised. "Let's wait for Nick, so I won't have to repeat it." He paced restlessly around the room, thinking it through again. It ought to work; *it ought to*.

WHEN Cantrella arrived, he turned on the two men. "Listen, both of you." He tried not to sound too eager. "If I handed you a piece of living tissue with a percentage of oxygen enzyme—and I don't mean traces, I mean a *percentage*—where would we stand in respect to…" He halted up the cautious complicated phraseology. "Hell, what I mean is, could we manufacture OxEn?"

"The living virus?" Gracey asked. "Not crystallized OxEn processed for absorption?"

"The living virus."

"We'd be a damn sight better than halfway along the processing that the Kelsey people do in Louisville. They grow the first culture from the Rosen batch, then they cull out all the competing enzymes, then they grow what's left and cull, for hundreds of stages, to get a percentage of the living virus to grow a pure culture they can crop and start crystallizing."

"How about it, Nick?" Tony demanded. "Could the Lab swing a job of crystallizing a crop from that and processing it for absorption?"

"Sure," said Nick. "That's the easiest part. I've been reading up on it since we talked about it before."

"Look here," Gracey exploded, "where do you think you're going to get your living virus from? You have to keep getting it, you know. It always mutates under normal radiation sooner or later, and you have to start over again."

"That's my end of the deal. I have a hunch I can get it. Thanks, both of you." He went into the nursery and told Polly calmly: "I'm taking your youngster away again—just for a few minutes, though. I want to check his lungs in the hospital. Anna?" She was already taking the baby from Polly's arms. Tony picked up the wrapped marcaine-box and started out.

"Hey, Doc, what goes on?" Gracey demanded.

He brushed past Nick and the puzzled agronomist. "Tell you later," he called back.

On the street, Anna turned a worried face up to his. "Tony, what are you *doing?* You can't operate on a five-day-old baby...can you?" she finished, less certainly. "You seem so—so happy and *sure* of yourself."

"I am," he said shortly, and then relented enough to add: "The 'operation,' if you want to call it that, won't hurt him." But he wouldn't say any more.

MIMI and Brenner were in Tony's living room. The woman said hopelessly: "Hello, Tony. Mr. Brenner's made an offer—Oh! It's Sunny!"

"Hello, Mimi," said Tony.

"The youngster, eh?" Brenner said genially. "I've heard about him."

With a brusque "Excuse me" to the drug manufacturer, Tony said to Anna in an undertone: "Rig the op table, sterilites on. Get out the portable biopsy constant-temperature bath and set the thermostat to Sunny's blood temperature. And call me."

She nodded and went into the hospital with the baby. Tony dropped his bundle into his trunk and began to scrub up.

"What's been going on, Mimi?" he asked.

"Mr. Brenner's offered five million, five hundred thousand dollars for Sun Lake's assets. I said the Council would put it in formal shape and call a vote."

The descent from his peak of inspiration was sickening. Nothing had changed, then, Tony thought.

"Ready," Anna said at his side. He followed her silently into the hospital, slipped into his gloves and said: "Sterilize the Byers curette, third extension, and lubricate. Sterilize a small oral speculum." He spoke quietly. Graham was asleep in the bed across the room.

Anna didn't move. "Anesthesia?" she asked.

"None. We don't know their body-chemistry well enough."

"No, Tony. Please, no."

He felt only a chill determination that he was going to salvage some of the wreckage of Sun Lake, determination and more confidence than he knew he should feel. Anna turned, selected the instruments and slipped them into the sterilizer. The doctor stepped on the pedal that turned on the op lights.

Anna put the speculum into his hand and he clamped open Sunny's mouth. The prompt wail of protest turned to a strangled cry as the sinuous shaft of the Byers curette slid down the trachea into the left bronchus. One steady hand guided the instrument, while the other manipulated the controls from a bulb at its base.

"*Hold* him," Tony growled as Anna's hands weakened and the woman swayed. Bronchus, bronchia, bronchile, probing and withdrawing at resistances—and there it was. A pressure on the central control that uncovered the razor-sharp little spoon at the tip of the flexible shaft and covered it again, and then all flexure controls off and out. It had taken less than five seconds, and one more to deposit the shred of lung tissue in the biopsy constant-temperature nutrient bath.

Hank was at the door. Anna, leaning feebly against the table, straightened to tell him: "Go and lie down, Hank. It's all right."

"Keep him away from me," warned Graham from the bed. "He was going to jump me before."

"I just wanted to see the baby," Hank said apologetically.

Tony turned to the intercom, buzzing the Kandros'. "Come on over," he told them. "You can have your baby back for keeps now. Is Gracey still there? Joe? I think I've got that tissue specimen for you. How fast can you get a test?"

"For God's sake, Tony, where did you get it?" Gracey was demanding on the other end.

"From a Brownie." He couldn't resist it. "That's what I said. Lung tissue of a Brownie."

He hung up.

"A Brownie? It *is* true. There are Brownies, aren't there?"

Tony turned to find the Kandros' standing by the examination table. Polly already had her baby in her arms.

Jim patted her shoulder. "He doesn't really mean it, Polly. Do you, Doc?"

Graham was grinning openly. Tony turned from one to the other, not answering.

There was a commotion in the living room and Brenner burst in, carrying a familiar box. "He just dived for it, Tony," Mimi said. "He said it was…"

"Careful," said the doctor. "You'll spray marcaine all over the place. Put it down, man."

BRENNER did, and unwrapped it with practiced precision. "My stuff, Doctor," he said. "Think I don't know my own crates? Mrs. Jonathan, my price for your assets has just dropped to two and one-half million. And I am now in a position to prosecute. I hope none of you will make difficulties."

Jim Kandro said, "I don't know what this is all about, but we need that stuff for Sunny."

"You don't *believe* that, do you?" the drug maker asked scornfully.

"I don't know what to believe," said Kandro. "But he's— different. And it makes sense. He doesn't have to take OxEn, so he has to take something else. You better leave it for us, Mr. Brenner."

The drug maker looked at Jim wisely. "It's okay, Mac," he decided. "If you've got the habit and you can't kick it, why don't you come to work for me? I can use you. And you don't have to take so much. The micron dust in the air takes your edge off—"

"That's not it," said Kanrdro. "Why don't you listen to me? We need that stuff for Sunny. The doctor says so and he ought to know. It's medicine, like vitamins. You wouldn't keep vitamins from a little baby, would you?"

Graham snickered.

KANDRO turned and lectured angrily: "You stay out of this. There hasn't been anything but trouble since you got here. Now you could at least keep from braying while a man's trying to reason with somebody. You may be smart and a big writer, but you don't have any manners at all if you can't keep quiet at a time like this."

He turned to Brenner. "You know we don't have any money here, or I'd offer you what we had. I guess the box is yours, and nobody has a claim to it except you. But Polly and me can get permission from the Council to go and work out whatever the box would cost. Couldn't we, Tony? Mimi? The rest would let us, wouldn't they?"

"I'm sorry, Mac," the drug maker said. "I wish I could make you understand, but if I can't, that doesn't matter. This box is going with me. It's evidence in a crime."

"Mr. Brenner," Jim Kandro said thickly, "I can't let you out of here with that box. We need it for Sunny. I told you and told you. Now give it here." He put out one huge hand.

"How about it, Mrs. Jonathan?" Brenner seemed to be ignoring the big man's menacing advance. "Two and a half million? It's a very reasonable price, all things considered. Your new father here would be glad to take it."

"I'll take it, all right," growled Jim. "Hand it over. Right now." He was a scant four feet from the drug maker; Brenner's eyes were still fixed mockingly on Mimi Jonathan.

Kandro took one more step forward and Anna cried faintly: *"No."*

Brenner stepped back and there was a large pistol in his hand. "This," he told them, "is *fully* automatic. It keeps firing as long as I hold the trigger down. Now for the last time listen, all of you. I'm going, and I'm taking my box with me. If you try to stop me, I have a perfect right to use this gun. You know better than I do what fingerprints the authorities will find on the box. You're caught red-handed and I won't have any trouble proving it to my man Bell. If you people decide to be reasonable instead, you better let me know— soon."

Mimi Jonathan said clearly: "So you're going to throw us off Mars, Mr. Brenner?"

"If necessary," he said, not following.

"You mean you're going to kick us out and we'll never see Mars again? And all the sacrifices we've made here will be a joke?"

He didn't get what she was driving at. "Yes," he said irritably. "You're quite right—"

He was cut off by Hank, broken at last under the goading. The youngster sprang, raving, at Brenner, bowling him over as the pistol roared in a gush of bullets that ripped Hank's body.

And then there was a silence into which Sunny Kandro shrieked his fear and dismay. Mimi leaned against the wall and shut her eyes. She wanted to vomit. She heard Tony's awed whisper: "smashed his trachea...broke his neck...belly shot clean out..." She shuddered, and hoped and feared that she'd carry this guilt alone to the grave.

# CHAPTER TWENTY-SIX

"COME on, Polly. You come out here." Kandro led his wife, still carrying Sunny, out to the living room.

Faces were peering through the hospital window and they heard Nick Cantrella shouting: "Let me through, damnit! Clear away from that door!" And he was in, latching the door from the street. He snapped the curtains shut with an angry yank. "What in God's name happened? I was coming for that tissue culture and now this—"

"Don't worry about it," said Graham drily and with effort from the bed. "Just a little useful murder. Hank Radcliff, hero of the Colony, gives his life to save the world, from Big Bad Brenner—sweet Jesus," he swore in awed delight. "*What* a story. 'The Killing of Hugo Brenner'—an eyewitness account by Douglas Graham. Swee-eet Jesus. Didn't Brenner know who I was?"

Mimi started. "I guess not," she realized. "I never told him."

"You're plenty beat up," Tony pointed out. "He wouldn't have recognized you. Hey, Nick, let's get those bodies out of here."

"Beat up is right," Graham chortled, "and it was worth it. Thank *you*, my friends, whichever one of you—or how many was it?—did that job on me. I thank you from the bottom of my poor old gunther's heart. Just to be able to lie here and listen to all *that*."

"I don't know who did it last time." Nick took one menacing step toward the bed. "But, by God, if you're starting on another of your yarns, I know who's going to..."

"Nick, wait a minute. You don't know what he heard."

"Hey, Cantrella, I need a hand here."

"'I *know* who did it." Anna had to shout to make herself heard above Mimi and Tony, both talking at once. In the sudden silence, she said: "Didn't I tell you, Tony? I guess it was while you were away that I found out. *They* did it. I think he was planning to hurt the baby. Or they thought he was."

"*They?*" the writer asked contemptuously. "Brownies again? You're a good second-guesser, Miss Willendorf, but you missed out this time. The only designs I ever had on the Kandro kid were to get him back to Earth where he could be properly cared for—instead of getting marcaine dosed out to him to cover up for Mama."

"LISTEN, you lying crimp." Nick continued his arrested advance on Graham. "If you think you're safe to turn out more of that kind of stuff just because you're laid up in bed, you better start thinking all over again. I've got no compunctions about kicking a rat when he's down.

"Nick! Stop it!" Swift and sure and deadly sharp, Mimi's voice came across the room like a harpoon. "Give him a chance. You didn't hear what *he* heard—what Brenner said. I don't see how anybody could get a story against Sun Lake out of it."

"Thank you kindly, ma'am." Graham grinned painfully. "Good to know somebody around here is still sane. Don't tell me you go for this Brownie nonsense too."

"I—don't know," she said. "If I'd heard it from anybody but Tony and Anna, I wouldn't believe a word of it. But they *did* get the baby back."

"Back from where?"

Tony realized for the first time that Graham didn't even know about Sunny's kidnapping. And the others, for that matter, still didn't know what had happened in the cave.

"Listen," he said. "If you'll all take it easy for a few minutes, Anna and I have a lot to tell you. But first…Nick, help me move them to the living room floor. Anna, get blankets to cover them."

"Wait a minute." She went into the living room. "All right," she called back a moment later, and Tony and Nick together carried what was left of Hank through the door. "I wanted to get the Kandros out first," Anna explained, locking the front door again.

They laid out Brenner's body next to Hank's, and covered them both with blankets. The two men started back to the hospital, but Anna laid her hand on Tony's arm to stop him.

"Could I see you a minute?"

"Of course." He let Nick go ahead, then asked, worried, "Ansie, darling, what's the matter?"

She closed the door firmly between them and the others in the hospital.

"Tony, we can't tell them," she said. "Not now."

"Why not? They've got to know."

"Don't you *see*? We shouldn't have talked as much as we did. We shouldn't have said or done anything in front of Graham, but he doesn't believe it yet. If we convince him— Tony, the Brownies are terrified of people. They've kept away from people all along. For a reason. Don't you *see*?" she asked urgently. "Think what would happen to them. *Think*. I got just a flash from Graham's mind when I said *they* did it, before he decided to be skeptical. It was brutal. They'd be exterminated..."

He did see it. She was right. He thought of Hackenburg over at Pittco, and Brownies being worked in the mines—"native labor." He thought of what an Earth power would give to have telepaths in its military intelligence. He thought of the horror and hatred people would feel for the "mind-reading monsters." He thought of Brownies in zoos, on dissecting tables...

HE thought of Sun Lake, still facing a charge of theft; of the difference it would make in Graham's story if he knew it *wasn't* Sun Lakers who attacked him. He thought of what the existence of the Brownies would mean to medical and biochemical research. And he made up his mind.

Anna looked away with anger in her eyes, hopelessness in the set of her shoulders.

"*Why?*" she begged. "They're—oh, Tony, they're *decent!* Not like most people."

"Because *we* know about them, that's why. Because you can't— you just *can't* keep a secret like that. Because it means too much to men, to all men, to mankind, or whatever part of it survives the end of Earth, Anna. Sun Lake may not be the answer to our future—the Brownies may be. Have you thought of that? They need us, they need to learn some of the things our civilization has to offer—and we need them. That piece of tissue I took from Sunny's lungs may mean the end of dependence on Earth for OxEn, and that's just one first thing. There's no knowing how much we can learn, how they can help us to adapt, what new knowledge will come out of the contact. We *can't* keep it to ourselves. That's all there is to it."

"There's no use arguing, is there?"

"I'm afraid not," he said as gently as he could. He opened the door. "Are you coming back?"

She hesitated, then followed.

\* \* \*

"THAT'S it," Tony wound up the narrative of their visit to the cave, and then repeated, this time to Graham: "That's it. But I think you ought to know that Anna was trying to persuade me not to tell this story in front of you, to let you go on not believing in Brownies. She was afraid of what people would do to them once it became known. I'm afraid too. What you write will have a lot to do with it." He paused. "What *are* you going to write?"

"I'm damned if I know." Graham tried to lift his head, and decided against it. "It's either the most ingenious yarn I've ever heard—it covers every single accusation against you people, from marcaine theft to mayhem on my person—or it's the biggest story in the world. And I'm damned if I know which."

He relapsed into a thoughtful silence, broken suddenly by the roar of a large plane. An instant later there was the noise of a second, and then a third. One at a time they came closer, and died out.

"That would be Bell." Mimi stood up wearily. "I don't mind saying I'm confused. What do we do now?"

"He's coming," Tony reminded her, "to help Mr. Graham. Perhaps we should leave it up to our guest to tell the Commissioner whatever he sees fit."

The writer was silent, stonyfaced.

"There's a slight matter of a couple of stiffs in the living room," Nick reminded them. "The Commish might want to know about them. Strictly inter-colony stuff."

"You know," Graham broke in suddenly, "if I was dumb enough to believe your story about Brownies—and if your little experiment with the kid's lungs works—Sun Lake could get to be quite a place."

"How do you mean?" Gracey asked.

"The way Mr. Brenner had it figured, your Lab is practically made to order for marcaine manufacture. And I gather you think you can turn out OxEn too, if that lung tissue is good. If there's anything behind all this Brownie talk—well, you've got a deal that looks worth a trillion. You can supply OxEn to all of Mars at what price? It wouldn't cost you anything compared to Earth-import..."

He looked around the circle of astonished faces.

"Don't tell me none of you even *thought* of that? Not even *you?*" he appealed to Mimi.

She shook her head. "That's not the Sun Lake idea," she said stiffly. "We wouldn't be interested."

Anna smiled, very slightly, and there was a violent banging at the front door.

\* \* \*

TONY went slowly through the living room. The door was beginning to shake under the blows.

"Cut that out and I'll open it," he yelled. There was silence as he swung the door open. A sergeant of the guards, three others, and Bell, who was well in the rear. He must have known there'd been shooting.

"What's been going on?" the Commissioner began. He sniffed the air and his eyes traveled to the covered bodies. "Graham? If it is, we might have a murder arrest. His dispatch gave you people plenty of motive."

"No. Brenner," Tony said shortly. "And a young man named Hank Radcliff."

Bell, starting for the figures, recoiled. "Sergeant," he said, and gestured. The non-com gingerly drew back the blankets, exposing the drug maker's face. The Commissioner stared for a long moment and said hoarsely: "Cover it, Sergeant." He turned to Tony. "What happened?"

"We have a disinterested witness," said the doctor. "Douglas Graham. He saw the whole thing."

TONY led the way into the hospital. The sergeant followed, then the Commissioner. Graham said from his bed: "Visiting a dead friend?"

Bell snapped: "It's an inter-colony crime. Murder. Obviously I can't take the word of anybody who's a member of this community. Did you witness the killing?"

"I was a witness, all right," said Graham. "Best damn witness you ever saw. Billions of readers hang on my every word." He made an effort and raised himself on one elbow. "Remember the chummy sessions we used to have in Washington Bell?"

On the Commissioner's forehead, sweat formed.

"Here's the story of the killing," said Graham. "Brenner pulled his gun on a man named Kandro during a little dispute. He threatened to kill Kandro, went into some detail about how fully automatic that gun was and—let me think—his exact words were 'spray the room.' With a babe in arms present. Think of it, Bell. Not even you would have done a thing like that; not even in the old days. The Radcliff kid jumped Brenner and took all the slugs in his belly. I guess they were dumdums, because the gun looked to me like a .38 and none of them went through. Only the Radcliff boy squashed Brenner's neck before he knew he was dead. Reminded me of a time once in Asia—"

Bell cut him off. "Did Brenner die right away? Did he—say anything before he died?"

"Deathbed confession? Delirious rambling? No."

The Commissioner relaxed perceptibly.

"*But*," said the newsman, "he talked quite a bit *before* he pulled the gun. He didn't recognize me with my battered face and I didn't introduce myself. He thought it was just a bunch of Sun Lakers in here and that nobody would believe a word they said about him. Brenner talked quite a bit."

"Sergeant," Bell broke in. "I won't be needing you for a while. Wait for me in the other room. And see to it nobody touches those bodies."

THE door closed behind the non-com, and Graham laughed. "Maybe you do know, eh, Commish? Maybe you know Brenner liked to refer to you as 'my man Bell?'"

The Commissioner's eyes ran unhappily around the room. "You people," he said. "Get out. All of you. Leave us alone—so I can take a statement."

"No," said Graham, "they stay here. I'm not a strong man these days, but Brenner talked quite a bit. I wouldn't want anything to stop me from getting the story to an eagerly waiting world."

Bell looked around hopelessly.

Tony saw Nick's face twist into a knowing, malevolent grin; like the others, he made an effort to imitate it.

"What do you want, Graham?" asked the Commissioner. "What are you trying to get at?"

"Not a thing," the writer said blandly. "By the way, in my statement on the killing, should I include what Brenner had to say about you? He mentioned some financial matters, too. Would they be relevant?"

Tony tried to remember what financial matters Brenner had discussed, aside from the price he offered for the Colony. None—but Graham was a shrewd bluffer.

The Commissioner made a last effort to pull himself together. "You can't intimidate me, Graham," he rasped. "And don't think I can't be tough if you force my hand. I'm in the clear. I don't care what Brenner said; I haven't done a thing."

"*Yet*," said the writer succinctly. "Your part was to come later, wasn't it?"

Bell's face seemed to collapse.

"Still think you can get tough?" Graham jeered. "Try it, and I guarantee that you'll be hauled back to Earth on the next rocket, to be tried for malfeasance, exceeding your authority, accepting bribes and violating the narcotics code. I can also guarantee that you will be convicted and imprisoned for the rest of your life. Don't try to bluff me, you tinhorn sport. I've been bluffed by experts."

THE Commissioner began shrilly, "I won't stand for—" and cracked. "For God's sake, Graham, be reasonable. What have I ever done to you? What do you want? Tell me what you want!"

The writer fell back on the bed. "Nothing right now, thanks. If I think of anything, I'll let you know."

The Commissioner started to speak, and couldn't. Tony saw veins of tension stand out. He saw, too, how Anna's lip curled in disgust.

Graham seemed amused. "There *is* one thing, Commish. An intercolony matter under your jurisdiction, I believe. Will you remove those carcasses on your way out? You'd be surprised how sensitive I am about such things."

He closed his eyes and waited till the door was shut behind the departing guest. When he opened them again, all the self-assurance was gone out of them.

"Doc," he moaned, "give me a shot. When I got up on my elbow something tore. God, it hurts…"

While Tony took care of him, Joe Gracey said: "It was a grand performance, Mr. Graham. Thank you for what you did."

"I can undo it," the reporter said flatly, "or I can use it any way I want to. If you people have been lying to me…" He sighed with relief. "Thanks, Doc. That's a help. Now if you want anything out of *my* man Bell—show me one of your Brownies."

## CHAPTER TWENTY-SEVEN

GRAHAM'S challenge fell into a silent room. Everyone waited for Tony to speak; Tony waited for Anna.

"I don't see why not," she said at last. "I guess they'd do it." She looked despairingly at Tony. "Is this the *only* way?" she pleaded.

"It's the only way you're going to beat that marcaine-theft rap," Graham answered for him.

"All right. I'll go out there in the morning. I think I can talk them into it."

"If you don't mind, Miss Willendorf, I'd rather it was right now. In twelve hours, your hot-shot engineer here could probably *build* a Brownie."

"I can try," she said. "But I can't promise. Not even for tomorrow. I only think I can talk one of them into coming here. I don't know how they'll feel about it."

Graham grinned. "That's about how I figured it," he said. "Thanks, folks. It was a good show while it lasted."

"We're going," Tony said grimly. "And we'll bring you back a Brownie."

"Still not good enough," the writer said. "If you go, I go with you. You mind if I'm just a little suspicious?"

"It's ten kilometers to the Rimrocks," Tony told him. "Most of it by half-track, the rest by stretcher for you."

"The hell with your humanitarian sentiments. It's your medical opinion, if any, that I want."

"You'll live. No danger of that."

"All right," the writer said. "When do we start?"

Tony looked questioningly at Anna, who nodded. "Right now," the doctor said, "or any time you're ready." He opened a cabinet and fished out a patent-syringe ampoule. "This should make it easier." He started to open the package.

"No, thanks," Graham said. "I want to see what *I* see—if anything." His eyes went swiftly from one face to another, studying them for reactions.

"If you can take it, I can," the doctor told him. But he dropped the package in his pocket before they left.

IN THE rattling half-track, with Anna driving and Tony in the truck body beside Graham, the writer said through clenched teeth: "God help you if you tell me the Brownies aren't biting tonight. It's a damn-fool notion anyway. You've been telling me Brownies are born of Earth people. Why aren't there any born on Earth?"

"It's because of what the geneticists, call a lethal gene. Polly and Jim, for instance. Each one of them had a certain lethal gene in their heredity. Either of them could have married somebody without the lethal gene and had ordinary babies, on Earth or on Mars, because the gene is a recessive. On Earth, when Polly's lethal gene and Jim's lethal gene matched, it was fatal to their offspring. They never came to term; the gene produced a fetus, which couldn't survive the womb on Earth. I don't know what factors are involved in that failure—cosmic rays, the gravity or what. But on Mars the fetus comes to term and is—a Brownie.

"A Brownie is a Martian. They don't just *accept* Mars air like an Earthman with Marsworthy lungs. They can't *stand* Earth air. And they need a daily ration of marcaine to grow and live. That's who stole Brenner's marcaine. That's why they slipped marcaine into Polly Kandro's food. They wanted her to pass it to Sunny in her milk. When we put Sunny on the bottle, they stole him so they could give him marcaine. They surrendered him on our promise to see that he got it."

"And that's a perfect cover-story for a dope-addict mama," scoffed the writer. "How many Brownies are there supposed to be?"

"A couple of hundred. I suppose about half of them are first-generation. There must have been a very few in the beginning, children of homesteaders abandoned on a desert ranch when their parents died, who crawled out and lived off the country, chewing marcaine out of the weed. And they must have 'stolen' other Brownie babies from other homesteaders when they grew."

Graham swore against the pain. "The Kandro kid looks as normal as any other baby. How are the Brownies supposed to know he isn't? Does he give them a password?"

Tony explained wearily: "They are telepathic. It explains a lot of things—why they're only seen by people they want to see them, why they could steal Brenner's marcaine and not get caught. They can hear people coming—their thoughts, that is. That's why they beat up Big Ginny; she was aborting a Brownie baby. Why they beat the hell out of you. Why they sensibly keep away from most Earth people."

"Except Red Sand Jim Granata, eh?"

"Granata was a liar. He probably never saw a Brownie in his life. He heard all the Brownie yarns and used them to put on good commercial shows."

Anna maneuvered the half-track around a spur of rock picked out by the headlights and ground the vehicle to a stop. "It's too rugged from here on," she said. "We'll have to carry him the rest of the way."

"You warm enough? Another blanket?" asked Tony.

"You're really going through with this, aren't you?" said the writer. "I'm crazy to play along, but *if*—*if* this is a story and I get beaten on it—Oh, hell, yes, I'm warm enough. Stretcher ought to be easier going than this tin can."

ANNA led, with Graham swaying between them on a shoulder-suspended litter that left the bearers' hands free. The writer's weight was not much of a burden in this gravity. Both she and Tony used torches to pick their way among the scree that had dribbled, for millenia, one stone at a time, down the weathering Rimrocks. They smelled the acrid fumes of Pittco across the hills, fouling the night air, and Graham began to cough.

"Anna?" asked the doctor.

She knew what he meant, and said shortly: "Not yet."

Another hundred meters, and Tony felt her begin to pull off to the right. Her "homing" led them to the foot of the mesa-like hills a few meters from a cave mouth. They headed in.

"Quite soon," said Anna, and then: "We can put him down."

"Be very quiet," Tony told the writer. He himself felt the faint, eerie "touch" of a Brownie in his mind. "They're very sensitive to…"

"*Gargh,*" shrieked Graham as a Brownie stepped into the beam from Anna's light. It clapped its hands over its ears and fled.

"Now see what you did," raged Anna in an angry whisper. "Their ears—you almost deafened him."

"Get him back." The writer's voice was tremulous.

"I don't know if I can," Anna said coldly. "He doesn't have to take orders from you *or* me. All I can do is try."

"You'd better. It scared the hell out of me, I admit, but so did the

Brownies in Granata's Interplanetary Show, and they were fakes."

"Man, didn't you *feel* it?" asked Tony incredulously.

"What?" asked Graham. "Please be quiet, both of you." They waited a long time in the cold corridor before the thing reappeared, stepping warily into the circle of light.

Suddenly Anna laughed. "He wants to know why you want to pull his ears off. He sees you thinking of pulling his ears and the ears coming off and he's as puzzled as he can be."

"Shrewd guess," said Graham. "Do I get to pull them?"

"No. If you have any questions, tell me, and I'll try to ask him."

"I think it's a fake. Come out from behind those whiskers, whoever you are. Stillman? Gracey? No, you're too short. I'll bet you're that little punk Tad Campbell from the radio shack. I'd like to get my hands on those flapping ears just for one second."

"This isn't getting us anywhere," said Tony. "Graham, you think of a person or a scene or something, the Brownie will get it telepathically, give it to Anna and she'll say what it is."

"Fair enough," said the writer, "I don't know what it's supposed to prove, but it's some kind of test. I'm thinking."

A moment later Anna said evenly: "If you weren't beaten up already; I'd slap your face off."

"I'm sorry," said Graham hastily. "I was only kidding. I didn't really think it would—but it did, didn't it?" With mounting excitement he said, "Ask him who he is, who his people were, whether he's married, how old he is—"

Anna held up her hand. "That's enough to start. I can't think of any way to ask his name. His parents—not Brownies, homesteaders—a shack and a goat—a kitchen garden—tall, tall people, the man wears thick glasses—Tony! It's the Tollers..."

"That's impossible," he said. "Their son's on Earth. He never answers their letters," the doctor remembered. "They keep writing, and— How old was he when he left?"

"I don't know," she answered a moment later. "He doesn't understand the question."

"I felt it," said the writer, suddenly, in a frightened voice. "Like a thing touching you inside your head. Is that him?"

"That's him. Just don't fight it."

After a long silence Graham said quietly: "Hell, he's all right. They're all-right people, aren't they?"

"Do you want to ask him any more questions?" asked Anna.

"A million of them. But not right now. Can I come back again?" asked the writer slowly and heavily. "When I'm in better shape?" He waited for Anna's nod, then said: "Will you say thanks to him and get me to the 'track?"

"Pain worse?" asked Tony.

"No, I don't think so. Hell, I don't know. As a matter of fact, I'm just worn out."

The Brownie glided from the circle of light. "'By, fella," said Graham; and then grinned weakly. "He said good-by back at me."

Swaying between them on the litter on the way back to the 'track, the writer said at last; "Two System beats. Eyewitness account of Drug King Brenner's death, and the first factual eyewitness account of extraterrestrial intelligent life. One newsman per century gets one story like this. *And I've got two.*"

They loaded him into the half-track. He broke silence only once on the bumpy trip back to Sun Lake, saying with a chuckle: "I think he *liked* me." And then he fell quietly asleep.

\* \* \*

GRACEY and Nick and half a dozen of the biochem lab boys were waiting for them at the hospital. Joe must have been watching out the window, because he ran out to meet them.

It was late, and the lights were already out in most of the double row of rust-brown huts. But Joe Gracey, the quiet one, the gentle ex-professor, possessor of eternal calm and detachment, came flying down the dim street, shouting: "Doc! Tony! *We've got it!*"

"Sh-h..." Tony nodded toward the dozing man on the shoulder litter, but Graham was already opening his eyes.

"What's up?" he asked mushily. "What's all excitement?"

"Nothing at all," the doctor tried to tell him. "We're back in the Colony. And you're going to bed. Hold on just a minute, will you, Joe?" He knew how Gracey felt; it was hard enough to restrain his own jubilance and keep his voice in neutral register. But Graham had had enough for one night, and Tony had to get his patient back to the hospital bed before he could take time to listen even to such news as Gracey bore.

Joe helped them get the writer comfortably settled, and waited impatiently while the doctor made a quick check for any possible damage done by the trip. Finally, Anna pulled up the covers, and the three of them started out.

"Oh, Doctor..." Tony turned to find Graham up again on one elbow, wide-eyed and not a bit sleepy. "I was just wondering if I could have my typewriter." Before Tony could answer, the elbow collapsed and Graham smiled ruefully. "I guess not. I couldn't work it. You don't have anything as luxurious as an Earthside dictatyper in the place, do you?"

"Sure," Tony told him. "We've got one in the Lab office. You get some rest now, and we'll set it up for you here in the morning."

"I'm okay," Graham insisted. "There's something I'd like to get on paper right away. I won't be able to sleep anyhow if I don't get it done."

"You'll sleep," the doctor said. "I can give you a shot."

"No." Graham was determined. "If you can't get the dictatyper out here now, how about some pencil and paper? I *think* I still know how to use them."

"I'll see what we can do. Anna, will you come with me?"

TONY led her, not to the living room where the others were waiting, but into the bedroom. "How about it?" he asked in a whisper. "How's he feeling?"

"It's a funny mixture, Tony," she said, "but I think it's all right. He's not nearly as excited as he was before. He's eager, but calm and—well, it's hard to express, but *honest*, too."

"Right." He tightened his hand swiftly on her shoulder, and smiled down at her small earnest face. "A man could get too used to this," he said. "How do you suppose I got along before I knew about you?"

He strode into the living room and consulted briefly with Nick, after which two of the men from the biochem section tramped out to the Lab, and brought back the machine for Graham to use.

Through the living room door, Tony heard the writer's voice droning on, dictating, and the soft tapping of the machine. But what was going on in the hospital didn't seem important.

THE thing that mattered was the tiny pinch of pink powder Nick and Joe had been waiting to show him.

"Tony," said Nick, exultantly, "look at this stuff. It's damn near oral-administration OxEn. Took it through twelve stages of concentration and we'll take it through exactly three more to completion when Anna blows some hyvac cells for us. I tried and all I got was blistered fingers."

"It works?" asked Tony.

"It's beautiful," said Gracey.

"The Kelsey people must have fifty contaminants they don't even suspect are there. Now I want to know where that sample tissue came from and where you're going to get more. And what did you mean about Brownies?"

"Didn't Nick tell you?" Tony looked from the puzzled face to the startled one, and chortled appreciatively. "You mean you've been working together on this thing all evening and you never…?"

"He didn't ask," Cantrella said defensively. "Anyhow, we weren't working together. We weren't even in the same Lab."

"Okay," Tony grinned, "here goes again. You gave me the idea originally, Joe. As much as any one person or thing did. You were talking the other day about lethal genes. Remember, I tried to ask you about it this afternoon?"

"When Mimi blew up? Sure."

"That's when it hit me. I got that lung tissue from Sunny Kandro, Joe. After we brought him home. He's a Brownie…the result of a Mars-viable gene that's lethal on Earth."

"And there are more of them?" Gracey leaned forward excitedly. "Are they cooperative? Will they answer questions? And submit to examination? When can I see one?"

"They're cooperative," Anna said, smiling. "The reason you haven't seen one yet is that they can't stand humans—too uncooperative to suit them. Examinations? I don't see why not, if your intentions are honorable. They're telepaths, so they'd know you didn't mean to harm them."

"Telepaths…" Gracey breathed the word as Nick exclaimed it. "What other changes," the agronomist started to ask, then said instead: "No sense you telling me. I *will* see one? Soon?"

ANNA nodded. "Why not? They were willing to talk to him." She motioned to the closed hospital door.

"How about new tissue then?" Joe asked her. "Can we get it when we need it? You know how this stuff works? The old culture keeps mutating, and you have to start it over again. We can't keep taking slices out of Sunny all the time."

"I don't know," she had to admit. "I don't know if they could understand what you want it for, or why you're doing it."

"I don't think we'll have any trouble," Tony put in. "Nick, our Lab is equipped to turn out marcaine, isn't it?"

"Well, hell—yes, of course, but what for?"

"Marcaine and OxEn both? Do we have the facilities for it?"

"Sure. Processing the OxEn won't take up much."

"Then I'm sure we can get our lung-scrapings," the doctor said. "What do you say, Ansie?" The name slipped out, and he never even noticed the sudden startled exchange of looks between the other men. He did notice the woman's slight hesitation and half-hidden smile. "Will they do it? After all, you're the expert on Brownies."

"They like us," she said thoughtfully. "They trust us, too. They need marcaine. Yes, I think they'd do it."

"Doc!" It was Graham, calling from inside. Tony opened the door. "There anything left in that bottle of mine?"

"Hasn't been touched."

"Pour me a shot, will you? A good, long one. I'm not in such hot shape. And pass the bottle around."

Tony filled a glass generously. "Take it and go to sleep," he ordered. "You're going to feel worse tomorrow."

"Thanks. That's what I call a bedside manner."

Graham grinned and tossed off the drink with a happy shudder. "I've got some copy here," he said. "Can Stillman get it out tonight?"

TONY took the typed paper from the dictating machine and paused a moment, irresolutely.

Graham laughed sleepily. "It's in the clear," he said. "No code. And you can read it if you like. Two messages and Take One of the biggest running story of the century."

"Thanks," said Tony. "Good night." He closed the door firmly behind him.

"Story from Graham," he said to the group. He buzzed Harve.

"Read it," said Nick. "And if that lying rat pulls another—"

Tony gathered courage at last to run his eyes over the copy, and gasped with relief.

"'Message to Marsport communications,'" he read. "'Kill all copy previously sent for upcoming substitutes. Douglas Graham.' And 'Message to Commissioner Hamilton Bell, Marsport, Administration. As interested lay observer strongly urge you withdraw intended application of Title Fifteen search cordon to Sun Lake Colony. Personal investigation convinces me theft allegations unfounded, Title Fifteen application grave injustice which my duty expose fullest before public and official circles on return Earth. Appreciate you message me acknowledgment. Douglas Graham.'"

NICK'S yell of triumph hit the roof. "What are we waiting for?" he demanded. "Where's Mimi? We have packing to do!"

"What's the matter with him?" asked Harve Stillman, coming in.

Tony was reading the last of the messages to himself.

Anna told him: "You'd like that one best of all. What's in it?"

He looked up with a grin across his face. "I'm sorry," he said. "This is how it starts: 'Marsport communications, sub following for previous copy, which kill. By Douglas Graham. With Brownies, lead to come.' Harve, what does that mean?"

The ex-wire-serviceman snapped: "It's additional copy on a story about Brownies—the first part isn't ready to go yet. What's he *say*, Tony?"

The doctor read happily: "'The administrative problems raised by this staggering discovery are not great. It is fortunate that Dr. Hellman and Miss Willendorf, co-discoverers of the Martians, are persons of unquestioned integrity, profoundly interested in protecting the new race from exploitation. I intend to urge the appointment of one of them as special Commissioner for the P.A.C. to take charge of Brownie welfare and safety. There must be no repetition of the tragedies that marked Earthly colonial expansion when greedy and shortsighted—'"

"Damn, that's great," muttered the radioman. "Let me file it."

The doctor, with the grin still on his face, handed over the copy and Harve raced out.

"I told you," said Anna.

Joe Gracey said: "Well, I certainly hope whichever one of you turns out to be Commissioner is going to give us Lab men a decent chance at research on the Brownies. I was thinking I could probably work out a test for the lethal gene, or Brownie gene, better call it.

Spermatozoa for a male, a polar body or an ovum from a female and we'd be able to tell—"

"No," said Anna hysterically. "No, no!"

The others were shocked into silence.

"I'll take you home, Ansie," said Tony

He took her arm and they walked out into the icy night down the Colony street.

"Ansie, I've been sort of taking things for granted. I should ask you once, for the record." He stopped walking and faced her. "Will you marry me?"

"Oh, *Tony.*" The name exploded from her in fear and desire both. "Tony, how can we? I thought—for just a little while after I told you about me, I thought perhaps we could, that life could be the way it is for other people. But now this. How *can* we?"

"What are you afraid of?"

"Afraid? I'm afraid of our children, afraid of this planet. I was never afraid before, I was hurt and bewildered when I knew too much about people, but—Tony, don't you *see?* To have a baby like Polly's, to have it grow up a stranger, an alien creature, to have it leave me and go to its—its *own* people…"

HE TOOK her hand and began walking again, searching for the words he needed.

"Ansie," he began, "I think we will be married. If you want it as much as I do, we surely will be. And we'll have children. And more than that, the hope of all the race will lie in our children, Anna. Ours and the children of the other people here. And the children of the Brownies. Don't forget that.

"They look different. They even think differently, and nobody knows more about that than you. But they're as human as we are. Maybe more so.

"We've made a beginning here at Sun Lake tonight. We've cut the big knot, the knot that kept us tied to Earth. Brownies helped us do that, and maybe they can help us lick this planet in all the ways that still remain. Maybe they can help us cure the next Joan Radcliff. Maybe they can keep us from going blind when the protective shots from Earth stop coming through."

"But maybe they can't."

"Ansie, if our children should be Brownies, we'd not only have to face it, accept it without fear—we'd have to be glad. Brownies are the children of Mars, natural human children of Mars. We don't know yet whether *we* can live here; but *we know they can.*

"They're gentle. They're honest and decent and rational. They trust each other, not because of blind loves and precedents, as we do, but because they know each other as Earth humans never can. If blind hates and precedents end life on Earth, Ansie, we can go on at Sun Lake. And we can go on that much better for knowing that even our failure, if we fail, won't be the end."

He stopped at her door and looked down at her, searching for the understanding that had to be there. If Anna failed, what other woman would comprehend?

"I'll ask you this time," she said soberly. "Tony, will you marry me?"

## THE END

*If you've enjoyed this book, you will not want to miss these terrific titles...*

## ARMCHAIR SCI-FI & HORROR DOUBLE NOVELS, $12.95 each

**D-71**  **THE DEEP END** by Gregory Luce
**TO WATCH BY NIGHT** by Robert Moore Williams

**D-72**  **SWORDSMAN OF LOST TERRA** by Poul Anderson
**PLANET OF GHOSTS** by David V. Reed

**D-73**  **MOON OF BATTLE** by J. J. Allerton
**THE MUTANT WEAPON** by Murray Leinster

**D-74**  **OLD SPACEMEN NEVER DIE!** John Jakes
**RETURN TO EARTH** by Bryan Berry

**D-75**  **THE THING FROM UNDERNEATH** by Milton Lesser
**OPERATION INTERSTELLAR** by George O. Smith

**D-76**  **THE BURNING WORLD** by Algis Budrys
**FOREVER IS TOO LONG** by Chester S. Geier

**D-77**  **THE COSMIC JUNKMAN** by Rog Phillips
**THE ULTIMATE WEAPON** by John W. Campbell

**D-78**  **THE TIES OF EARTH** by James H. Schmitz
**CUE FOR QUIET** by Thomas L. Sherred

**D-79**  **SECRET OF THE MARTIANS** by Paul W. Fairman
**THE VARIABLE MAN** by Philip K. Dick

**D-80**  **THE GREEN GIRL** by Jack Williamson
**THE ROBOT PERIL** by Don Wilcox

## ARMCHAIR SCIENCE FICTION CLASSICS, $12.95 each

**C-25**  **THE STAR KINGS**
by Edmond Hamilton

**C-26**  **NOT IN SOLITUDE**
by Kenneth Gantz

**C-32**  **PROMETHEUS II**
by S. J. Byrne

## ARMCHAIR SCI-FI & HORROR GEMS SERIES, $12.95 each

**G-7**  **SCIENCE FICTION GEMS, Vol. Four**
Jack Sharkey and others

**G-8**  **HORROR GEMS, Vol. Four**
Seabury Quinn and others

*If you've enjoyed this book, you will not want to miss these terrific titles…*

## ARMCHAIR SCI-FI & HORROR DOUBLE NOVELS, $12.95 each

**D-91**  **THE TIME TRAP** by Henry Kuttner
**THE LUNAR LICHEN** by Hal Clement

**D-92**  **SARGASSO OF LOST STARSHIPS** by Poul Anderson
**THE ICE QUEEN** by Don Wilcox

**D-93**  **THE PRINCE OF SPACE** by Jack Williamson
**POWER** by Harl Vincent

**D-94**  **PLANET OF NO RETURN** by Howard Browne
**THE ANNIHILATOR COMES** by Ed Earl Repp

**D-95**  **THE SINISTER INVASION** by Edmond Hamilton
**OPERATION TERROR** by Murray Leinster

**D-96**  **TRANSIENT** by Ward Moore
**THE WORLD-MOVER** by George O. Smith

**D-97**  **FORTY DAYS HAS SEPTEMBER** by Milton Lesser
**THE DEVIL'S PLANET** by David Wright O'Brien

**D-98**  **THE CYBERENE** by Rog Phillips
**BADGE OF INFAMY** by Lester del Rey

**D-99**  **THE JUSTICE OF MARTIN BRAND** by Raymond A. Palmer
**BRING BACK MY BRAIN** by Dwight V. Swain

**D-100**  **WIDE-OPEN PLANET** by L. Sprague de Camp
**AND THEN THE TOWN TOOK OFF** by Richard Wilson

## ARMCHAIR SCIENCE FICTION CLASSICS, $12.95 each

**C-31**  **THE GOLDEN GUARDSMEN**
by S. J. Byrne

**C-32**  **ONE AGAINST THE MOON**
by Donald A. Wollheim

**C-33**  **HIDDEN CITY**
by Chester S. Geier

## ARMCHAIR SCI-FI & HORROR GEMS SERIES, $12.95 each

**G-9**  **SCIENCE FICTION GEMS, Vol. Five**
Clifford D. Simak and others

**G-10**  **HORROR GEMS, Vol. Five**
E. Hoffman Price and others

*If you've enjoyed this book, you will not want to miss these terrific titles…*

## ARMCHAIR SCI-FI & HORROR DOUBLE NOVELS, $12.95 each

**D-101**  **THE CONQUEST OF THE PLANETS** by John W. Campbell
**THE MAN WHO ANNEXED THE MOON** by Bob Olsen

**D-102**  **WEAPON FROM THE STARS** by Rog Phillips
**THE EARTH WAR** by Mack Reynolds

**D-103**  **THE ALIEN INTELLIGENCE** by Jack Williamson
**INTO THE FOURTH DIMENSION** by Ray Cummings

**D-104**  **THE CRYSTAL PLANETOIDS** by Stanton A. Coblentz
**SURVIVORS FROM 9,000 B. C.** by Robert Moore Williams

**D-105**  **THE TIME PROJECTOR** by David H. Keller, M.D. and David Lasser
**STRANGE COMPULSION** by Philip Jose Farmer

**D-106**  **WHOM THE GODS WOULD SLAY** by Paul W. Fairman
**MEN IN THE WALLS** by William Tenn

**D-107**  **LOCKED WORLDS** by Edmond Hamilton
**THE LAND THAT TIME FORGOT** by Edgar Rice Burroughs

**D-108**  **STAY OUT OF SPACE** by Dwight V. Swain
**REBELS OF THE RED PLANET** by Charles L. Fontenay

**D-109**  **THE METAMORPHS** by S. J. Byrne
**MICROCOSMIC BUCCANEERS** by Harl Vincent

**D-110**  **YOU CAN'T ESCAPE FROM MARS** by E. K. Jarvis
**THE MAN WITH FIVE LIVES** by David V. Reed

## ARMCHAIR SCIENCE FICTION CLASSICS, $12.95 each

**C-34**  **30 DAY WONDER**
by Richard Wilson

**C-35**  **G.O.G. 666**
by John Taine

**C-36**  **RALPH 124C 41+**
by Hugo Gernsback

## ARMCHAIR SCI-FI & HORROR GEMS SERIES, $12.95 each

**G-11**  **SCIENCE FICTION GEMS, Vol. Six**
Edmond Hamilton and others

**G-12**  **HORROR GEMS, Vol. Six**
H. P. Lovecraft and others

*If you've enjoyed this book, you will not want to miss these terrific titles…*

## ARMCHAIR SCI-FI & HORROR DOUBLE NOVELS, $12.95 each

**D-111**    **THE MOON ERA** by Jack Williamson
         **REVENGE OF THE ROBOTS** by Howard Browne

**D-112**    **SON OF THE BLACK CHALICE** by Milton Lesser
         **SENTRY OF THE SKY** by Evelyn E. Smith

**D-113**    **OUTPOST ON THE MOON** by Joslyn Maxwell
         **POTENTIAL ZERO** by S. J. Byrne

**D-114**    **OUTPOST INFINITY** by Raymond F. Jones
         **THE WHITE INVADERS** by Ray Cummings

**D-115**    **TIME TRAP** by Rog Phillips
         **THE COSMIC DESTROYER** by Alexander Blade

**D-116**    **THE OTHER SIDE OF THE MOON** by Edmond Hamilton
         **SECRET INVASION** by Walter Kubilius

**D-117**    **DANGER MOON** by Frederik Pohl
         **THE HIDDEN UNIVERSE** by Ralph Milne Farley

**D-118**    **THE WAILING ASTEROID** by Murray Leinster
         **THE WORLD THAT COULDN'T BE** by Clifford D. Simak

**D-119**    **THE WHISPERING GORILLA** by Don Wilcox
         **RETURN OF THE WHISPERING GORILLA** by David V. Reed

**D-120**    **SPECIAL EFFECT** by J. F. Bone
         **WARLORD OF KOR** by Terry Carr

## ARMCHAIR SCIENCE FICTION CLASSICS, $12.95 each

**C-37**    **THE GREEN MAN RETURNS**
       by Harold M. Sherman

**C-38**    **THE SHAVER MYSTERY, Book Five**
       by Richard S, Shaver

**C-39**    **MARS CHILD**
       by Cyril Judd

## ARMCHAIR MASTERS OF SCIENCE FICTION SERIES, $16.95 each

**MS-9**    **MASTERS OF SCIENCE FICTION AND FANTASY, Vol. Nine**
       Poul Anderson, "The Star Beast" and other tales

**MS-10**    **MASTERS OF SCIENCE FICTION, Vol. Ten**
       Robert Moore Williams, "Time Tolls for Toro" and other tales